To Blake

Heres to Dante Justice

COLD
SLITHER

AND OTHER TALES OF THE
WEIRD WEST

David J West

DAVID J. WEST

DAVID J. WEST – COLD SLITHER

Please visit http://www.kingdavidjwest.com/
And sign up for the newsletter

LOST REALMS PRESS

DAVID J. WEST – COLD SLITHER

For Bear

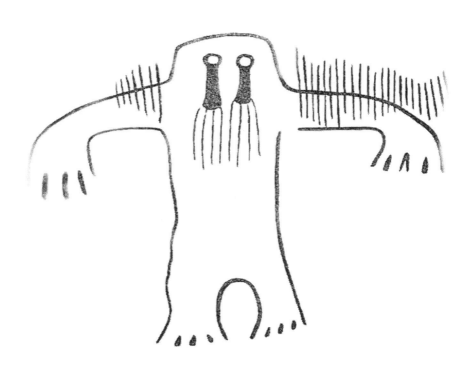

Acknowledgments:

Thanks to Nathan Shumate, Jason King, Jaleta Clegg, John Palisano, Eric Jepson, William Morris, Michael R. Collings, Frank Holdaway, Deborah Talmadge, Joel Jenkins, M.R. James, Robert E. Howard, Karl Edward Wagner, David Grant Stewart Sr., Douglas Dietrich, Steve Shaffer, Kerry Boren, David Hatcher Childress, Loren Coleman, JC Johnson, Melissa Adrina West and everyone else that has inspired and or encouraged me to write these tales.

Contents

"*In his build he was a gladiator; in his humor a Yankee lumberman; in his memory a Bourbon; in his vengeance an Indian. A strange mixture, only to be found on the American continent.*"
— Fitz Hugh Ludlow on Orrin Porter Rockwell

Cold Slither

"There was also the snake story, reported by the early explorers, both Spanish and American, and believed ever since: that this tribe was peculiarly addicted to snake worship, that they kept rattlesnakes concealed in their houses, and somewhere in the mountain guarded an enormous serpent which they brought to the pueblo for certain feasts. It was said that they sacrificed young babies to the great snake, and thus diminished their numbers."

— Death Comes for the Archbishop ~ Willa Cather

1. Son of Thunder

Stark white mountains rose jigsaw against an ashen sky. The frozen valley was mute but for hooves crunching against the shallow ice covered snow. The pale horse, its nostrils fuming out like dragon's breath, stepped carefully across the untrustworthy ground. The rider, a dark clad man with exceptionally long hair, brooded in the saddle, listening. So far as he knew, he—Orrin Porter Rockwell—, could very

2

well be the first white man in this high mountain valley. He had studied the maps of Jim Bridger, Jedidiah Smith and even Father Escalante and this valley was not upon any of their charts. If not for the freak blizzard shooing him off course, Porter might not have found it himself.

"Whoa Hoss," Porter whispered, tugging a halt on the reins. He ran a frostbitten hand over his beard shaking away some of the webbing of ice.

The horse stamped impatiently.

Somewhere beyond the thick wall of frosted pines, a scuffle came filtering through. A muffled cry and the equine scream of a horse in distress.

Porter readied his pistol. Something was coming this way.

An emaciated pony, half frozen to death with ice and blood on its snout, burst through the tree line and bolted past Porter.

In the opposite direction, a man cried aloud as a wild shot rang out. Porter gave spurs to his mount, and its hooves stomped through the gleaming snow as he sped toward the danger.

Breaking through the barrier of woods and snow, a pair of shots echoed almost simultaneously through the frozen valley. Porter responded in kind to this leaden welcome.

Charging while holding the reins in his teeth, Porter's .44 Colt Dragoons were alternately belching smoke, fire and lead.

Two men in their very last moments—had each fired from a pair of old flintlock's. They had missed by a mile and Porter wasn't about to let them loose their arrows at this point. He shot them down quick as anything when they reached for their more primitive weapons.

Steam issued from their grievous wounds like spirits passing into the next world.

Porter eased up, careful-like, on a trio of dead men. All three were Indians. Two desperate horseless Shoshone and the other a curiously foreign looking man.

What happened was apparent enough to a skilled tracker like Porter. The Shoshone had been after the foreigner's pony and supplies. They shot him as he came riding through the opposite tree line. Likely they were so impatient and cold that in their haste to rob the man; the pony had escaped in the ruckus and ran for its life down the valley. Porter was so cold himself, he wasn't sure he wanted to pursue the starved animal either.

He looked again at the dead foreigner who was surely no Ute nor from any other semi-local tribe. The exotic and strange clothing made even the well-traveled Porter curious as to where the dead man was from. Ornaments of copper and a leopard skin were terribly out of place here in the Territories. Snake-like tattoos covered his exposed neck and arms along with an incredible heap of scars all over his hands and face. He also had severe frostbite burns.

"Wheat! Son of a bitch has been through a whole lotta pain," Porter muttered, to his horse as much as to himself.

The animal was looking over his shoulder at the rising steam from the dead men's bodies. Maybe it really was their spirits passing on.

Reaching inside the foreigner's bulging leather bag, Porter found a large jade idol that weighed perhaps twenty pounds. Intricately carved, its body looked like a voluptuous woman, yet with snakes in place of her hands, feet and heads. The head of the thing, or rather both conjoined heads, were serpents looking either way Janus-like. The figure was perched on a thick grooved rectangular base of white quartz that sparkled despite the grey overcast sky above.

"This is the damndest idol I've ever seen," he said, again to his horse. It neighed, welcoming the company as well.

The bag also contained a bit of jerky, some roots Porter didn't recognize, a pipe and some dried herbs likely for smoking during a ceremony. But the real find was and a magnificent obsidian dagger that was as much a work of art as a weapon. The gold handle looked like a crouching man embracing a bolt of lightning or perhaps a snake for a blade. It was a vicious looking thing and testing it out, Porter cut clean through a thick leather strap like it was butter.

"Sharp as slander," said Porter, to the horse again. For the sake of curiosity, Porter decided he would keep the items in his saddle bags and show them to someone soon as he got back to civilization. Wouldn't hurt to have the strange things to barter for later on, he figured.

The ground was too frozen to bury the dead and Porter wondered if any more Shoshone might be in the vicinity. Unlikely, as these two had been horseless but it wouldn't do to sit still and invite trouble. The ringing sound of the gun fight bounced off the mountain peaks relaying location vibrant as any smoke signal. He covered the dead men with the foreigner's multicolored blanket. It was the best he could manage in the circumstances and as much as he figured the bushwhacking Shoshone deserved. Too bad about the alien looking Indian, but not much else he could do in this bitter cold. If he didn't find shelter soon, he would be joining them in the happy hunting grounds.

A babbling stream ran dark and serpentine, cutting a path down the valley. Porter let his horse drink a moment before urging her on. The wind suddenly whipped up; a phantom robber tearing at Porter's woolen coat. Shivers reached inside sprouting goosebumps before he could pull the flaps closed again.

A mournful crow cawed from a dark pine branch.

Porter's revolver flew from his pocket at the unexpected sound. "Wheat bird! I almost killed ya!" Chuckling, he returned his sawed-off Colt Dragoon to its preferred pocket.

He felt foolish for still being jumpy but an uneasiness hung over him, akin perhaps to a predator knowing when it is being stalked by another.

Porter watched his mare's tracks, wary of the ice cutting her forelegs. Like it or not, he had to admit to taking an unplanned route in the storm. He was never lost. He had just never been here before.

The tallest peak to the north resembled the semi-familiar Mount Nebo, but this angle gave Porter pause. He must have traveled farther afield than expected and was now likely well within Ute territory. This in itself was no worry, Porter was on friendly enough terms with Chief Walker and the Utes—but that was always with an interpreter, his friend George Bean. Porter himself didn't speak Ute, he hardly knew more than a few key words. Still, perhaps he could communicate with someone and learn the quickest route from the high valley before his horse became crippled and they were both in danger of freezing to death.

The snow was coming down again in big flakes, swirling about like a serpent squeezing the life from a man. Porter wondered again about someone following his back trail in the aftermath of the fight but didn't feed the idea too much worry. Soon enough, his trail would be invisible again. He *did* have to find shelter, though. The blizzard was a lot more likely to kill him than any unseen stalker. Sure, he had been blessed by a holy man that no bullet nor blade could ever harm him but what about a simple snowflake? Those tiny white bladed stars could eventually cut through any man alone out here without shelter.

Porter prayed aloud at what he ought to do and where he ought to go. He heard nothing but the eerie moaning of the wind in return. The sound raced across the snows like a banshee and didn't grant no comfort.

"Thanks' a lot, Lord," he grumbled.

Then he saw a wispy string of smoke rising from a hillock not a few miles south.

"Forget my complaint. I'm just a fool, a learning your mysterious ways," he said, before making his way for the wavering gray finger, cautious as ever.

2. Keeper of the Sacred Flame

It was nigh on dusk, by the time Porter made it to the big rounded hill. Wisps of smoke still rose from some small fire, but were swiftly carried away by the north wind. Looking about for a teepee, Porter was surprised to spot smoke issuing from a cave high on the south cliff-face. Like a skulls gaping socket, it was ominous and foreboding, and like an eye, the flickering lights of flames inside promised life within. But cold as that night's storm promised to be, he had to find shelter regardless, so Porter pressed on.

It took him a few moments to carefully guide his horse up the windswept slope. Just to the leeward side, the rock gave way to a short cliff with fingers of granite reaching up from the snows.

"Hello in there," Porter called out, wanting to be sure he didn't startle anyone, even if they did not speak English. Wouldn't do to take a bullet just from spooking somebody.

Porter peered into the orange splashed gloom, wondering if it was now unoccupied, when a wrinkled gray-haired Indian stuck his head out the cavern's opening. He looked as if he were eagerly expecting someone, but seeing only the black-bearded white man, he made a crude gesture for Porter to leave.

Porter beckoned at the rapidly darkening sky and made his own show of force, if not his willful stubbornness known. "Come on Chief, ya crotchety old bastard," he grated, through his teeth. "It's mighty cold."

The old man again shook his weathered face.

"I'll share my whiskey," said Porter, dangling the bottle outward. "Name is Porter."

The old Indian took another look up at the charcoal shaded clouds and buffeting snowflakes again before finally giving Porter a reluctant nod.

The cavern's mouth was just large enough to guide Porter's mare inside after them, and the old Indian did not seem opposed to letting the horse in.

A fire burned at the far end of the oblong cavern, right beside another small tunnel leading further on into the gloom. The smell inside was disagreeable but better to endure that than the storm. Weird pictographs of cinnabar and ochre were splashed across the walls. They looked like visions of serpents entwined and inhuman horned men in communion with one another. The cave floor itself was littered with debris and char, the remnants of eons of continued use. A wide variety of tokens, herbs, fetishes and what Porter knew were sacred medicines hung on the walls. This was a sacred place. He tried to remember the Ute words for horse and apologies but slipped over himself like fresh cow pies on a rainy spring day.

"I speak Mericat, plenty good," said the old Indian, using the Ute term for Americans. "Horse is fine."

"Well, thanks much, Chief. Looks to be a cold night and I didn't want to—,"

"I did not say to keep talking, Mormonee," snapped the old man.

Porter scowled but went silent, figuring the old man would talk when he was ready. Besides, he obviously knew at least a little about Porter being in this territory, what with the Ute term for the Mormon's being handed out like that.

Instead of saying anything more, the old Indian proceeded in taking stones and walling up the doorway-like tunnel at the far side of the cave. He pounded tiny wedges and sticks into the spaces further tightening his stone handiwork. He then plastered mud over the whole of it making it nearly invisible. When finished, he fed the fire again and took a branch of sage, let it take light until it smoked and wafted the incense about the cave while muttering a chant Porter couldn't hope to understand. He then sat down staring at Porter.

Quite some time passed and Porter watched the storm roll in and cover the white land outside with darkness. Wind tore inside but the cave stayed tolerable thanks to the old man's fire.

Finally, Porter had enough of the silent treatment. "You know Chief, we could keep a bit warmer if we moved that fire a little more central. Away from the entrance and your sealed tunnel there."

"Sacred fire must stay where it is."

"What's in there anyway? Some kind of Indian treasure? Not that I have interest in what's yours," said Porter, holding his hands up.

The old man narrowed his gaze at Porter. His eyes were like seas of flint, dark and mysterious. "You should not be here," he said, accusingly.

"Yeah, I get that a lot. But here we are. You want any of that whiskey yet, Chief?"

The old man gave him a cross look but reached for the offered flask and took a swig, then another and another and finally said, "At daybreak you must leave. Forget this place." He took another few swallows. "Go back to your children and wives."

"Ha! Chief, you get a little more neighborly with a square drink in ya," laughed Port. "And you speak Mericat awful good. Better than some pukes I used to deal with in Missouri."

The old man gave a sarcastic half grin and took another swallow of whiskey. "I have spoken to your brother, Isaac Morley, many times and learn from him of your language and customs."

Porter capped his hands together. "Well that's real good, we have friends in common then."

The old Indian held his hand up to silence him. "I only allow you to stay the night because of the storm. In the morning, you must leave and forget this place."

"Why? Is it cursed or something?" Porter laughed, but the deadly serious look on the old Indian's face gave him pause.

The old man took a bit of sage and again let it catch flame and wafted the holy incense about the chamber. "The curse contained here is more deadly than any storm."

"Curse? That why you're tending this fire instead of being with Walkara and the tribe?"

"I am no Ute. I am Mexica. What you Mericat's and Mormonee call Azteca. I have tended the sacred fire of Coatlicue for many moons, as my fathers before me. The goddess must stay here. She must be allowed to sleep."

"She must be some gal."

The old Indian stifled a laugh, shook his head and took another drink of whiskey.

Pointing at the sealed tunnel, Porter asked, "What's in there? What are you afraid of?"

"I fear I am the last," the old man said, taking another swallow.

"The last what?"

"To keep the sacred fire burning and to keep the Blood Gods asleep. I am old and await the coming of the next shaman who shall tend the sacred fire. I fear he will not come. Those who remember the old ways dwindle and those that respect them—even fewer." He then gave a soft laugh, born out of sadness not mirth. The whiskey was taking hold and a solitary tear came rolling freely down his face.

"That reminds me, Chief," said Porter, as he pulled the jade idol from his pack. "The next shaman, did he carry this?"

The old man's savage eyes opened wide in a rage at sight of the idol. His gnarled hand wrapped around the knife hilt at his belt. Shouting incomprehensibly, he launched himself panther-like at Porter.

In a contest of strength, the old man would be no match for a human grizzly bear like Porter, but the sacrificial obsidian knife carried a thousand years of respect.

Porter dodged the first few wild slashes, then as the old man over extended himself, Porter struck like unchained lightning. The powerful blow sent the old man flying—releasing his grasp on the volcanic knife. The black blade shattered as it struck the cave wall.

Struggling to his knees, the old man wiped at the blood oozing across his swollen lips and nose.

"Sorry 'bout that Chief, but you need to listen afore you try that again. I didn't kill the man who carried this. Shoshone horse thieves did. I took this damnable idol so that I might find out who he was."

The old man scratched at his face asking, "What did the dead man look like?"

Porter propped his hat back saying, "Well, he was foreign looking. He had a leopard skin tunic, copper arm bands and a whole mess of snake tattoos over his exposed skin. Even his neck and face. Did you know him?"

"No. He must have been one of the servants of Coatlicue. He was alone?"

"So far as I know. Course the storm blew me off course, maybe he was lost too?"

The old man lit a pipe and thought for a long moment before saying, "My son's name was Mazatl. He must surely be dead if that man was carrying the idol here. My son was to take my place here and keep the spirit of Coatlicue contained, that she might never return to Tenochtitlan."

"Sorry, Chief, I truly am. But is that such a bad thing? Some spirit returning?"

The old man nodded and slumped against the cave wall. "I know now you are not a servant of the Blood Gods. But for a moment, I was afraid, I thought maybe you were."

Porter took a swig from his flask. "Good. I don't know whatever could have given you that idea."

"When you held the vessel of Coatlicue, I could see blood glowing on your hands." He shrugged, "I panicked."

Porter nodded. "Lord knows I got blood on my hands, but it was all blood that needed spilling. What's with the idol?"

"There are dark forces that wish a return to cruel gods. But I remember the blood debt they demand and I will not exchange them for even the hated Spanish. Men can be overcome . . . but gods . . . much more difficult."

The old man stood and threw branches on the fire and as the sparks flew up and smoke curled from the green wood, Porter could almost see the bloody tale the old man began.

"This world is a wheel, what has come before, comes again. Sometimes all that stands before evil conquering is one good man."

Porter couldn't help but look at the sealed tunnel behind the fire, it contrasted with the howling wind and swirling snows outside the cave.

The old man continued, "Ages before Monctezuma, a wise man, a good man, called Madoc, came from far across the sea. He was a herald of Quetzalcoatl and became king of my people by banishing the cruel Blood Gods. Madoc stopped the human sacrifices and ended the evil ways of the Blood Gods. He was the first to succeed in that since the Blood Gods began their reign under True Great Jaguar Claw a thousand years earlier, beginning the Age of Chaos."

"Forgive my saying so Chief, but weren't your people sacrificing to the Blood Gods again when Cortez came rapping at their door?"

The old man nodded soberly. "The priests of Tezcatlipoca, Huitzilopotchli and Coatlicue tried for years to bring back the favor of the Blood Gods. It was a mixed blessing for both Cortez and my people that the magic didn't work anymore. Because Madoc had banished the Goddess Coatlicue and the other Blood Gods too far to be recalled—yet."

Porter took another swallow. "Can they ever come back?"

"Their return is difficult but not impossible. I have stood watch for many moons, keeping the sacred flame burning. Keeping the Snake Goddess and her servants asleep."

"You mean in there?" Porter gestured to the tunnel. "What's in there? Evil spirits?"

"Worse."

The sealed doorway beckoned, inviting all of Porter's curiosity and wonder. He stood and went to the edge of the walled up tunnel. There was yet a tiny space left open where a draft flowed. Air coming from the very top portion, was musty, foul and reptilian. Yet something tugged at Porter's senses, asking, no, pleading with him to loose the stones and look inside.

The Chief wagged his finger at Porter. "You go in there—you never come out."

Porter swallowed the last drop of whiskey and stared into the abyss for a long moment. "You're right Chief, you are old. What happens when no one is around to keep that fire burning? Do these Blood Gods escape? Can they roam free?"

The old man shook his head. "They still need a vessel to touch our world. Evil men, would want that," he said, pointing at the idol of Coatlicue. "It is a bell to wake them. If they could take it down into depths to wake the Blood Gods, they would. The only reason my son would have brought it here is because it was too dangerous to remain in the south."

"You asking me to get rid of it?"

The old man nodded. "My son is gone and my people have fallen. That is the reason you are here. To protect the way. To keep them

11

asleep."

"You want me to throw it off a cliff? In a lake?"

Chief shook his head. "No, they would find it and bring it here. You will take it to your chief, the great Brigham, let him keep it safe. Then *you* return and keep the sacred fire safe. That is enough."

"Look, I got a lot of responsibilities, and I can't be sitting in no cave the rest of my days. If someone has to tend the fire and the idol it should be your people . . ." Porter realized he was talking about the old man's dead son as if that were still a possibility, he felt bad and tried to change the subject. He laughed hoping to lighten the mood. "Hey! At least we got the idol now right? They can't use it now huh?"

The old man shrugged again. "Let me show you the magical way of the old ones." He beckoned for Porter to come closer. He took hold of the jade idol of Coatlicue and rubbed his hand vigorously along the grooved white quartz base. A slight snapping of electricity and the very idol itself began to glow bright as a lantern.

"That's amazing," exclaimed Porter.

"In elder days, many such items were in use in the lands of my birth. They were gifts from the gods. But this one is cursed and is only to be used to wake the Blood Gods." He covered it in a deer hide and tucked it beside a cairn of stones. "This must be taken far away and hidden away."

Porter rubbed his chin. "Sure, Chief. I could do that."

The old man nodded, looking quite pleased. "Then return and take up your watch as the keeper of the sacred flame."

"I told you, I can't do that, Chief. I've got other responsibilities."

The old man shook his head in confusion. "Why else would the Great Spirit guide you here when my son was slain? You are the one to take possession of this honor."

Porter frowned. He had a lot of duties and not a one of them included sitting in a cave like a damn hermit. "Look Chief . . ."

The old man interrupted him, asking, "Are you sure it was Shoshone that killed the man that carried the idol?"

"Sure, I'm sure," answered Porter.

"Then who are they?" asked the old man, pointing out into the windswept moon-covered gloom.

3. The Servants of Coatlicue

Porter glanced around the cavern wall and outside, he looked down the slope. At least a dozen tall lanky men, shadows taller than their souls, were approaching uphill through the snow. Three or four had rifles, the rest were armed with clubs, tomahawks and bows while the largest intruder had a full sized ax; though he was so big himself it looked like a tomahawk in his clenched fist.

"They followed you," said the old man, gravely.

"Sorry, Chief."

"It's all right. They would have found me eventually anyway."

Dark as it was, silver moonlight stole through the clouds and caught the swirling snows granting ghostly definition to the marauders, who sure didn't look to be Shoshone. They were dressed as alien as the dead man Porter had found earlier that day, spotted jaguar pelts wrapped about their loins, brightly colored feathers decorated their hair and copper armbands betrayed their foreign source. Once they knew they had been spotted they split in multiple directions, some disappearing into the frosty murk others remained as sentinels facing the cave. Their intent was murderously clear.

One in a dark cloak called out in a language Porter couldn't fathom.

The old man replied in the same tongue. Porter still couldn't understand a word but the old man's message was clear enough. He told them off and they weren't happy.

The leader shouted something menacing again, then shrunk back into the shadows.

"Who the hell is that?"

"Ichtaca Eztli, he is the Blood Gods Brujo. He asks that I give up and put out the sacred flame, extinguish it. I told him—."

Porter stopped him with a wave of his hand. "I know what you told him and I support you all the way. We had better get ready to throw down with 'em." He checked his pockets and felt the comfort of having four extra cylinders ready for his Dragoon's. It made reloading in a gun fight a whole lot faster—and faster counted in leagues out here.

"They mean to wake the Blood Gods. There are more men out there than you can see. Might be more on their way here."

"I'll be dipped," Porter spat. "Sure hope you've got some supplies in here so we can wait them out. At least the bitter cold is on our side."

"They won't wait. They come for blood." The old Indian folded his arms.

"I was afraid you'd say that." Porter checked his two Dragoon's then motioned to his rifle. "Man that Springfield musket, Chief. If they rush us you can get at least one or two, I'm sure."

The old man took the rifle in hand. It was a flintlock musket that Porter had bartered from a veteran of the Mormon Battalion. He hadn't used it much yet but it was reliable and would sure do the trick.

The gale howled outside the cavern. Porter expected to hear the cry of attack, the unnerving yipping and yowling of braves on the warpath, but instead there was no sound but the mournful wind.

"What are they waiting for?"

"Ichtaca Eztli is wise as a serpent and he waits for our nerve to drop so that his men may attack us unexpectedly."

Porter grimaced, but kept both Dragoons trained on the entrance. His mare nickered. He responded to her, "It might get loud, Hoss. You gotta have some patience too."

An hour passed and though the storm subsided, the roiling skies with pinpricks of stars overhead only made it all the colder. Not to mention that the wailing wind hadn't let up either. Their fire was waning against the relentless tide of wind.

Porter spit to the side. "And you said they wouldn't wait."

"I just meant that my supplies wouldn't matter for this confrontation. It will be decided by morning."

"Maybe you ought to let that fire go out. They won't be able to see us too well in here, if you think they're coming before daybreak."

The old man shook his head, though he never took his eyes away from the threshold. "I must keep the fire burning. The evil ones must be held at bay."

Porter cursed under his breath, but couldn't help but respect that the old Chief's complete devotion to his charge. The old man had lived out here as a hermit shaman for who knew how long anyway? Years? Decades? Now that was dedication!

DAVID J. WEST – COLD SLITHER

The wind ripped a freezing blast into the cavern, hushing the fire dangerously low. The coals flared bright red while the flames themselves vanished. In a panic, the old Chief put down the rifle and cast more twigs and sage atop the glaring embers. Smoke roiled up and the blaze snapped awake in a flickering yellow-orange dance accompanied by castanet-like snaps.

Then warriors were at the entrance. First one, then another and another until their muscled tattooed bodies blocked out the cold light of the stars.

The old man made a dash to grab the rifle and fire at the intruders but arrows sprouted from his chest like pins in a cushion. He fell backward over a cairn of stones.

Porter blasted both Dragoon's and took down the bowman assassin as well as the warrior beside him. The chamber filled with a healthy gout of smoke and flame from the guns and echoed the throaty retort. A hidden rifle just beyond the border of the cavern belched acrid flame and smoke. The ball buried itself in stone just above Porter's head.

The mare's scream echoed into the canyon as arrows ricocheted from the ceiling above. One shaft buried itself into the animal's shoulder blade. Snorting and kicking in pain, it reared, snapped its reins and dashed out into the night, carrying Porter's supplies and ammunition with it.

Somewhere out into the licking darkness, a trio of rifle shots rang out and the mare's screaming stopped.

Porter returned fire in kind, though he no longer saw anyone to aim at. All was again silent again as the grave. Cold blackness beckoned like a spurned lover outside the flame-lit cavern. Porter found it to be a curious paradox. He stood amidst swirling smoke and snow, the juncture of cold and heat, flame and ice, life and death.

Shallow breaths escaped from the old man who lay bleeding a few paces from the fire. Porter went to him, turning the old man so that he laid flat on his back in order to examine his wounds.

"Keep the flame burning," he wheezed as blood bubbled over his lower lip. Several wicked shafts protruded from his chest and stomach, leaking blood into a veritable river that rolled across rock floor.

"We got other worries, Chief. I'm a little shy on ammunition now.

You haven't bartered any have you? Out here as the shaman mystic?"

The old man, coughed up blood, smiled and said, "I've been a fool many years but I recognize now that a new blood and people had to come here, had to hold back the darkness. My time is over. It is you and your people's duty now. You must keep the Blood Gods asleep. You must keep them contained."

"No old man, you got time left. This is your job, not mine," Porter argued. But the old man's spirit was already wind-walking its way up to the stars.

A crunch of snow outside the cavern brought the Dragoons up again, blasting lead balls at unseen opponents. A startled cry and the crumpled sound of groaning and tumbling down the hillside in the snow told Porter he had hit someone.

A deep throated voice called something infernal out in the vast palpable darkness, but Porter had no idea what was said. A scuffle near the entrance made Porter blink. Another rush was coming. He quickly reloaded his pistols and had three cap and balls in the first pistol when they came.

War whoops shattered the silence. Two wild shots rang out and then men were inside the cavern.

The titanic ax man, face splashed with black and white war-paint meant to resemble a deaths head, strode into the cavern. He swept his vicious weapon at Porter's head.

Porter lunged backward to avoid the death stroke. The ax head bit into the unforgiving stone wall and sparked as fragments chipped off.

Rolling away from another blow, Porter fired twice, barely missing each time. He held off his barrage on the last shot. It had to count.

A screeching wild man with bright feathers in his hair and raccoon-like eye makeup, loosed an arrow at Porter but miraculously missed. Falling to his backside, Porter scooted away from another hammering blow of the ax man.

As the wild man took another arrow from his quiver, Porter aimed the Dragoon and fired. It split the wild man's head like a canoe.

Porter had just enough time to duck as the ax man swung again, but his hat wasn't so lucky. It was taken right off Port's head by the ax man's terrible maul.

Another tattooed warrior was at the entrance, then another and another, tomahawks and bows in their skilled hands.

Porter grabbed the flintlock musket from beside the fire. He swung it up just in time to shoot the ax man square in the chest as his own weapon hung perilously overhead. The .69 caliber ball threw the big ax man against the cave wall; where he slumped down, leaving a ghastly red smear behind.

Using the musket like a club, Porter swung and jellied the brains of the nearest attacker. He charged at the two warriors remaining in sight shouting like a man possessed.

The two warriors at the door stared stupidly at their ruined comrades and at the angered white man. Shaking themselves out of their shock, their self-preservation got the better of them, and they turned and fled into the night. They tumbled down the snowy embankment in a mad rush to escape his wrath.

Porter halted beside the sheer edge of the hillside, watching the warriors retreat. Remembering he had to reload, he fumbled in his woolen pockets for more caps and balls, hoping he could pick them off before they got too far away.

A sudden crunch in the snow behind him brought him wheeling about just in time to catch a crack to his skull and then swift blackness on dreamy wings spun from spider-webs took him far, far away.

Porter fell twenty feet off the leeward side of the exposed cliff, right between two jutting fingers of stone.

From the top, Porter's opponents looked down at his body. He wasn't moving.

4. Blood Brujo

Porter's face was numb, his eyelids nearly frozen shut. He awoke face down in pink snow. He raised his head and slowly looked about, relieved that most of the blood in the snow wasn't his own. One of the men he had shot in the night was broken atop one of the two pillars of granite he had landed between. Thankfully, there was quite a cushion of snow where he'd met the ground. It seemed his enemies believed him surely dead. His mare lay less than a hundred yards away with fields of hoar frost sprouting over her stiff body. The rosy finger of dawn was just teasing at the backside of the mountains, but Porter couldn't see any light issuing from the cavern above.

He slowly perked his head up to look about for any foes. None it seemed were outside any longer and he listened a long while before moving. Far down and around the hillside, he saw more than a dozen picketed horses. One man lay nearby the animals as if on watch but Porter guessed by the way he sat at a near dead fire that he was asleep.

The others must be in the cavern going through the old man's things. Not that there had appeared to be much that he could recollect. They must be after the idol and going into that sealed tunnel.

Cold as he was, he needed a drink. He took a mouthful of snow and washed it down with his flask. He would get the jump on those men soon enough, but he needed more ammunition. Scooting to his dead horse, he felt inside a saddle bag and grasped a handful of caps and then his lead balls. He loaded his one remaining Dragoon. Both had fallen in the snow with him, but he couldn't find the other one. Whomever had bushwhacked him must have taken it and his knife. He reached for the spare in the saddle bags and found the sacrificial obsidian knife from the dead man. Lighter and shorter than his favored blade, the knife was still a mean contender.

Deciding he didn't want anyone coming up behind him again, he slunk toward the lone sleeping guard with the horses. Stepping silently through the snow was difficult and the foreigner's horses were suspicious of his hairy countenance. They knew their riders were tall dusky red men, and Porter looked more like a wild animal. The horses neighed and jostled and Porter softly nickered back to them.

Just as Porter was almost upon the sleeper, the man's eyes shot open. Porter's hand clamped over his mouth before he could yell, but the muted man drew a blade of black obsidian. They tumbled into the snow wrestling with their knives and sheer will. Porter slammed the man into a tree trunk but lost his own footing and fell backward. The enraged guard was so intent on stabbing Porter that he didn't yell an alarm but lunged forward. Porter rolled and caught his opponents arm and rolled over it bringing him into a deadly embrace on the ground. Still holding the arm with the knife with his own left, Porter snapped the man's neck between his right arm and right knee. He then placed the man near enough as he had been beside a tree, to look as if he still slept on his watch.

He watched a long moment to be sure their tussle hadn't drawn the attention of the others. Still there was no motion or sound coming from the cavern, so Porter sped over the bleak snowy distance back to the gaping socket-like entrance.

As he neared the cavern's mouth, he drew his guns and slowed his pace. There was no longer a sacred fire burning nor any other sound. Porter crept through the entrance. Bloody drag marks went from the mouth to the cliff-face. The dead, including the old man, had been drug out and tossed over the side of the cliff. Porter would give the old man a respectable ceremony and internment once the matter at hand was dealt with.

The cave den was ransacked. Clearly the marauders had been looking for something and they found it. The deerskin beside the cairn was lying open and the idol was missing. The once sealed doorway was broken open, the stones and mortar cast aside.

Porter approached the doorway and looked into the stygian darkness. A fetid, disagreeable, reptilian smell slithered out. It was overwhelming. Tracks in the dust showed that the men had ventured inside and followed the tunnel into the waiting abyss.

Whatever these men hoped to accomplish was demonic. They had killed the innocent old man for it and would have killed Porter had they been able too. Porter resolved that while he wasn't about to become the keeper of the sacred fire, he sure wasn't going to let these servants of evil get away with disrespecting it. He stepped through the threshold.

Inside it was black as pitch and Porter couldn't see his hand in front of his face. The air however was hot, fetid and uncomfortable, almost as if something was breathing directly in front of his face. He stepped careful and felt his way along the gloom. The tunnel abruptly sloped downward and no hand holds were readily apparent.

He had to turn back.

The light of day beckoned somewhere far behind; it seemed a mile away and even with that guide Porter tripped a number of times on invisible stones and once, something else that moved beneath his boot. Whatever it was clawed at his foot but could do nothing against the thick ox hide and moved on.

Back in the original chamber Porter found a wand of sage and the sacred pipe that the old man had smoked. By fashioning a smoldering wand of sage to the bowl of the pipe and blowing when needed, he was able to fashion a dim orange light. He wanted to keep it dim so that his lighted approach wouldn't give himself away to the servants of Coatlicue.

With the dim orange glow, Porter carefully watched his steps. Whatever it was he had stepped on a few moments before was gone now. He wondered if it had been a hand or foot of one of the servants of Coatlicue but if that had been the case surely they would have ambushed him by now. It must have been an animal, but what kind could have lurked in this perpetual darkness?

Porter went beyond his initial exploration until he came to a fork in the passage. He decided to go left—as that was the direction the boot prints in the dust lead—and the tunnel sloped downward for some distance. His pipe lamp's glow cast shadows but the light was soon swallowed by the hellish black. Searching for handholds, Porter slowed and gingerly made his way down the tunnel. Small lumps in the rock gave slim purchase and he continued down for some time. Then it ended.

His makeshift lamp revealed a sudden drop off with no visible bottom. Listening brought no answer either. He concluded he had been wrong about the direction the servants of Coatlicue had gone, and made his way back up and soon found an off shoot tunnel that veered off to the left. It had been invisible coming down from the top and Porter couldn't have seen it on his original pass. Scuffs upon the stone revealed that indeed men had passed this way. But how long ago? Porter wasn't sure.

He followed this second route for only ten feet before a hole met him. It cut straight down to unknown depths. There was a narrow ledge going round it, but Porter felt it was too narrow. Being that it was only a four-foot jump across, Porter leapt. Passing the deep defile, the tunnel remained horizontal and made for easier travel, but it also had dozens of abrupt nooks and hollows. Lurking shadows made Porter constantly look over his shoulder expecting an attack at any moment. There were too many places to hide, too many eyes he felt rather than actually saw watching him.

Sweat dripped from his face and the foul air was stifling. There was no sound but the beating of his own heart and once he confused the sound for that of a kettle drum. The long tunnel ended with a cave in of boulders.

Determining he had made a circuit of the entire tunnel and yet found nothing, he went back the way he had come. The initial tracks had been lost on the stone floor and he knew which way to return to the surface but not to pursue his enemies. Deciding he had to carefully watch his back trail just as he did on the slanted route for the sake of yet another hidden passage, he blew into his pipe lamp for the best glow possible to see the telltale scuffs of dust marking human passage. Sure enough, almost back to the defile he had to leap over and there was another twisted back passage defying his sight to find it.

This way also had a hole but it was only about five feet deep. Dropping down in, Porter saw that it continued much like the one above and so he journeyed on, hoping to spy tracks in the dust.

After another short distance, he found the tunnel again had a hole this time almost ten feet but this was easily clambered down as the stones themselves remained uneven enough as to form a natural ladder of sorts. Then it pancaked out to just a little over a foot and a half high and Porter was forced to crawl on his belly for some twenty feet.

It was midway thru that Porter came face to face with a sister of what he suspected he had stepped upon earlier. The rattle was shaking like a Mexican maraca while the wedge shaped head of the rattlesnake was swaying back and forth yet looking him dead in the eye. It was a big one, maybe six or seven feet long. Its tongue flashed out tasting the air. Porter stared at it right back, frozen as the ice above ground.

Unsure how to break the standoff without giving his position away with gunfire, Porter blew into his pipe lamp flaring a bit of flame and heat into the rattlers face.

It slithered past him, otherwise heedless.

Once he was sure the snake had gone its own way, Porter continued his crawl to where the passage opened up. There were lights here and there, torches crackling venomous orange light while belching hellish black smoke. A chanting was droning from somewhere unseen yet none too far off accompanied by the relentless throb of a skin drum.

Porter got up and dusted himself off, wary to watch for more rattlers. There was enough dim light now that he extinguished his own lamp and put it into his pocket for later. He guessed he was close to only having enough fuel for his return journey anyhow.

Here the cavern roof raised up and was almost lost in its cathedral like loftiness. Pillars of living rock, stalactites and stalagmites met in twain touching the floor. Porter looked about in wonder. The torches left by the wayside led toward yet another even greater chamber. Beyond that threshold, weird greenish light reflected upon a black sea of infinity. He couldn't tell what gave off that unusual light but he was sure that there was a great underground lake beneath the old man's sacred hill!

Cautiously passing from one great chamber to another, Porter marveled at the scope of this amazing sight. But any amount of wonder was dimmed by the awful glimpse of the servants of Coatlicue and their blasphemous ceremony.

The high priest, the one the old man had named Ichtaca Eztli, the Blood Brujo, was the source of the chanting. Beside him, two kneeling warriors drummed with bare hands, keeping a primal rhythmic beat. At least six or seven warriors stood sentinel-like nearby. They were almost black in the shadows, so outlined by both the guttering torch light and the bright illumination from the idol of Coatlicue.

The idol was operating just like the old man had shown Porter, it was activated and giving off the most intense yet eerie green light he had ever beheld. It sat upon a short pillar and shone upon a vast section of the domelike cavern. It almost seemed to glow brighter in time with the throb of the drum, waxing and waning to the terrible beat.

A woman's sudden scream woke Porter from the horror of the pounding drums.

5. The Purloined Princess

On the other side of the chanting Blood Brujo, stood a large rectangular altar of cyclopean stone and upon that lay an Indian maiden, writhing in palpable fear. Her hands and feet were bound to the altar by some means Porter could not yet ascertain. Her back arched as her cries of terror and pain created a horrifying counter-measure to the Blood Brujo's droning chant. Just beyond the altar a forbidding precipice waited. Dark gulfs which could not be plumbed by the idols intense glow lapped at the shore of eerie light.

Porter made his way closer, stepping ever so carefully, wary that one of the warriors might sense his presence.

The maiden wailed aloud again as the Blood Brujo increased his own voice in a majestic yet terrible fervor.

Porter thought that over the din of the chant, the wails and the drums, he could hear something stirring within that awful precipice. Had the old man been right? Were there really Blood Gods sleeping here? If so, this sound and fury would surely wake them.

One way or another, he was gonna stop this abomination.

Porter stalked up behind the furthermost warrior and slammed the knife handle down on his head, cracking his skull. He caught the warrior as he crumpled and laid him down beside a boulder, hoping none would look back and notice. Regardless he had to give himself better odds before letting them all know he was there.

The drum beat boomed throughout the cavern and a sickening rumble answered back, echoing off the distant walls from across the black lake.

Creeping up beside the next warrior would be riskier, this one wasn't that far from the next man beside him and the odds of one or the other noticing Porter would be high. But he would gamble on taking them both out quick.

The Blood Brujo's chant grew louder and wilder as did the drums and shimmering idol. Some strange thing gasped from below in the unknowable pit and Porter's hackles washed over him in a tide of both awe and disgust.

He had to move as swiftly as he ever had in his life. He was lightning, he was the son of thunder, he had to be.

Porter slammed the handle of the knife on the back of the warrior's skull, just as the other turned around shouting warning to his companions. The servant of Coatlicue launched himself at Porter with his own blade high like a scorpion's stinger.

The Blood Brujo halted his dirge in angered shock. He commanded his men to respond.

Porter caught the leaping attack and hammered the warrior into a stalagmite, and heard the man's spine crunch against the primeval pillar like a dry log splitting. He drew his Dragoon and shot the two closest attackers. They collapsed with savage cries escaping their lips. The others swiftly retreated into the shadows like roaches.

The drums and chant were silenced but a dull vibrating echo still sounded throughout the magnificent chamber. First sounding like it was above, then behind and then below.

Porter moved cautiously toward the unholy altar. The maiden was silent and watched Porter expectantly with fearful eyes. He held one hand up to try and make her understand that he was there to help while also keeping his Dragoon at the ready for the attack that would surely come from the remaining servants of Coatlicue. He was surprised in that she didn't quite look like Paiute as he had expected, but instead resembled the tall litheness of the foreign Mexica Indians; granting too that she was also a beautiful maiden.

"It's all right," he said. "I'm here now. I wish you could understand me. I'm gonna get you out of this."

He waved the pistol about as the sound of a rock fell somewhere behind him, slowly chipping and rattling over the smooth stone floor.

Nothing was there.

Shadows warped and retreated somewhere beyond his range of vision. The closer Porter got to the altar and the closer he got to the idol the more he was blinded from seeing what was behind him.

The maiden suddenly gasped.

A warrior charged from the black with a ghastly bone tomahawk raised at Porter's head. The Dragoon blasted taking the warrior in the chest but another charged from the other side.

The servant of Coatlicue took Porter to the ground, trying to bash his brains in with a stone. Porter lost his grip on the Dragoon but not the sacrificial knife. He stuck the attacker in the ribs and ripped out. The obsidian blade cut through flesh and bone and even the jaguar skin tunic of the warrior like it was feasting on him. The warrior gave a weak cry, as he lost all breath.

Porter grasped his Dragoon and fired a warning shot at a retreating shadow. A shriek told him he had at least wounded his opponent. Porter gauged there were at least three or four more of the servants of Coatlicue hidden in the inky blackness. He kept his back toward the altar and watched.

The vibrating hiss was stronger now though Porter couldn't determine what was causing it. An earthquake?

Porter backed into the altar and felt the maiden struggling against her bindings. He turned to look at her saying, "You can't understand me, but I'm here to help."

"I can understand you. We must hurry and escape this chamber," she said, urgently.

Porter was surprised, "You speak English?"

"Cut me loose!" she insisted, holding her bindings toward him as far as she could manage.

The binding appeared to be snakeskin of some sort and Porter was perplexed as to how such a reptilian rope could have been fashioned, but his sacrificial dagger cut through them like nothing. "What's your name?"

"Call me Waving Grass."

"I'm Porter."

"Behind you!" she shouted.

Porter turned with the Dragoon and knife just in time to face three foes.

His first shot knocked one away, but the next pull of the trigger was a disheartening click!

Both warriors were upon him in an instant and he bashed one in the face with the empty pistol while thrusting the knife at the other. He caught the one in the face with the muzzle of the Dragoon but the other dodged the blade.

The one with the bashed face came back and struck Porter with his war club, but it was a glancing blow as the other warrior had caught Porter in an arm bar and was trying to stick him with his own knife.

Wheeling about, Porter slammed the warrior who trapped his arm against the stone altar and beat his face to a pulp against the corner stones. He lost the knife however and it went flying away into the shadows. Waving Grass disappeared after it.

An arrow skittered across the altar, letting all three men know that the Blood Brujo didn't value any of their lives, so intent was he in ending Porter's.

One of the warriors shouted something to the darkness.

Porter kicked the shouting one and let fly a crunching blow into the face of the other.

The kicked warrior raised his war club and was about to dash Porters brains in when he fell back in an awful gasp.

Waving Grass stuck him with Porter's lost knife. "We have to get out now!" she cried.

Another arrow skittered across the stones nearby having just barely missed. They each took shelter behind the altar.

The booming voice of the Blood Brujo taunted them.

"What the hell did he just call me?" asked Porter, as he traded the cylinders in his Dragoon.

"He isn't calling to us. He is trying to awaken the gods in darkness. The Blood Gods of the Mexica," she said.

"Well, thanks for your help. That warrior would have stuck me with his club if it weren't for you."

She nodded. "How did you find me?"

Porter finished loading and glanced around the side of the altar. "I've been in the wrong place at the wrong time for the last few days. It just keeps getting better and better. Good luck for you I suppose."

"We can't stay here," she urged.

"I know but we can't have you getting stuck by one of his arrows."

"Better that than what is waking behind us," she said, looking back fearfully.

Porter took a moment to glance back at the precipice. He couldn't see anything down there but the vague twisting movement of shadows but clearly that was where the rumbling, buzzing, hissing sound came from. Something strange and unknowable was writhing down there and it seemed to be rising.

"If we stay here, it will devour us," she said, standing up to run.

Porter shouted, "Hold on, least let me cover you!" He fired a couple of blind shots in the direction he thought the arrows had come from.

He must have guessed wrong because one flew perilously close to him, he felt the wind of it part his long wild hair. Waving Grass ducked back down behind the pillar of the idol.

"Do you know anything about all this?" Porter asked her.

She nodded. "Some of what they said on the journey here. Some my fathers of old have spoken of."

That was curious to Porter, he hadn't thought yet about their incredible journey just to get her and perform the ritual he had interrupted. He spoke softly now, hoping she would barely hear him above the rising hissing sound. "Y

"You hold tight, I'm gonna shoot that idol and see if I can't bring back the darkness that is only helping him and hurting us."

She had been keeping a lookout and only half listening to his words, but when his suggestion dawned on her, she turned and cried out, "NO!"

But it was too late. Porter squeezed off a shot at almost point blank and hit the idol dead center.

Time seemed to stop for a moment as Porter looked at the shock and terror on her face. He could swear he actually saw the bullet hit the illuminated jade idol and suddenly fracture like a spider's web across a mirror.

Blooming like the noon day sun, a gargantuan bright explosion followed by a crackle of electricity radiated outward from the idol as it vanished in a million tiny shards. A gust of wind slapped Porter and Waving Grass end over end and they found themselves on the edge of the precipice, though they still could not see into it as the light had been snuffed out save for a few guttering torches some distance away.

That weak orange light flitted as if between great fingers of shadow barely reached them but the intense hissing was almost right at their feet. Without being able to have any sight of the precipice, Porter could sense the deep gulf behind him, like the very air was being sucked downward.

Porter helped Waving Grass to her feet. "Sorry, bout that. I just wanted to even the odds," he said.

She was sobbing, trembling, and shaking her head, "The Blood Gods are awake."

6. The Blood God Wakes

Something unseen yet big around as his arm, moved beside Porters left foot. He kicked it away. "Let's get moving then. We have some concealment now if not cover."

He had to pull Waving Grass along as the explosion had almost sapped her will and sense. They had only taken a few steps when Porter's cat like reflexes caught the arc of a blade aimed at his throat.

Dodging back, the invisible obsidian blade stole a button from his collar. The Blood Brujo snarled in maddening anger at having missed.

Porter's hand shot up and he caught the return swing of the knife and racked the priests arm back, before slamming him against the altar. He pounded the hand against the multi-angled stones until the knife dropped from the wicked priests grasp.

But the priest had a few tricks of his own. He swept his leg out and dropped Porter against the altar so he could slither out of his hold. He then blew a handful of some mystic dust into Porters face.

As dark as it was, Porter was now completely blind. His senses reeled with the loss of sight, the stink of reptiles and the deafening sound of echoing hisses and rattles. His Dragoon was knocked from his hand.

The Blood Brujo struck again and again, hammering blow upon blow against Porter, as he twisted serpentine, attacking from a new angle at every moment. Finding a tomahawk from one of his fallen warriors, the Brujo picked up the deadly weapon and raised it for a death blow.

Porter, blinking madly, prayed in this most dire hour and it was answered.

Shaking off her dazed fear, Waving Grass, plunged the sacrificial knife into the Blood Brujo's back all the way to the hilt.

Stricken, the dark priest wheeled, slapping her away, sputtering some Aztec curse but he could not reach the knife handle halfway down his back.

Porter stumbled and caught hold of the Brujo's cloak and yanked him down. Still blinking and with tears running down his face, Porter picked him up again only to punch him, sending the priest flying across the altar.

Tears fell like rain and sight had almost returned. He felt the gentle hand of Waving Grass, the purloined princess, at least that's what he now thought of her. "You royally saved my rump, Sister."

She helped him stand, guiding him away from the altar. "We must hurry," she said.

"Yeah, I'm coming."

Something grabbed Porter's right foot and pulled.

Turning about, terribly off balance, Porter could barely see the dark shape of the Blood Brujo. The wretched priest wasn't out of this fight yet. He twisted Porter's foot forcing the half-blind gunman off

28

balance.

Despite Waving Grass holding him with her left shoulder, Porter went down as the Blood Brujo shot up.

Leering with a broken face, the Blood Brujo drew a copper knife from his belt and slashed at Waving Grass like he was swatting flies.

Porter kicked him from the ground and the Brujo went staggering back.

Waving Grass screamed, this time in rage, a particularly dire curse.

Porter found the Dragoon in the dust, he smiled wickedly and pointed at the shadow he thought was the Brujo. He faltered suddenly, he couldn't take a chance of accidentally hitting Waving Grass. Unable to get a clear shot yet because of his watering eyes, Porter struggled to his feet, ready for his opponent. It was hard enough for Porter to see him in the dim light but the clotted blood color of the dark priest's cloak helped him remain invisible.

The hissing, buzzing sound in the pit grew louder, faster.

"We must flee!" shouted Waving Grass.

"Hang on," gasped Porter, "I can't leave that polecat behind us. Gotta finish this."

The Blood Brujo lunged out of the spider-haunted gloom at Porter with his copper knife.

Porter batted the blade aside and fired, narrowly missing his target. The Blood Brujo knocked his shoulder into Porter and he lost the Dragoon again. No knife or gun stood between them any longer.

Tumbling across the altar, they rolled and gained their feet only to batter each other again.

"The Blood God wakes!" shouted Waving Grass.

But Porter and the Blood Brujo couldn't hear her, they were grappling against one another.

Struggling to the far side of the altar, Porter sensed they had slipped closer to the precipice. The sound of turmoil within was growing. Darkness swirled over itself, black on black, shadow melting into shadow.

Straining against one another, the two men were matched like titans on the brink, neither yet overpowering the other. The Brujo's right palm crept over Porter's face in a vain attempt to tear out his eyes. Porter's hand in turn found the stuck sacrificial blade in the Brujo's back.

Porter twisted and ripped it out.

The Brujo screamed and his hands shot away from his body, then cringed like claws. He fell backward, yet grasped Porter as he did so, pulling the gunman into the abyss after him.

Porter felt the sudden absence of earth. He was enveloped by flowing darkness. Falling into the black.

The Brujo screamed shrilly below and was silenced by a soft thud and then a sickening crunch. The terrible echoing song of rattles grew louder.

Desperate hands reached and Porter caught the lip and strained to hold on, let alone climb. His handhold broke and crumbled. He caught another but was slipping ever closer to the yawning black doom below. The hissing, the buzzing, the very sound of the earth vibrating, rattled his teeth.

The stone lip in his right hand puckered and broke free in a kiss of death. The fraction of a second that Porter was falling seemed a cruel eternity.

"I've got you!" Waving Grass caught his hand, granting just enough time for Porter to kick his feet and find purchase on the precipice. He struggled to climb as she yanked him upward. Just over the rim and something tugged at his heel. It slipped off and he looked back into the pit.

It was rising, or they were rising, he couldn't be sure. There was too much movement, variations of crisscrossing shadows swarming over the outline of a massive bulk. Larger than an ox, larger than a wagon the thing rose up. Rattles and hissing and groaning's from more than a thousand fanged mouths.

Porter could never be sure of what he saw within that maddening gloom, it had the appearance of a great ball of rattlesnakes entwined as all snakes do for the winter but also it had the outline of a man or woman. As if there was gigantic person made of snakes. In just the right—or wrong—light it almost looked as if it had two heads and was looking right at him. Then the rising pile collapsed and the snakes slithered forward in droves.

What he had thought might have been the double heads of a giant were instead the heads of two giant rattlesnakes, big around as tree trunks.

"Let's go!" Porter shouted, as he picked up his Dragoon and the

30

gold handled sacrificial knife.

Waving Grass said, "I told you the legends were true."

He tugged at her, directing her to run with him back the way he had come into the chamber of horrors.

A colossal hiss and the pile of snakes seemed to be tumbling if not slithering after them all at once.

Porter wasn't sure what was worse, not being able to see them very well in the gloom of the pit, or being able to see them now that they had run as far as the next chamber where the guttering torches remained. He gathered up as many of the torches as he could.

There were thousands of rattlesnakes, but they weren't acting natural, they were entwined with one another, moving together almost like they were one giant snake.

Porter and Waving Grass reached the end of the open chamber. He handed her a torch saying, "Crawl thru until you get to a tunnel like a chimney going up! I'll be right behind you!" He handed her a torch and ushered her on.

Facing the oncoming snakes, he fired his Dragoon a few times into the serpentine morass. But there was no discernable effect. The flood of rattlesnakes would soon drown him in their dripping venom.

7. Coils of the Serpent

Waving Grass crawled ahead and Porter was right behind, albeit a bit slower as he was scooting three torches behind himself in a desperate plan to hold off the snakes.

The wedge-shaped heads hissed and snapped and struck. Porter wasn't sure himself how the foremost rattlers had missed him.

Porter reached the chimney passage, he left the three torches to defend his position and started climbing up. He knew the rattlers could maneuver up it themselves, he just hoped he was faster than they were along with the three torches holding them at bay for just a bit.

He was dependent on Waving Grass's torch for light and hoped she didn't get too far ahead of him when she reached the top. She waited.

"I don't remember which way they brought me down," she said.

"This way, come on," said Porter, as he cast a look at the shaft. The hissing and rattling were rising albeit slower than the initial slithering charge but he knew the snakes would be at their heels in a moment. Searching the gloom for a moment, Porter saw a few good sized boulders. It would be all he could do to move them but it might be their only chance. "Here," he called to Waving Grass.

Together, they rolled and shoved a massive stove into the chimney. It fell halfway, lodging tight and likely crushing a few reptiles with it. They gathered a few more loose stones and threw those in to help plug the open spots. Then they found a larger stone and moved it over the top.

"Let's get going, before any small ones get out."

Porter led the way and soon enough they were almost back to original defile that he crossed. Porter jumped first then took the torch and let Waving Grass jump. They moved around the edge of the deep slanted tunnel when they each heard a buzzing rattling, deep from down in the black.

"I didn't see that bottom to that when I got here but I think I know where it leads to now. Move!"

Porter helped Waving Grass up the steep slope. A reverberating hiss had him look back. Waving his torch, Porter saw the dim flame light catch the yellow around the black slits on a gigantic set of eyes that slithered back and forth up the incline. He pulled the Dragoon and let loose a few deafening shots but the monster snake didn't slow down at all.

Just a few paces above Porter, Waving Grass had her feet braced up against a massive stone. She was pushing as hard as she could. Porter joined her and together just as the snake was a few paces from them, the boulder went free, tumbling down at an awful crooked pace.

It caught the snake god full in the mouth and the monster fell back away into the dark.

They hurried the rest of the way out and came to the original cavern entrance. Soon as they passed through, Porter started trying to light a fire.

Waving Grass, gathered fuel from around the inside and the smoke started to tickle into flames just as a mess of regular size rattlers started through the passage. They weren't nearly so difficult to manage but it was unnerving. They either shot the serpents or flung them out into the snow outside the entrance.

Between dealing with the dozen or more rattlers, Porter got the fire roaring in front of the serpent's doorway. No more snakes came, and there was certainly no sign of the giant ones.

Shadows appeared at the door. Two servants of Coatlicue. They pointed their rifles at Porter and Waving Grass, barking orders.

"They say to drop your gun belt and get against the far wall," said Waving Grass.

Porter slowly undid his belt and cast it at their feet. He was ready to lunge soon as one of them leaned down to pick it up and the other took his eyes off him for even a second. But that chance never came, they ignored the gun-belt and shouted at Waving Grass.

She reluctantly gathered snow from outside the cave mouth.

"What are you doing?" asked Porter. The servants of Coatlicue shouted at him.

"They said for you to be quiet. They asked where their master is. I told them he is below. They told me to put the fire out or they will kill us."

"We put that out and we're all dead," argued Porter.

One of the servants of Coatlicue approached and struck Porter with his rifle butt and said, "I speak 'Mericat. I know the white talk good. I tell you the source of all life will die if we don't feed the gods blood. It must be done."

"Lemme guess who's blood you're gonna feed 'em."

The servant of Coatlicue said nothing but gave a cruel smile and nodded at Porter.

Waving Grass made eye contact with Porter then dumped an armful of snow in the fire and it sizzled and steamed in a great splash.

Each of them lunged at their captor's. Porter knocked the one that could speak English into the dying fire and at the serpent's doorway. The man shot up screaming in pain from the steam burns and coals and was further afflicted with waiting snake bites from the other side of the doorway. He stood up but fell over again.

Waving Grass grabbed the rifle barrel of the other. It went off as they wrestled for it but since it was a single shot Remington, it could be dealt with.

Porter tackled the servant of Coatlicue after he shoved Waving

Grass aside, and they rolled outside the cave mouth through the snow, sliding down the hillside at a greater rate than anyone would have guessed.

The sun was beaming and snow melted just enough for the ground to be wet and slick.

Waving Grass grabbed Porter's Dragoon and raced outside after them.

The short-lived slide down the hillside came to an abrupt stop at a boulder and Porter throttled the servant of Coatlicue. He looked back up the hillside and shouted at Waving Grass, "Get away from that cave, Sister!"

She turned to see the head of the second of the two giant rattle snakes, gingerly flicking its tongue in the outside air. Its massive wedge-shaped head was bigger than a horses. It slithered through the breach and outside into the sunlight and gleaming snow.

Waving Grass faced it but slowly backed away. She tossed the Dragoon to Porter behind her. He snatched it up.

The giant snake watched her intently. It started to move forward, its head higher than Waving Grass was tall.

Three quick shots took it in the head or thereabouts, then Porter had to reload a cylinder. "Move it, Sister! Off the cliff! Jump! There's snow!"

Waving Grass understood and ran to the cliff face on the leeward side. The great snake followed her swift as the wind.

She leapt, arms wide as if she could take flight.

The snake god's mouth opened wide, its fangs more than a foot long extended, and struck—and missed Waving Grass by a hair's breadth.

She hit the snow twenty feet below and lay still. The snake god pondered a moment if it should follow down into the snow or back toward the man who was getting ready to shoot at it again?

Then it saw the horses.

Slithering through the snow it left a trail like a ship's wake going over the sparkling white. The horses had been tied up to the trees, some might have been hobbled, Porter wasn't sure, but they saw the giant snake coming and screamed trying to break their tethers. It wasn't enough. The monster struck. It bit and slammed with its tail and destroyed them.

Porter went up the hill but watched in horrid fascination as the snake god swallowed one of the animals whole. Its belly swelled and now it left an even wider trail through the snow.

Waving Grass stood up out of the snow and signaled to Porter.

He kept his hand low, signaling her back to remain where she was, relatively out of sight. The wind shifted and blew from Porter toward the great rattler.

The snake god swung its colossal head back and watched Porter standing halfway up the hill.

Its massive tail curled closer to itself and Porter could not count the rattles at the end. It seemed there were dozens in great folds of its bone-like material. This monster must be hundreds of years old.

He had no more cap and balls, no more cylinders, he had nothing anymore but the sacrificial knife. But he would not go down without a fight. Porter clutched the blade, figuring he would tear out the monster's insides if he was swallowed whole like the horses.

The snake slithered closer, covering yards in seconds despite its huge bulk. It came right up on Porter eyeing him like dessert.

Porter stared back, hard and sharp as the obsidian in his hand.

The snake god's tail slipped around behind Porter. There would be no running away, no place to hide, no place to flee. He was trapped but good.

Porter didn't have a lot of options but he would never give up. He fingered the obsidian blade and backed away until he was bumping into the tail. The snake readjusted a few times but Porter moved with it. Once the tail bumped him purposely in an attempt to make him stumble but he kept his footing.

"Well, come on! Let's throw down!" Porter shouted.

Just past the myriad rattles the tail coiled about Porter holding him fast. Only his arms were free. Then it struck, the massive fangs dripping venom. Porter did his damndest to bring the blade up and position himself between the spear-like fangs.

The two fangs went either side of his body but the outstretched right arm with the sacrificial knife stabbed into the roof of the snake god's mouth. It drew back in an instant with the knife still stuck to the top of its palette. Flailing wildly, the tail whipped up and down across the snows, slamming down with enough force to smash trees to kindling. It coiled and knotted, distended and spat. Porter dodged and rolled in a superhuman effort to evade the maddened reptile. The tail whomped down a number of times almost crushing him but for rolling through the snow inches away just in time.

Waving Grass called trying to distract the snake god but it was too disturbed and in pain to pay any attention.

As the snake convulsed in an effort to be rid of its insufferable thorn, Porter escaped and ranged back toward Waving Grass and the cave. "Did any horses make it?"

She shook her head, saying, "Maybe, but if they didn't get bitten they are far away."

"We can't stay here, we better head off after them." Porter motioned back to the cave, "We can look for any supplies the old man left and start hunting then."

"What about the snakes?"

"I think we killed one with that boulder, but ain't nothing more I can do about that other one there."

The snake god was slowly making its way down the valley in terrible writhing motions.

"I don't want to stay here but I don't want to go back in there," she said.

Porter breathed aloud. "Then wait here while I gather what I can," he said, in a huff. He trudged back up the hill, slipping once or twice on the melty slick hillside. Once inside the cavern, he found a store of jerky and a few more caps and balls and one full cylinder he must have dropped in any number of the melee's encountered. One of the Remington rifles was still good so he took that and searched one of the recently dead servants of Coatlicue for more ammunition.

Porter was aghast at what he found. The man had disintegrating blackened flesh from the terrible snake venom. The big one must have bit him as it exited the tunnel. He was glad now that Waving Grass didn't have to see this.

Stepping outside he worried for a moment. Two dozen Indian warriors on horseback were at the bottom of the hill speaking with Waving Grass. The most troublesome thing was they appeared to be dressed similar enough to the servants of Coatlicue with bright feathers, jaguar skins and copper ornaments. Why weren't they attacking? At least they didn't seem to be wearing the sinister war paint that the servants of Coatlicue had.

She saw Porter and motioned for him to come down and that everything was all right.

He slipped down the hillside to be by her side, rather reluctantly.

She spoke rapidly in Uto-Aztecan to the Chief, then she turned to Porter. "Porter, this is Amoxtli. He is my brother."

"Brother?"

She nodded. "I was stolen when I was a girl by Mescalero Apache and sold as a slave. I learned English from a white woman who was also a slave. When Ichtaca Eztli came north to wake the Blood Gods, he recognized me in the city of Avanyu. He bought me so I could be used as a sacrifice here. I told my brother of your bravery and facing down Ichtaca Eztli and the servants of Coatlicue."

The brother nodded to Porter and beat his chest.

"That explains how well you can speak but now what? Will they give me a horse?"

The brother understood well enough and shouted for a someone to bring Porter and Waving Grass a horse. He spoke quickly and fiercely to Waving Grass and she reluctantly nodded.

"What is it now?"

She said, "We must follow the snake god and try to redeem it and return it to the cave."

Porter laughed out loud. "That ain't gonna happen. Why do they wanna do that?"

The brother looked incensed and Waving Grass said, "The snake god is one of the most powerful gods of my people. If we can contain it, we can grow in power. We don't want it to go back to the ruins of Texocanocan and bring back the other Blood Gods. There are too many. It took Madoc years to defeat and banish them."

"I've heard that story before, but I still don't see how it can be done."

"We must try."

Porter rubbed at his forehead and nodded with a big sigh. "All right. I'm with you."

Waving Grass repeated that for her brother and he and the other braves gave a mighty war whoop and together raced their horses after the wide trail of the snake god.

8. People of the Snake

Porter stared a moment at the bizarre zig-zag trail. It almost looked like someone had paddled a canoe over the snows, such was the bizarre track. The massive snake had made good time, even if it was writhing in crazed pain at the tiny blade affixed to its mouth.

Waving Grass, her brother and her people were hardy and though they came from a southern clime they were relentless in their pursuit of the snake god.

They stopped a babbling creek to water their horses and give them a much needed rest.

"So if you're Mexica, what is your real name?" Porter asked.

Waving Grass said, "My birth name was Coaxoch, it means Serpent Flower as I am the princess of my peoples. But the Mescalero's and then my masters in Avanyu called me Waving Grass. I never told anyone that I was the heir of Moctezuma. But Ichtaca Eztli, he recognized me and took it as sign that he was favored by the Blood Gods to find me after so many years, and he said that my blood would be spilt to awaken the new dawn of the Blood Gods."

Porter rubbed at his beard, "All that makes sense enough to me, I suppose, but what are we gonna do when we catch up to the giant snake?"

"We must coax it to return with us. To sleep and let that dark red day come in the end of times, not now. If we have the god contained, we keep its power with us. My people will thrive again. We can drive the Spanish out of our homeland. It will be ours again."

Porter shook his head. "It's just a snake, the biggest damn snake in all of creation but it's just a snake. It's no god."

Waving Grass's face darkened and she snarled, "Don't speak such things. You whites cannot understand our way. I shouldn't have told you anything."

"It's no god," said Porter. "Take my word for it."

She shook her head. "You have your beliefs. You have your god. I have mine."

"We aren't gonna talk a snake into nothing but killing."

Her brother Amoxtli rode up beside them and said what

amounted to 'what's wrong' and 'we need to hurry'. Waving Grass told him something that had him frown at Porter.

Waving Grass mounted her horse, saying, "You have wrestled with the gods. You have seen Coatlicue face to face down in the underworld. You met her eyes and still you don't *believe*? I *do*. I *know*. If you will not help us, then go back to your lands and your own *gods*."

"Hey," said Porter, "I'm still here to help you. I don't want anything bad to happen, not after what you've already been thru."

She sniffed and rode away followed by her brother and the other People of the Snake. They whooped like mad men as they rode on.

"Horse chips!" snarled Porter, as he mounted his horse and rode after them.

Hours went by and they had not caught up to the monster yet, the one comfort was that it was still moving as the trail through the snows and smashed underbrush was wide as an ox and unmistakable. This wasn't something they couldn't find eventually. This was something that couldn't hide.

As they came down the mountain passes and were entering a lower valley canyon the snows were turning to mud and the creeks would soon converge into a river. Dusk was painting the sky a brilliant scarlet overhead and Porter couldn't help but see it as a bloody sign of what might lay in store for all of them against the snake god.

Damn, even he was starting to think of it as a snake god now.

The two lead trackers for the Snake People proclaimed that it couldn't be that far ahead of them judging by the sign across the creek bed.

"We ought to be cautious going through this canyon. That thing could be around ay one of these blind curves," he said.

"Keep your loud white advice to yourself," said Waving Grass, dismissively, as she urged her horse ahead.

"Women," Port snarled, and kicked his mounts flanks to catch up to the lead.

Tiny tributaries splashed down the canyon walls catching the fading golden sunlight in their descent. Gradually they collected and the creek bed at the bottom was at least ten feet across though none too deep.

Porter had a good idea on round about where they were now and he knew a valley and river weren't that far off, and where the river met the mountains he was pretty sure there would be a Ute village too. "We ought to hurry, I'd rather we find that thing before it finds anyone else."

Waving Grass's brother said something in a derogatory tone and Waving Grass didn't bother to translate it, but glanced apologetically at Porter.

"I got the gist of that one, still we need to hurry and act on whatever it is you think we can do."

Waving Grass gave a shrill cry and kicked her horses flanks again and they raced on following her lead. They splashed through the creek and through the marshy river bottoms and over sandy dune like hillocks. Pines were scattered thick here and there along with a few quaking aspens and willows.

The unmistakable snakes trail weaved through the bottoms like it was on the hunt. The valley opened up here at the base of the mountains and Porter could see and smell the smoke of a village not far to the east. He kicked his horse and raced ahead.

They reached the village taking in the carnage of the snake god attacking the people and horses. Dog's fled, babes cried, and horses screamed as Ute warriors tried to shoot arrows into the monster only to be cast aside like mice. They could not stand against the leviathan.

Porter joined in, firing his six shots from the Dragoon and then reached for the rifle.

"No, we must try to coax it away!" shouted Waving Grass.

"Care to explain how?" shot back Porter. He was angered that the Snake People merely watched the frenzied attack rather than joining with the Utes against the great rattler.

Waving Grass had a faraway look on her face and seemed to Porter that she was listening to someone that wasn't there. "I know my purpose now," she said, serenely as she dismounted from her panting spooked horse. "I was born for this, but did not remember until the gods awoke it inside me. Thank you for sparing me that I might do this duty for my people."

She walked purposefully toward the coiled monster. It sat within a clutch of destroyed teepee's and ruined cook fires. Men and horse were strewn about in reckless abandon. A child cried somewhere, invisible in the gathering gloom.

"Waving Grass, no!" cried Porter, as her ran after her into the camp but her brother and another pair of warriors held him back.

They took his gun belt and knife and cursed in their foreign tongue at his struggles.

Waving Grass strode to the incredible snake god, stripping off her coat and buckskins. With her arms raised to the square on each side, she began a song as enchanting and melancholy as anything Porter had ever heard. The words were lost in the mists of time but sweet as honey and sad as a dying newborn's last cry. Her long black hair was flowing in the wind and somewhere Porter could have sworn he heard pipes playing in rhythm along with her melodious voice.

The snake god's forked tongue flicked out, tasting her scent, feeling her heat. It swayed back and forth in time with her bodily movements. Porter couldn't have guessed whether beauty or the beast was the more hypnotized between the two of them.

Porter ripped free from her brother's hold asking, "What is she doing? What is gonna happen?" And just as quickly the braves took hold of him again.

Amoxtli took a moment to answer, as he was himself transfixed at the spectacle. He stared at Porter and answered in quick staccato verse but not a word of it could Porter understand.

The snake god swayed watching with its great yellow eyes. The long black tongue jetted out and in. Its thick body was breathing in a relaxed manner and Porter wondered if Waving Grass had truly tamed the monster.

Then the rattle thrummed mightily and the snake god's mouth wretched open with a hiss the size of the mountains.

9. God is a Bullet

"Please, take me," cried Waving Grass. "Claim me, I am yours!"

"What the hell?" shouted Porter. "NO! Woman!" Porter tried to break free but Amoxtli and the other braves of the Snake People held him. If he could just extricate himself, he would do something. He didn't know where his guns were any longer but a single shot rifle lay only a few steps away in a splash of river water.

"She must do it! She must sacrifice herself for our people. She knows what she is doing!" said a brave, standing beside Amoxtli.

The great snakes rattle shook beating the strangest dirge, its head rose up even higher, as the tongue flicked in and out.

"Like hell!" Porter struggled and punched and kicked to escape so that he might shoot the monster.

Waving Grass stood before the snake god pleading with it to devour her.

Porter couldn't hear anything as he fought Amoxtli and the other Snake People. Red rage clouded over him in a thunderhead and he put everything he could into the fight. He couldn't let Waving Grass throw her life away to the monster.

The monstrous snake brought its head down to Waving Grass's level, til it was looking her right in the eye and its tongue nearly kissed her face.

"Please," called Waving Grass. "Claim me, I am yours."

Porter knocked the teeth from a brave and kicked another end over end. He took hold of the rifle that lay soaking in the puddle and swung it like a club keeping the men back.

The braves of the Snake People hit their knees in supplication, the one who spoke English crying aloud, "Please, let her sacrifice herself! It is the only way to appease the gods and have them return to us."

Porter ignored them and brought the dripping rifle to bear as he whispered a prayer through gritted teeth that his aim might be true.

"Please, take me," pleaded Waving Grass.

The snake suddenly turned away from her and its great slit of an eye met the gunfighter's. Man and monster looked at one another across the field of ruin, a demon god versus a heroic cowboy king of the earth. Each must have innately known the deadliness of the other and while the snake god could call upon none higher than itself, Porter could. His stare burned like a brand into the snake's soul and the words of his prayer raised like an incense to the heavens.

The snake god's mouth wretched open in a furious hiss.

That's when Porter's eagle eyes caught sight of that sacrificial dagger still stuck to the roof of the snake's mouth. The dagger hung like a black stalactite in its palette.

Porter pulled the trigger and the wet cartridge fizzed in a whispered hush with almost no smoke or flash.

Anyone else might not have even believed that it had fired but it did, the lead ball silently streaking through the night and finally snapping the dagger loose at the hilt. The obsidian blade fell and plunged down the snake's gullet.

Porter could only guess, but it seemed to him that the snake was quite disturbed at that sudden development. Like it was choking. Maybe that sacrificial dagger was cutting up its insides real good.

The massive snake suddenly turned away from Waving Grass and slithered into the river. The banks overflowed with brown murk as the giant slid into the dark waters. It twisted and just before it vanished into the deeps it looked like it went belly up.

Porter wondered. Did God hear his urgent prayer and aid in a silent bullet? The massive reptile vanished into the cold waters just as swiftly as the stars appeared in the sky and then it was gone.

One of the Snake People snatched the rifle away from Porter and shouted unintelligibly.

Waving Grass dropped to the ground, weeping. Porter ignored the Snake Peoples wrath and ran to her side. "The gods have rejected me. They have rejected us. We will fade away," she said, between sobs.

Porter didn't know what to say, what to do. He put his arm on her shoulder but she seemed unaware. Looking to the river there was no trace of the giant snake. The brown waters surged on, heedless of the death and destruction that had so recently taken place upon its shore.

Waving Grass looked to Porter asking, "Why did he reject me? Why wouldn't he take me so I could fulfill my destiny? I was to be the sacrifice. I would have covenanted with the Blood Gods on behalf of my people. Now we shall fade away, never to regain our lands and positions. We have lost all." Tears streamed down her face.

Amoxtli and the other Snake People were on their horses sneering down at Waving Grass. He barked something unkind at Waving Grass and the translator repeated the words in English for Porter's benefit. "You have failed us. The Blood Gods rejected you and now we do as well. Do not come back to Texocanocan. You are not my sister." Amoxtli spat and they rode away vanishing into the darkness.

Porter was confused to say the least. He had saved her from death that she had so freely offered herself up to and was in turn rejected by her own people. None of this was her fault as he could see it. Life sure ain't fair. It seemed a cruel blessing but no one realized he had slain the monster; it hadn't just given up as they all seemed to believe.

"Well, they left us a couple of horses, we best get moving on to a safer campsite," he said, hoping they didn't find the snake god dead downriver and return in anger.

She didn't move. He had to pick her up and put her on a horse as she wasn't about to move on her own volition. Ranging back toward a hollow along the route they had come, he made a campfire.

"Why?" She asked again through the freely flowing tears. "My sacrifice could have saved my people."

Porter scoffed, after all he wasn't the most sensitive of men, though he did always speak the truth. "How? By covenanting with a Blood God? That would have made you the same as that Blood Brujo. No, you gotta make your own way in this world. Struggle that it is."

"I could have saved my people. Now without the snake god to grant us favor, the hard times will just be that much harder."

Porter thought on his own people's trials and tribulations and all they had been through. This life after all wasn't about ease, it was about experience and struggle so that you could appreciate—nay savor the sweet with the sour, know the light from the dark and love from the hate, pleasure and pain but all that came out was, "Awww, don't beat yourself up about it. Sometimes the best you can do in these situations is just survive."

Black Wings in the Moonlight

Dusk revealed uncaring stars as the moon cast its ghostly image upon Old Man River. Bats flitted chasing mosquitoes, as darkness weaved against the swaying shoreline. The riverboat, *Golden Phoenix*, chugged upriver as if chasing the silvery moon light.

At the bow stood a taciturn, broad shouldered man with long dark hair erupting out from under his slouch hat. A black beard covered his face, but there were a number of laugh lines about his pale blue eyes. He had a brace of pistols leering from his vest as well as a bowie knife upon his belt. Holding a long hemp rope, he watched the shrouded eastern shore with interest until one of the crewmen, a steward, gave warning.

"It's not safe to be out at night on this stretch of the river, Sir." With eyes wide and fearful, the steward glanced up in the star flecked night rather than at the shoreline. "We'll be coming up on the bluffs soon and I've already heard tell that two dozen men have been taken by the monster bird, the Piasa."

The long haired stranger grunted, "Piasa, huh? Well, that's why I'm here."

"You must be Mr. Porter then."

"That's right," answered the long haired man, as he tied one end of the rope to the iron riggings that were themselves stoutly anchored to the deck. "Captain Jack asked for my help."

"I'm sorry sir. Thought you would be taller. I mean . . . after some of the stories I've heard."

Porter either chuckled or growled at that, it was hard to tell.

The steward watched the gathering gloom above saying, "Some of those lost were hunting for the Piasa too. They had buffalo guns and one brought a whaling harpoon. Have you got a harpoon to go with that rope?"

"Nope."

The steward wrinkled his curious brow as Porter finished a massive knot and tested it by pulling his full body weight against it. "Excuse me, but what do you plan on doing against the Piasa? It's a bloodthirsty beast, Sir. Swoops in and devours men alive. Plenty have tried to shoot it. But it has slain them all. The Governor even said we may have to limit river traffic to daylight only when the monster don't come out."

Porter fashioned a noose with the opposite end of the rope, just listening and nodding.

"The Indians say this is a monster that goes back to the old times. That it's been gone for centuries but just come back lately. But I say what if the monster bird has a clutch of eggs? What then? Limiting river traffic won't stop a pack of starving thunder birds."

"Thunder bird's?" questioned Porter.

"That's what old chief Deecoodah calls it. The thunder bird that drives the storm. But everyone else calls it the Piasa, the bird that devours men."

Porter nodded and coiled his rope. "Deecoodah said that?"

"Yeah, he did. You mind telling me why you're so darn light-hearted about this? You stay out here tonight and you're gonna die. What can any man do against a monster bird that bullets can't harm and with a twenty-foot wingspan?"

"So you've seen it?"

"No, I haven't. But Kofford told me, he seen it not two weeks ago aboard the *Samaritan*, when it ate the Johnson brothers."

Porter guffawed, "You know Kofford is the biggest liar and drunk

46

on the river."

"I can't deny that, Kofford is a thief and a cheat, but them Johnson's is dead and the Piasa is what ate 'em."

Stretching this way and that, Porter said, "I've heard tell the Piasa has a ten-foot wingspan upwards to fifty feet. Seems some people just aren't accurate witnesses. I suspect closer to ten and the thing scares men into jumping in the river, where they drown."

The steward shook his head fiercely, "No sir, Billy Barnett was torn apart and everyone knows that. The Piasa ate 'em up and spit out the mean indigestible parts."

"Yep, that would've been most of Billy alright."

The steward looked warily over his shoulder to the comfort and protection of the wheelhouse. "You sure I can't convince you to come inside for the night? Your trap could work without you, couldn't it?" He gestured at the rope.

"Nope."

The steward shook his head, "I heard a lot of wild stories about you Mr. Porter, but this seems crazy. Why you doing this? The glory? Think you can succeed where everyone else has failed? You think you're better than all those others that died trying?"

Porter wheeled on him, "You wanna know why? Not for them that died trying to kill it. But for those women and kids that never saw it coming. The ones that had no chance, that's why."

The steward tipped his cap and made the sign of the cross at the mention of the dead women and children, they had been the first to die only a few weeks back. "I hope you can do it. But I'm still afraid the Piasa is gonna ate you up tonight."

Porter grinned, "We'll see."

"See you on the other side then, Mr. Porter." The steward tipped his hat and hurried back to the wheelhouse.

Rummaging through his equipment, Porter put together a scarecrow and stood it upright in a waist high barrel. About the scarecrow's shoulder he coiled the wide noose, he then eased the rope back and away to a canoe on deck, from there the rope was knotted to the rigging firmly attached to the deck.

Crouching, Porter hid in the canoe with a worn piece of canvas to conceal himself. He knew the Mississippi and that the riverboat would be coming up on the bluffs between the towns of Alton and

Grafton soon enough. He had but to wait.

It was a warm night, the mosquitoes hardly buzzed in Porter's ears and the chug of the riverboat paddles lent a soothing rhythm. Porter's eyes drooped and with nothing happening, he felt sleep swoop in on soft feathered wings and he dreamt of happier times in his youth.

A cacophony of shrill squawks roused Porter from deathly slumber. A strong breeze washed over him, sending the canvas that covered his hiding spot flying away into the humid murk. Hovering in the darkness, a massive shape tore into the scarecrow and cried at the trick. It was assuredly angry at the lack of flesh and blood.

Blinking with surprise, Porter yanked on his rope and caught . . . nothing. The noose glided toward him on the deck with naught but a hint of straw and the scarecrows hat to show for it.

But the movement caught the monster birds amber colored eye. It croaked at Porter who still sprawled in the canoe, as it landed upon the deck. Covered in thick black feathers, it was doused in shadow and gloom. The pink hued head was almost bald of feathers but for a trace of midnight between it's terrible eyes. Its twisted beak was curved, an instrument made for the tearing of meat and rending of bone. Standing perhaps eight feet tall, Porter could only guess at what the monster birds wingspan must be.

The sound of its talons scuttling across the deck broke Porter's surprise. From his vest he pulled his horse pistol and shot a .58 caliber ball into the breast of the Piasa.

It hardly noticed. If there was a wound, there was no blood.

Porter rolled out of the canoe just as the murderous beak crashed. Screeching, the Piasa stepped upon the canoe, tilting it over as Porter scrambled away.

A pair of shots were fired from the wheelhouse and the monster bird was momentarily distracted. Porter got to his knees, then ran behind the cover of a stack of crates.

The Piasa lifted into the air. Porter felt the beat of its wings as it melted into the night overhead.

Watching, Porter reloaded the horse pistol. A crash and scream from the rear of the riverboat told him he had precious moments left. Racing back to his scarecrow, he lifted what was left of it up and readied the wide hangman's noose. His trap likely would not work a second time but he wanted to be prepared.

The monster bird had ignored the first shot of his horse pistol, but it was a living breathing creature and Porter didn't believe any animal could ignore bullets forever. If he could trap it, he and the crew could surely overwhelm it with lead. He would try for a head shot the next time.

The familiar beat of wings echoed overhead. Porter shouted, "Down here! Ya overgrown buzzard!"

The Paisa's awful call rocked the night. It swooped over the deck not far from the remains of the scarecrow.

Porter sent his lasso flying but he missed the monster bird.

Aboard the riverboat, near everyone had doused their lamps so as not to attract the birds notice. Porter wondered if there was even a pilot any longer or if they might run aground.

Black wings glided overhead.

Porter sent the noose flying again, a silent prayer upon his lips.

Still it missed.

Cursing, Porter stepped out from beside the ruined scarecrow. "Here I am! Come on!" He fired his Navy revolver twice at the airy phantom.

Still no blood appeared, but the sounds did anger the monster bird. It swung its massive gnarled head about and champed its pointed beak. Swooping in for the kill, it screamed.

Porter held his ground against the Piasa, swinging the noose.

Talon's flared and wings spread wide, the Piasa screeched an unholy dirge.

Porter dodged aside at the last second. Talon's ripped Porter's shirt. He swept the noose at the reaching feet.

The noose caught one foot and held fast.

Porter jerked on the rope hoping to send the monster bird reeling. But the Piasa remained airborne, tugging at its thick restraining tether.

Porter hoped it would wear itself out in the struggle or perhaps even have a heart attack and drop dead in its battle. The monster had likely never been caught before and it didn't know how to react to being a prisoner.

A line of more than one hundred feet into the dark stretched taut as the monster bird cried.

Then the rigging started to creak.

A nail popped from the deck and the rigging flexed skyward on one corner. Porter jumped and stood upon the anvil-like rigging hoping to weigh down the monster. He held to the rope and watched warily to be sure the monster didn't circle back.

There was a pop and a burst of wind made Porter close his eyes.

Then the line went slack. Then it was tight again. The wind slapped Porter in the face.

And the realization struck Porter. He was riding the rigging as the Piasa carried him into the night sky. Looking down, he was far above the riverboat. The wide Mississippi shrunk and they were soon over the trees.

The Piasa circled to see what it was carrying, but it couldn't dive at Porter because like a kite tail, whenever it dipped, he did as well. The constant spinning made Porter queasy.

Sensing that it could not attack its unwanted passenger in the air, the monster bird came up with a new plan for its dogged antagonist.

Losing altitude, the Piasa took Porter into the treetops. Tiny branches slammed his body as if he were beaten with stout rods of iron. Leaves slapped like leather and then Porter saw the stony bluffs. Either he would be taken to the nest to be fed to the Piasa's ravenous chicks, or the monster would crush his body at high speed against the limestone cliffs.

Guessing any option was suicide, Porter did the only one that gave him a modicum of choice. He waited for a thick looking clump of trees and leapt into the aether.

Hurtling through the trees, Porter slammed into myriad branches and brambles, each breaking his fall while threatening to make bread of his bones. The earth greeted him by expelling the fraction of whatever air was left to him.

Lying on his back, he heard something falling through the branches above. Was it the Piasa? He couldn't breathe yet and here came the monster bird.

No, this was smaller.

Silver glinting and spinning through the air with captured moonlight. Singing through the night air, his own Bowie knife landed blade down, sticking in the soft earth only inches from Porter's face.

He glimpsed the reflection of his own eyes in the Damascus blade. Somehow, he managed a mute nervous chuckle.

Above, the Piasa shrieked its displeasure at losing a meal.

Rolling onto his stomach, Porter attempted to get his stolen breath back. Feeling for his weapons, he discovered he had lost all but the bowie knife that almost killed him.

The Piasa squawked overhead, circling. Porter watched its dark form high above the trees as it blotted out the stars. The rope and rigging still trailing from its taloned foot. It appeared unwilling to land on the forest floor and hunt for Porter. Guessing he had a small amount of time, Porter glanced about for his pistols, hoping to find at least one of the three. He found them. But one was broken, one was lost and the last, his big horse pistol, only had a single shot left. He searched again for his cartridges but could not find them in the moldy undergrowth.

Porter resolved that he must slay the monster bird. Finding its lair might yield answers, so he watched the Piasa circle, and then followed it to the bluffs ahead where it disappeared.

Crags of stone rose up from the forest floor, giving a commanding presence over the Mississippi.

Porter watched and listened a few moments before even attempting a climb. The Piasa had been silent some twenty minutes now. Perhaps it was bedding down after its eventful night or maybe it waited in ambush for an easier meal. Either way, Port knew he had to finish this tonight. His trick on the riverboat would never work again. But if he hurried, maybe he could take advantage that the rope was still attached to the avian leviathan.

The cliffs were almost vertical and Porter had to hunt a moment to find a long crack that would provide good handhold's. He scrapped and prodded his way up, attempting to be as silent as possible while also knowing he failed at that. His breath was labored in the climb and twice he cursed in frustration at the lack of good purchase.

A long ledge afforded some relaxation. It ran horizontally along the bluff until it disappeared around an outcrop of fractured stone. Porter slumped and looked over the river below. He wasn't nearly to the top of the bluffs yet but even so he had a magnificent view. This place was an ideal aerie for the Piasa.

Movement caught Porter's eye and he thought he glimpsed a tall dark man at the far end of the ledge. The stranger was concealed by the gloom of night; did he wear a black robe? Was he a priest? Porter had to wonder at whom else would be fool enough to be upon this monstrous cliff at night.

Stepping careful and keeping a hand upon the face of the bluff, Porter edged toward the dark man. Over a dozen yards away, Porter would have sworn the man was looking directly at him. Then the man turned and vanished around a bend. Porter continued and cautiously went around the bend.

It was dead end.

The sheer cliff face offered no answer as to where the dark man could have gone but to the ground below. Porter saw no one in the jumble of rocks below. Where could the black robed man have gone?

A rampaging squawk stole down like haunted thunder. The Piasa flew straight at Porter with its talons outstretched and beak snapping.

On pure instinct Porter drew his horse pistol and aimed for the monstrous head. The horse pistol boomed a deafening crack at almost point blank range and yet the Piasa was unfazed. Talons tore at Porters legs as the vicious beak snapped at his head and arms. The wings beat the air like a hurricane, holding the Piasa in a stationary position to attack. Porter dodged and held his arms up to evade the deadly assault when he lost his balance on the cliff face. He twisted to avoid the talons and footing vanished.

Then he was falling.

A rope brushed his face and Porter grabbed hold for all he was worth.

The Piasa still had the rope attached to its foot and Porter yanked the flying behemoth down as he took hold.

Screeching, the monster flapped wildly as Porters hands burned sliding down the rope.

The ground hit harder and sooner than expected.

The rigging leapt past Porter's face as the Piasa went upward, cawing its discontent and anger.

Porter took stock of what had just happened. He was sure what he had seen was a man and not the Piasa itself, where could the dark man have gone? Could the Piasa have eaten him silently? Even more disturbing, the massive .58 caliber horse pistol had done virtually no damage to the monster bird at even point blank range. What could harm such a monster?

Porter lay still a moment pondering when movement caught his eye. It was a man, an Indian by the look of him striding through the forest. He was old with white hair and pale colored buckskins. He greeted Porter with his arm held up to the square and he smiled with no guile behind it.

"Hello?" said Porter, surprised at the old man's sudden appearance.

Nodding, the old man said, "I have watched you in your attempt to slay the Piasa and am here to offer my help. Your guns cannot harm a monster with such strong medicine protecting it."

"Yeah, I noticed," said Porter.

"My name is Ouatoga and I can help you."

Extending his hand, Porter said, "I'm Porter and I'd be obliged for whatever you can suggest."

Ouatoga didn't take Porters hand, keeping back a pace or two but pointed to wide flat stone nearby. "Remove that stone."

Porter looked at Ouatoga, furrowed his brow but did as the old man suggested. He stopped to look skyward once to be sure the Piasa wasn't bearing down on them, then hefted the stone up. Like a lid to a box, the stone revealed a small chamber. Inside rested an unstrung bow and a handful of arrows in a fine deer skin quiver.

"You must use these to defeat the black medicine of the Piasa and the Mahan."

"Mahan?"

"The dark man you saw upon the cliffs. He is a sorcerer and witch and it is he who has brought the evil of the Piasa back to the land. His magic protects the Piasa. But with my bow and my blessed arrows you can defeat them."

Porter rubbed his bearded chin. "Bows and arrows aren't something I have any familiarity with."

"You will use them."

Porter picked up the bow and quiver. He strung the bow and tested its pull. It wasn't much, he had expected it to be more. The arrows were nondescript and all bore the same dull colored bands, owl feather fletching and obsidian flint heads. "This will do what a horse pistol couldn't?"

"It is blessed," answered Ouatoga, ending the questions. He turned and walked to the edge of the bluffs until he came upon a narrow saw tooth like weathering upon the stone face. "This is the way."

Porter shook his head and followed. The saw tooth notches allowed them to swiftly climb. It was farther up than Porter had climbed earlier. Then as they entered a narrow gorge, the mouth of a great cave loomed open.

"The Piasa is there now. You must enter and slay it."

Porter gave Ouatoga a shrewd look and wondered why this had not been done before, a long time ago. He was about to ask the old man when a sound within the cave alerted him to its angry presence.

Ouatoga offered encouragement again. "Keep your arrows ready. You must slay the demon bird. It knows you are here."

Porter nodded and stepped into the cave. He kept a loose draw on the bow and watched with eyes flickering in every direction. "Here birdy, birdy, birdy."

Moonlight splashed into the cave giving weak cold light. Bones littered the cave floor in a gruesome display of the monster's appetite.

Porter stepped over skulls only to crunch a ribcage. A loud flutter of wings threatened from somewhere in the gloom.

Porter looked back and Ouatoga was still there ushering him on.

A long black feather floated across the chamber, carried on the gulf of night.

What looked to Porter like a great nest sat against the far end of chamber. It appeared empty.

Where was the Piasa?

Porter watched his sides now more than the nest. Where could the monster lurk?

Almost to the nest, Port spun to face the mouth of the cave, Ouatoga was gone. Wondering if the nest held a clutch of gigantic eggs, Porter stepped closer to peer inside.

The bald head shot up from the nest and snapped in harsh clipping retorts.

Porter leapt back loosing an arrow wildly to the side, missing the mark by several feet.

Retreating to the far wall, Porter readied another arrow.

The gloom played tricks on him. Shadows swirled like phantasms in the pale moonlight. Voices in the dark whispered that he was a dead man. Dread welled up in Porter's heart and he almost dropped the bow to flee to the cavern's mouth. Doubt and fear crossed swords with faith and hope.

The Piasa croaked from somewhere in the darkness and that primal fear turned into anger.

Remembering his sacred charge, Porter renewed his vow and steadied his aim.

The Piasa squawked divulging itself and crossed a section of the cavern chamber in seconds. It's bloody amber colored eyes narrowed and with a snapping beak it came on, strong and loud as thunder.

Porter loosed an arrow into its breast. The first reveal of pain echoed from the big bird. With the cascading fire on him, Porter backed away.

The scuttling bird raised a mighty wing and batted Porter against the cavern wall.

Porter rolled away with the sharp snap of the beak close behind. Tripping and falling face first against a grinning skull, Port rolled again as a taloned foot smashed the grim trophy. He lost the bow.

The avian demon backed Porter up toward the cavern's mouth, its sharp beak snapping and lunging.

Weaponless, Porter felt in the darkness for a stone or femur to use as a club, useless as it may be. His strong hands instead caught the hemp rope and the rigging. He clutched the anchor like piece of iron and started it swinging like a shaft of whirlwind.

The Piasa paused briefly then lunged, getting the pig iron full in the face for its trouble.

Blinking and cawing it lunged again. This time Porter sent the rope and iron in a wider swing about the monster's narrow throat. The iron rigging swung around twice, slapping the monsters breast while also strangling it. A silent squawk came from a struggling beak.

Rushing back into the chamber, Porter searched for the bow upon hands and knees. He glanced back at the struggling Piasa as he searched, guessing he had but moments.

Then something crushed a bone only a step away.

Mighty hands grasped Port about his collar and tossed him aside as if he were a child. The dark man, the Mahan, rushed to strike him again.

Port rolled even as he spat blood. The Mahan was huge and could apparently see in the dark just fine. The most unnerving thing was his determined silence.

Another kick and Port was dazed almost beyond reckoning then his rough fingers found the quiver of dogwood shafts, the obsidian arrowheads.

Drawing one in his left fist, Port lurched to his feet.

The dark man crossed his arms daring Port to fight back.

Pretending to be even more woozy than he was Port sent an incredibly slow right hand punch at his foe.

The dark man might have laughed had he not been so silent. Coming in for his next excruciating attack, the dark man missed Port's feint and walked right into an obsidian assisted roundhouse punch.

Now the Mahan made noise as Port twisted the arrowhead. Staggering back, the Mahan twisted his black cloak over himself and vanished.

Rope snapped and the Piasa let loose its shattering call. Swinging its gruesome head, it eyed Port and clawed at the ground before rushing in.

Port dodged about a boulder and felt the bow of Ouatoga. Scooping it up in blind frustration, he knocked the arrow.

Porter aimed true and sent a blazing shaft into the Piasa's neck. It dropped to its crouching position and cawed, soft as rain. The monster flopped and jerked like a headless chicken.

A third arrow ended the monster. Then it was still. There was no sign of the Mahan, nor did the nest have any eggs and Porter was grateful for that. Monster bird or no, he didn't like the idea of smashing young un's.

Climbing back down the cliff face, Porter looked for Ouatoga, but the old man was gone.

Dawn rose soon afterward and Porter made his way to the river and waited for a passing flatboat.

Once aboard, news of the demise of the dreaded Piasa spread like a fever. A Quapaw Indian woman with a collection of woven baskets asked to see the final arrow Porter still retained. He handed her the dogwood shaft. She ran her hands across the fletching and simple bands of color on its length.

"Do you know who gave you this?" she asked.

"An old man, said his name was Ouatoga or some such. Don't know who he was or where he went."

"I know him."

Porter shrugged, "Well? Who is he?"

She sighed and answered, "Ouatoga slew the Piasa first and returned to help you do the same in his stead."

"In his stead? But he was there."

She shook her head, "Ouatoga slew the Piasa, yes. But that was more than a thousand moons ago."

Soma for the Destroying Angels Soul

Somewhere along the pony express trail . . .

Horseshoes slipped almost silently down the moldering wilderness road when Porter caught a glimpse of some phantasm skulking parallel to him in the wood. The ghostly image froze. Porter brushed aside his own long dark hair and narrowed his gaze straining to see the unexpected through the willows.

"I'll be dipped."

A ram bared its teeth, gave the most god-awful "Bah" and charged. Crashing through the saplings and mossy undergrowth the ram came on in a stilted unwholesome gait.

Porter spit in shock. He drew the Sharps rifle from the scabbard on his saddlebags and took aim.

His horse, Roman, unused to such a bizarre attack reeled backward when the ram was within twenty feet.

Porter missed.

The retort from the Sharps rifle did nothing to spook the oncoming beast and then it was too late. Lunging, the ram bit Roman on the neck before attempting to gore or bite Porter as well. Thrown to the ground in the ruckus, Porter drew his Navy Colt and fired all six balls into the rampaging spiral-horned head.

The mad creature didn't stop until the fifth shot.

Porter got up and dusted himself off. He scanned the woods,

watchful for anything more as he reloaded. He then checked the wound on Roman's neck and cleaned it with a bit of whiskey, even if he instinctively believed in the painful inevitable. Roman had been a good horse and didn't deserve to go out this way.

Porter put the barrel of his Navy Colt to Roman's head just below the ear and cocked the hammer. "Wheat! Why'd you have to go and get bit?"

Roman nickered and turned to look at Porter.

Holstering his six-gun, Porter muttered, "All right. I'll wait."

He glanced over the ram's carcass and wondered at its mangy coat. Wretched disease covered the animal from ear to hoof. Porter had seen this before, on more than a dozen pioneers headed west. He was grateful they were already dead by the time he had come upon them— but he was also sure they didn't get that way by accident. Someone or something caused this.

Before moving on, Porter lit a good sized fire over the top of the ram. He didn't want anyone or anything sampling the foul body.

By mid-afternoon Roman carried Porter into a small nameless town, but at a definitive effort. He wouldn't last much longer before going the maddening way. Port sniffed at the bite and was horrified to see a pale fungal infection seeping outward.

Calling to a stable boy, Port shouted, "Is there a horse doctor in town?"

The boy shook his head, "But Doc Mathers might could help."

"Obliged. Where is he?"

The boy pointed to a house on the opposite side of the blacksmith.

As Porter walked Roman toward the doctors, an obvious scarlet woman from a local bordello crossed his path. Bad luck like a black cat, Porter couldn't help but admire her figure while at the same finding revulsion in her sore condition. She covered herself with a frilly umbrella to match her provocative corset and bustle but still there was no mistaking the circular ringworm trails about her neck, shoulders and face. Her ebony eyes met his and a fear lingered there along with her scent. She disappeared into a slattern house with a sign that read Maison Rouge.

Porter shuddered especially when he saw a second soiled dove with a similar affliction and then an old man likewise marked. The old man had perhaps the worst case but seemed unperturbed, a fancy whiskey bottle with exaggerated embroidered lettering in hand might have accounted for that.

Knocking on Doc Mathers door, Port was met with a stream of vulgarity followed by, "Leave me be! I've no damn cure!"

Porter opened the door, "Pardon Doc, but you ain't even heard what I have to jaw at you about."

Doc Mathers, checked himself as he gazed upon Porter; a thick broad shouldered man with long black hair and a thick beard who stared back at him with the ice pale eyes of a killer. A Bowie handle and a six-gun in turn leered from Porters belt and the Doc had no doubt they had seen their use.

"You're Porter, the killer—"

"Yup. Now how about you take a look at my horse."

"You shot Frank Worrell, Quinn Kofford, Philip Jackson and Governor Boggs."

"Yup, 'cept the last one. Now let's take a look at my horse."

Stepping outdoors to examine the horse, the Doc kept a second eye on Porter. Glancing only briefly at the animal. "Like I said, I don't have a cure for this or any other fungal infection. You better put him down."

"Any other?" frowned Port.

"So you didn't shoot governor Boggs?"

"If *I* shot Boggs he'd be dead, the son of a bitch. Now what's this about other infections?" Porter gestured at yet another passing prostitute tattooed with the circular ringworm tracks. "What'd I see on them soiled doves?"

Doc Mathers shook his head. "Near everyone in town has come down with infections. Quite a few have gone insane and I can't do a thing. I could help with scarlet fever but not this pestilence."

"Just ringworm," Porter protested.

"That's the beginning. Soon enough, a few days maybe . . . they'll all have what your horse has. And I give your horse a day before it goes mad and attacks someone. We've already shot all the dogs in town. We locked up some people."

"What people?"

Doc asked, "What's a holy killer, a destroying angel like you care?"

"I ain't never killed anyone who didn't need killing."

"Say's you."

Ignoring that, Porter persisted, "Where?"

Doc pointed at a log cabin with a heavily barred door and said, "We put the worst of them in there, a bunch of easterners bound for Oregon. They stopped making noise last night. Now they just squat grunting, acting like rabid dogs."

Port grunted, "And you think I'm heartless?"

"There was nothing we could do, jail was full. At least we didn't shoot them."

"Any idea what caused this? Fever? Bad food?"

Doc shook his head. "Bad food? Naw, how could that do anything?"

Porter shrugged, "Just a hunch."

"No, this is a curse from runaway slaves and an old voodoo shaman named Bockkor."

"Bockkor?"

Doc gestured for Porter to follow him inside. "We got word from a traveling salesman, a tonic doctor, that some dangerous runaway slaves were heading this way. Real rough bunch out of the Caribbean, heard they killed their whole master's family down in Arkansas. We ambushed them at salt creek. We killed two and captured all but one, the witch-doctor name of Bockkor."

Porter rubbed a calloused hand over his midnight beard. "So he told you to let his people go just like Moses or he would curse the town?"

"Yes, well maybe."

"See any frogs?"

"Yes, well no. We never understood what he said in the darkness. He only shouted in French, but the tonic doctor, Silas Worthington he speaks French and he told us to watch out. He said we ought to kill them all for our own good, but Missouri state law says we need to try and apprehend them to return them to their rightful owners. It's the law. Maybe we should have listened to the tonic doctor because once Bockkor escaped, the curse started. Silas knew what he was saying, even sold us some medicine to take care and ease the pain."

Porter frowned, "Ease the pain?"

Doc Mathers raised his arm letting the shirtsleeve fall, revealing a grotesque spiral ringworm pattern down his upper arm. A white fungal fuzz crept over the maroon scab that itself covered most of his bicep. "We've all got it. And since your horse does as well, I expect you'll catch it in a day or two."

"Anyone try to capture this Bockkor?"

"Hell yes! But he has even infected the beasts of the field, a damn herd of sheep attacked us! Several men didn't make it. And no one could find a trace of Bockkor in the forests southeast of here, nothing but open plains to the north and west. Nowhere to hide there. He's a black magic piper that one. And we're dancing to the devils tune now."

Porter drew his flask and took a long pull before replying. "I'll find him and get to the bottom of this. Where are those slaves being held?"

"At the sheriffs, building at the center square, everything wheels around it. But listen, we looked for Bockkor for three days and nights. Over fifty men, half of which are too sick now to get outta bed. What are you gonna do by your lonesome that we couldn't with a pack of dogs?"

"Suppose I'll just have to sweet talk him." With that, Porter went out the door.

He was about to run a bare hand down Roman's muzzle and reassure the stallion that things would be all right, but considering the infection looming from the bite mark, he held back. Instead he nickered to his friend getting a similar response. "I'll be back soon."

At the sheriff's office, a dozing deputy jumped at Porter opening the door.

"Sheriff in?"

"No sir, he ain't. Can I help you?"

Port gestured to jail cells beyond. "I wanna talk to them slaves, see what I can do about Bockkor."

The deputy sniffed. "You won't get nowhere with them. They don't speak no English and ain't too kind on us anyhow."

"Then you won't mind if I try."

"S'pose not." Sniffing again the deputy asked, "Who're you anyway? Some kind of tracker?"

"Something like that. You agree with Doc Mathers? This is all a curse from Bockkor?"

"Yes, I do. Ain't none of those slave's sick, but the rest of us are."

"Everyone?"

The deputy sniffed and thought a moment. "Yeah, everyone but you—so far, them slaves and a couple travelers headed east, but the sheep got them. Oh, and the tonic doctor, yeah, everyone. Why?"

Porter just shook his head.

The deputy sniffed and sitting down, gestured for Porter to walk on down the hall. Ebon bodies were crowded into two rooms no larger than a wagon box. They did not bear the fungal infection, though their living conditions did not grant them any reprieve.

"Anyone speak American? Polly view English?" asked Porter, in his most barbaric of French pronunciations.

Dark eyes flickered though all remained deathly silent.

"I want to know what Bockkor knows."

The emaciated faces turned away.

Porter lingered, hoping one of them might say something. "I'll come back."

He recalled the sign over the local bordello, Maison Rouge, it was French. Maybe one of the soiled doves could speak it.

"I'm here for a woman—" growled Porter, as he stepped through the door.

"Ain't we all. But you're gonna wait your turn for the clean ones like everybody else," said a tall man with crooked teeth. A laugh erupted from the half dozen dirty men sitting about the parlor. Egged on by their approval, Crooked Teeth cast his toothpick at Porter and grinned.

Like buckshot, Porter grabbed Crooked Teeth by his lapels then slammed his right fist into Crooked's nose. A swift knee to the groin brought Crooked down and just as quick, Porter threw him out the door.

"—that can speak French."

"He can have mine," said one, of the six before ducking out the back door.

The Madame chuckled, "Oh, you'll like Sabine. Right down that hall honey."

"Have her get dressed and meet me outside," ordered Port, before he too went outside, stepping on Crooked Teeth's hand as he did so.

Sabine was the same striking woman Porter had seen when he first rode into town. She was curious and direct. "You're the first one who has asked if I could speak to the runaways. Do you think they could know anything?"

"Everyone knows something," grumbled Porter, holding open the door to the sheriff's office. The sniffing deputy waved them back. "Just find out if they know where Bockkor is."

Sabine rattled away in French and this time the slaves paid attention. One of the men seemed to argue a moment with her over some point that Porter could not follow.

"They said why should they help us?"

"Tell them that I swear to God, on my honor to get release for them and call them free, if they will help remove the curse. I ain't asking for them to harm Bockkor or do anything to him, just help me remove the curse. Fair enough?"

Sabine repeated Porters sentiments and was met with a stern reply. "They can't or they won't. There is no bargaining with them."

Porter ran a hand over his beard and contemplated a few moments in silence. "Did Bockkor curse them along with the town?"

"No."

"Then why do I see the beginning of the ringworm spiral on that one's arm?"

When Sabine stared at the man who had the affliction, he howled in fear and the others joined in. A chorus of shouts and cries echoed in the tiny jail and the sniffing deputy came running up. "Let's go," urged Port, ushering Sabine down the narrow hallway.

"What's with the caterwauling? They didn't do this when we locked 'em up."

Porter shrugged, and led Sabine out the door while the jailed slaves yelling grew louder. "Maybe Bockkor abandoned them or maybe he isn't behind the curse. Won't know until I get it outta him myself."

Sabine sighed, "This was pointless. You don't know a thing more on where to find Bockkor or lift the curse."

"With every blessing comes a curse. I have to think there's a blessing after every curse too. I just got to find it."

Sabine shook her head and drew a bottle from her coat pocket. She drank two swallows and offered it to Port.

He disliked the greenish hue of the liquor and asked, "What is that?"

Sabine giggled, "Its Doctor Silas Worthington's Nutritional Fantastical Medicinal Soma! I can't say it as good as he can, he's got this way of making it exciting. It's really good, he makes it himself. I almost don't feel the scabs and aches anymore."

"You getting better?"

"I think so. I hope so. At least I don't hurt like I did a day ago."

Porter nodded, "Small miracles."

"Where will you look for Bockkor?"

Looking up at the gathering stars and fading pink twilight Porter answered, "Don't know, maybe the woods below salt creek. I still need to talk to this Doctor Silas, or—"

"—Porter!" interrupted Sabine, tugging on his shoulder.

Standing not ten feet from them with a crazed grin and near glowing eyes was the man who must surely be Bockkor. A long wide blade dripped in his hand.

Porter shoved Sabine away as he reached for his Navy Colt. Bockkor leapt with his blade arcing. The knife knocked Porters gun off target, but this allowed Porter to push inside Bockkor's overwrought lunge.

Grasping at the knife wielding hand, Porter sent blow after blow into Bockkor's face and stomach. The frail-looking opponent threw Porter off as if he were a child. The strength coming from the older man was incredible.

Porter charged again fists swinging, all in an attempt to reach his

Navy Colt that lay in the dust at Bockkor's feet. After being thrown, Porter was sure he heard the old man's bones crack, but there was no reaction, no even faint grimace of pain.

Wheeling into the fray, Porter wondered if Bockkor even felt pain? Perhaps not, but he could still be broken, still be stopped.

Swinging back, Porter brought his full weight down on Bockkor's knee. There was a snap and change in Bockkor's gait but he made no sound and continued attacking, when he finally opened his mouth only a primal scream erupted out.

Porter heard Sabine screaming and briefly wondered if it was because of Bockkor's terrifying ignorance of pain, then he realized other bodies moved in the gathering darkness. Someone or something had opened the pestilent cabin that had caged the first victims of the disease.

Trotting with the same unholy gait Porter had witnessed the crazed ram use, people stumbled, some barely ambulatory toward he and Sabine. He strained in the darkness for the lost pistol.

Bockkor still attacked, snapping his jaws while he raked the air just in front of Porters face. His heel felt something solid in the dust. Dropping, his hand brushed over the familiar wooden handle. Springing back up, Porter shot Bockkor almost point blank in the chest.

Bockkor hardly responded, clutching at Porter once again despite thick bile gushing from his chest.

Porter shot again at what he guessed was the heart only to have Bockkor bat the gun away a second time. Retreating back to the sheriff's porch as he was surrounded, Porter heard a terrible scream from within.

Sabine glanced inside then slammed the door shut. "They killed him!"

Grasping a four-foot piece of timber railing, Porter swung at the oncoming horror to little avail. Bockkor raised his blade when a trumpet blared seconds before shots fired.

Wave after wave of gunfire birthed light to the darkness only to obscure it again with venomous smoke. Bockkor's body shook with the terrific violence of multiple shots.

Porter witnessed the insane ring-wormed victims take more hits than any human could possibly endure. Scrambling for his pistol, he instead dove for cover as shots were inevitably directed at him. Sabine screamed as she held her ears against the thunder of guns. Deciding on the lesser of two evils, Porter pushed Sabine back into the sheriff's office.

Three chained men stood over the deputy, who lay dead at their feet. Porter dove and grabbed a shotgun from the wall rack as the three charged. Porter was quicker, but held off pulling the trigger. "Back! Tell them to get back!"

Sabine repeated Porter's words in French and the three retreated. One of them protested and Porter understood their intent was freedom, not blood.

Porter snarled, "Tell them it's time for truth. The U.S. Cav is out front and Bockkor is dead."

Sabine repeated Porters words and the three opened up. "They say they can cure us if they are given the right ingredients."

"Out front the only cure is a bullet. They need a better story."

"I believe them," said Sabine, as one of the three took her Soma bottle away and cast it against the wall. "That was mine!"

One mixed salt and water in a coffee can as another began offering invocations to his god and lit a small fire. The third took keys from the deputy and unlocked all of their chains. Porter watched the door, dumbfounded at the terrible carnage inflicted upon the town's formerly sane residents.

Once the salt water was warm enough to steam, the three men took deep draughts and shared it with Sabine. "How about you?"

"I'm not sick, but if that works I'll want some salt water for my horse."

"Juma says—"

Porter interrupted, "Which one is Juma now?"

"He's the tallest one. He says you should drink it to be safe."

Porter grimaced. "Can't I just rub some on?"

"No, Juma says for the salt to work on Zuvembi, it must be eaten. They said something about Napoleon using salt on bayonets in Haiti and that it didn't work, that the salt must be ingested."

Porter reluctantly drank the foul brew, he then noticed the gunfire had stopped. Cracking open the door, he gazed upon a horrific scene of crawling broken monstrosities feeding and the retreat of the cavalry in the distance. "I'll be dipped. The U.S. Cav almost got something right, but they couldn't handle all of these—whatever you called them."

Before Sabine could answer, several thunderclaps announced fires igniting all over town.

Every direction Porter looked, flames encircled him. Worse, to escape the choking heat, the crawling staggering Zuvembi made their way toward the central sheriff's office.

"We gotta bar the door!"

Pushing all furniture and materials against the doors and windows seemed frightfully inadequate. Scouring the deputy's pockets and cabinets, Porter found no more than a couple dozen shotgun shells and perhaps fifty shells for the deputy's revolver.

"Better tell them to make more salt water," urged Port.

"There isn't any more," cried Sabine.

The creaking of the offices floorboards announced the Zuvembi's presence. All at once the windows and doors were broken and thrown open. A tangle of ring-wormed faces, some missing jaws or arms, others with gaping wounds all writhed together into the sparse room. Porter opened fire at select targets, attempting to slow down the horde. Through the broken windows, he saw the fires taking the town apart. Soon enough everything even half alive would be coming straight at him.

"Get the keys!" shouted Porter.

Sabine scooped them up just as the surging horde broke through Porter's rain of lead. Two of the slave men were taken down as they struggled against the reeking mass.

Pummeling aside staggering foes, Porter and Juma raced behind Sabine.

The cell door still hung open in unwelcome embrace. Slamming the door shut, they realized too late that it was not locked. Porter jabbed with the shotgun and fired his last two rounds as Sabine and Juma tried to crank the key without being bitten. It clicked and then the three of them retreated to the back wall as every single space for an arm, leg or face lurched against the bars. Reaching, clawing, straining, the horde never stopped.

They were safe, yet there was no sleep.

The night air burned with a putrid choking reek. Within the cell, Porter, Sabine and Juma could hear the crackling fires as the town burned down around them. They wiled away their time breaking a Zuvembi's arm or leg, anything to fight back so long as they could remain safe themselves.

"The Cav is out there, I just hope we get a chance to let them know we are here and they don't burn this place down to get these bastards."

Sabine was the go between granting conversation between Porter and Juma and explaining the root of the pestilence. "Juma says that they were bound as partial Zuvembi to the Tonic Doctor. Bockkor was his father, those others his brothers. All of them were taken in a raid off the coast of Haiti. They commanded a fine price between the occultists who knew their value."

"Value?" asked Port furrowing his brow.

"Beyond being slaves, because Bockkor was not his father's name but occupation. They create Zuvembi."

Porter shoved Juma, "You make them?" he shouted, kicking at another straining clawing arm.

Juma heatedly responded but Sabine intervened. "They were forced beyond measure to comply with the devil man. And they tried to thwart him by not giving the proper ingredients for the Zuvembi formula. But something went wrong, the new ingredient made it worse than usual. Made them uncontrollable."

"What ingredient?"

Juma laughed darkly.

"The mushrooms that grow in the buffalo dung."

"I'll be dipped."

Morning light shone through the haze of smoke and the Zuvembi retreated from the sheriff's office. Porter waited a good few moments in case it was a trick before he dared open the cell. He signaled Sabine to wait as he and Juma crept soft as shadows to the front room.

Out front, Porter heard men and horse. Glancing carefully around the corner, he saw the U.S. Cav running down or shooting the last few Zuvembi. They had learned their lesson in the night and shot out the legs of the Zuvembi before finishing them.

"Hold your fire! We're friendly's," shouted Porter, after he had instructed Juma to gain cover behind a thick oak desk. As Porter had guessed, his shout brought a volley of fire from the troopers. "You done yet? We're friendly's!"

"Who is in there?" came the cold reply.

Hardly above a whisper, Porter called Sabine to come forward before replying to the troops. "A waylaid Pony Express rider, a local proprietress and her slave." He mouthed, "You explain it to Juma, just for now."

Sabine nodded and Juma accepted the proposal.

"Hold your fire men, let them come out where I can see them," commanded a burly captain astride a fine roan mare. "Do any of you have that flux."

Porter stepped out first with his hands slightly raised, Sabine and Juma followed. "No we don't have the flux. As new travelers into the area we hadn't time to catch anything and holed up in the jail cells to keep those fiends off."

The captain looked them over and Juma's near nakedness convinced him that they were untainted. "My apologies Madame, but I'm afraid the town is a complete loss. But the scourge has been thoroughly eliminated."

"You sure?" asked Porter.

"Absolutely, you have the solemn word of the federal government," said the captain, as he curled his mustache. Behind him, troopers rummaged and looted what was left of the town. "Madame, if there is anything else I could do for you, you have but to ask."

Sabine asked, "How did you get here in the middle of this? Who told you?"

The captain puffed out his chest, "A traveling tonic doctor apprised us of the terrible maddening flux. Good man, risked his life."

"Much obliged then, it's all over," said Porter, tipping his hat to the captain. Sabine went to interject as she gazed over the destroyed town. Porter shook his head. "Let's bust a hump outta town before they want to know anything else."

Sabine whispered, "But it's not over, what about the tonic doctor?"

"True," Porter agreed, "but it won't be a help to have these trigger happy fools involved. Let them think they won and leave it at that. I'll get the tonic doctor."

In a pouring rain, Porter strode through the saloon doors. He shook off the storm and asked the barkeep for a drink. The whiskey was especially sour but it had been an awful week and anything was better than the mud-holes he had been drinking out of the last two days.

Though it initially had a foul tang, Porter felt better with another. All the ache in his bones was gone and even the sores on his feet went numb.

Numb. That was the difference. He wasn't feeling good; he was feeling numb.

"Put that on my tab friend," said a voice behind Porter.

Swiveling on his stool, Porter looked at the middle-aged, almost paunchy man with a sickening green vest and battered top hat. His face was unremarkable but a vile light burned in his eyes.

"Have some more, all of it on me."

Porter fought the numbness as it turned into a searing pain. "And you are?"

"Haven't you guessed yet? I'm Dr. Silas Worthington. And you Mr. Rockwell," he jabbed Porter in the chest to emphasize, "damaged my operation. I deemed it necessary to start over. But I had to clean up all my loose ends. The army was most helpful in that regard."

Porter was a master poker player but drugged as he was his face betrayed his sympathies. "Sabine?"

"That French whore of yours, and my former slave, yes they're gone now. Probably been dead since near the time you left them days ago. But you, you I wanted to know an excruciating pain before you left this world."

Porter doubled over in pain as his vision flickered to and fro. The top hat stretched and reached almost to the high ceiling of the saloon. The Tonic Doctors wicked grin spilt until it was almost as wide as the player piano.

"I prepared a very strong dose, you probably don't even see me as I am anymore."

Porter saw a demon-toad with a score of eyes wearing a top hat that glanced at its pocket watch and laughed. The mirror behind the bar loomed into eternity and black gulfs beyond beckoned like a satanic lover. The toad opened its mouth and a score of lashing violet tentacles grasped a crow-sized fly.

"You were a famous man in some circles, legendary even. Some tales said you couldn't be killed, neither bullet nor blade could harm you. Ah, but poison. I've given you enough to kill a dozen men," spoke the demon-toad.

Porter blinked at the pulsing taunting face and chuckled despite the crushing pain. "You think you got the sand to kill me? I'm blessed like Samson and I still got all my hair."

"You're finished," spat the demon-toad, through its maw full of teeth and tentacles. Its myriad eyes leered and its flabby slime covered hand slapped Porter. "You're done. No one in the world could bring you back now."

Sabine's ghostly form stood before Porter, her face folded revealing a puffball top. Spores rose like smoke and Porter knew he could read her thoughts, "More," she said "have more."

Porter reached for the brimming vessel of sloshing green ichor.

Silas taunted, "Yes, yes, have more you fool. Do you enjoy being driven insane?"

Dead friends reached across the divide and through the veil.

"Don't you get the joke? My soma was made from the destroying angel mushroom and you, the man called the destroying angel, is felled by such a simple thing."

Porter drank another ocean of soma and made peace with all the dead. All the bandits and mobsters, all the ignorant and overly educated, all the horse thieves and foul souls that had crossed his bloody path. Even all the friends and loved one he had failed.

"No more! No more!" cried the demon-toad. "Stop, you're taking too much."

Porter shook the dead hands and despite the differences he knew he was forgiven, that no one on the other side held a grudge. He saw Sabine, Juma and even Bockkor and beyond reason knew it was all good. And he drank another ocean of soma.

"Impossible! Still he stands!" gasped the demon-toad. "Fetch my rifle, Joshua!"

Porter blinked, his stomach growled, agitated and erupted like the fountains of the deep.

Doctor Silas took but a mouthful of the ejected brew and promptly collapsed in convulsions.

Porter blinked and the room stopped warping long enough for him to draw his Navy Colt on Joshua and put him down like the dog he was. Doc Silas writhed one last time, twitched and went still.

Out the back door Porter found the Tonic wagon, still loaded with bottles of soma. He rode the horses hard around the block and cut the team loose at the last possible moment, letting the momentum carry the gaudy wagon through the doors of the saloon. He lit a cigar and threw the match inside. Flames licked over the wagon and bodies.

Porter puffed once and turned away. "Lord, I'm thirsty."

Rolling in the Deep

San Francisco, 1855

A sharp hard rap at the door made the girl jump. She left her dutiful spot at the piano and crossed the parlor to peek out the window. A burly man stood there, not particularly tall but broad shouldered, very rough looking. His clothing was coarse. A gun was visible, its worn wooden handle leering from his woolen jacket. His hair was very long and dark, as was the beard. Glancing into the window he locked eyes with the girl. Volcanic blue, they seemed the eyes of a killer. Eyes that bore into her soul. She involuntarily gasped.

"What is it Ina?" her sickly mother asked, only looking up from her stitching because of the girl's gasp.

Ina backed away from the window as another knock struck the door.

"Well, who is it?"

"A murderous looking man. He has long hair and terrible eyes."

"Answer the door for him Ina."

"Mother?"

"Answer the door."

"Mother!"

"Answer the door."

Ina went to the door and without looking at the strange man, opened it to him.

"Agnes?" he asked.

"Come in Porter. I'm afraid you scared my daughter. It's been too long since she saw you last."

He entered, watching the young girl who still wouldn't meet his gaze. As he crossed the threshold, she disappeared down the hallway. "My apologies, Agnes. I just led a party through the Sierra's and thought I would drop by and pay my respects." Porter paused as he got his first gaze of Agnes.

She was wretchedly thin and bundled in the parlor with a scarf despite the relative outside heat. A bonnet upon her head did not conceal that the sickness had made her bald as an egg.

"What happened?"

"Typhoid. I lost my hair," she said, running a hand across the phantom locks.

Porter sat across from her, removing his hat. He blushed, knowing it only magnified his own lustrous head of hair. "Are you going to be all right?"

"Doctor Howard said I was recovering well, but . . ."

Porter stood, putting his hat back on. "Where is a barber?"

"I can't ask you to do that for me," she protested.

"You didn't ask Agnes." He smiled like a grizzly bear, "I'm offering you a gift. I ain't got any real money or gold dust yet, but I do have something else of value for you."

She shook her head slowly, "No, if your hair be cut, you'll be weak as a shorn Samson. Think of the promise you were given. Remember?"

"How could I forget? But a man has got to think of others, or what good is any talent he is given?"

"No, you can't."

He opened the door, looking back at the fragile woman. "Wheat! What kind of man would I be, to not help a widow in distress? I'll be back shortly."

Agnes argued again but he was already gone.

Only after his heavy jingling boot steps faded from the porch did Ina venture into the parlor. "Who was that terrible looking man?"

"He was a close friend of your late fathers. Appearances can be deceiving. As dark as he may appear, his heart is indeed golden."

Porter returned not an hour later with a wig made from his own once flowing black locks. He placed it like a crown upon Agnes head.

She wept.

He rubbed the short bristling top of his own head, he had even allowed the barber to trim his beard to match.

"You look like a Caesar now," said Agnes.

"And you look like a queen," he said, giving her a lopsided grin.

"I cannot thank you enough. But now I'll worry for your own well-being."

"Don't. Ain't nothing gonna lay this old wolf low," he laughed. "I'm gonna head on out now. There's some other folks to give greeting too, maybe catch a drink."

She frowned, "Porter, you really should abstain in your condition. I don't want you slipping back into any bad habits."

He smiled at her concern, "You take care. I'll be heading out soon enough."

"Porter, thank you. And take care, you hear?" With that he was gone and Ina returned again. A flash of realization crossed Agnes's face. "Ina! He is going to the saloons. Follow him and tell him I said to stay away from any of them on Davis Street. Hurry child!"

Ina nodded and rushed out the door and down the porch. She could still see Porter as he strode up to Portsmith Square. She could catch him, if she wanted too. But she didn't. She let him walk on and disappear into the swarming crowd. She went back inside and told her mother she had warned him.

Porter found himself on the corner of Davis Street and Chamber streets right near the water front. A sparkling newly painted sign advertising the Boston House saloon seemed inviting. He had avoided strong drink of late, but the temptation was overwhelming now, it uncoiled in his brain like a slow fire catching hold of oil. He went inside and ordered a whiskey.

A jovial red bearded man joined Porter at the bar. "Howdy friend, what brings you to town? You ain't from around here are ya?"

"Nope."

"I could tell. The haircut," laughed red beard.

Porter rubbed a hand over his head again.

"You just do that?"

"Yeah."

"I could tell. You a sailor?"

"Nope."

"Name's Kelly. This is my place and I like talking to everyone that comes in. I like getting the news of the world that way."

Porter grunted and took another swallow of his whiskey.

"Allow me to buy you another round and tell me something interesting about yourself," said Kelly, signaling to his barkeep.

"Now you're talking," said Porter. "What do you want to hear about? Crossing the Sierra's?"

"Naw. How's about that haircut? You got a pale neck, must have been pretty long before huh? Like an Indians."

"Yeah suppose so."

Kelly sneered, "Now why would a civilized man do a thing like that?"

Porter stared Kelly dead in the face and said coldly, "Whoever said I was civilized?"

Kelly gave a nervous grin.

"I cut it off for the Coolbrith widow. Had typhoid fever and needed a wig."

Kelly slapped Porter across the shoulder, "We got us a real saint here. Another round on the house."

Port grew more irritated by the moment at the boorish Kelly but found it hard to argue with free drinks. Soon enough he wasn't really hearing Kelly anymore just a buzzing coming out of the ginger haired man's mouth. But the free drinks kept coming and Porter indulged and indulged. He enjoyed himself winning a game of poker, then an arm wrestling match and finally a show with a fan dancer. He knew he had had too much but it was so hard to say no to free drinks. And they kept coming.

Until darkness took him.

A splash and mouthful of stinging seawater roused Porter from a throbbing headache. He knew in an instant it wasn't the whiskey. It was the back of his head. A goose threatened to emerge full grown from the egg centered on the back of the skull.

His senses reeled and he sat up blindly looking about at the dark form before him. Struggling to his knees, he thought to pitch over one way then the other.

"Well, get up you scallywag!" ordered a shrill voice. "We'll have no loafers on the *Dagon*, I can tell you that."

"*Dagon?*" Port wrestled with his senses. With the cry of the gulls, he thought for a moment was still on the waterfront. But the heaving twist to and fro told him otherwise.

He was at sea!

"Up! You lubber, afore Captain Quinn takes the lash to ya!"

Grasping a solid rope that dangled near his swollen hand, Port pulled himself erect, still blinking like a newborn pup.

"You look to have a strong back. Get sobered up and we'll have you assist with the rigging first. We'll be coming about soon," shouted the shrill voice. A bell rang out from somewhere behind and men's voices chanted a gloomy sea shanty as they worked.

Daylight crept into Port's eyes and looking in every direction, he saw naught but varying shades of blue as his eyes adjusted.

"I don't belong here. I signed up for no ship. Let alone one with a godforsaken pagan moniker," snarled Porter, toward the coming shadow he deemed must be the first mate.

It was not.

The butt end of a whip struck Port across the face. Uncoiling, the whip then struck his back, shredding his woolen jacket in three stinging bursts.

Porter felt for his guns and bowie knife but they were gone.

"I tell my men that we have the title of the original sea god *Dagon. He* even before Neptune," said the captain. "It is an honor to serve his namesake."

Porter thought that a truly bizarre thing to say, but kept it to himself.

"So I'll not have sacrilege mocking my ship. As to your duty . . . I am afraid you have already been paid for your contract and services. And I can't have you thieving."

Porter retorted, "I signed no contract."

"I have the document. Your X is here. Your beneficiary, a widow in San Francisco has been given your stipend. Overseen and witnessed by a Mr. Kelly. You now serve my ship for the duration of its voyage."

Kelly! fumed Porter. He would revenge himself on that ginger headed devil. "I signed no such thing! I'll have your stipend returned, but I serve no ship! And you will owe me for the whipping!"

Two towering sailors grabbed Port's arms and held him fast. He remembered a time he could have easily thrown off the louts, but now he was weak as a kitten. The strength he had counted on had all dried out and he was at the mercy of Quinn's cruelty.

The whip cracked and met Porter across bare flesh.

"You have no choice. We set sail at dawn, hours ago. We are bound for China, then Africa, England and finally New York. Then . . . we return to California. It will be two years. In the meanwhile, you serve my ship like every other man here. Or I, Captain Quinn, will shoot you like the dog you are. Men who shirk their duties don't last long aboard the *Dagon*. Mr. Bolan!"

"Aye captain!"

"Show him to his duties."

The first mate, Bolan helped tear off Porters ruined coat and shirt. "May as well throw those boots overboard, you shan't use them here."

Porter looked and near every other man was barefoot. But if he cast the boots aside it would be the same as giving up and accepting this dreadful turn of events and he couldn't do that.

Bolan shrugged and showed Porter to his duties, and directed him in several demeaning yet necessary shipward tasks.

Cursing, Porter set about them as he studied and plotted how he would revenge himself and escape. There were several life boats, but Porter knew nothing of sailing, nor even how far he was from land any longer.

He learned that the *Dagon* was a clipper ship, bound for China to trade opium for tea. The crew were either aloof or cruel, three times he fought them that first night. He grimly had to accept he was the lowest man aboard the cursed vessel.

Over the course of the next few days, he typically found his meager amount of food tainted. Twice, men tried to knock him overboard and each time he fought back, he was given the lash. No amount of explaining would ease Captain Quinn's whip. The man enjoyed inflicting tortures on the crewmen he disliked and Porter was foremost among them.

Porter lamented that he was in bondage like the Israelites of old and he too needed a deliverer. Being that there was no one he could expect to help him, he repeated inwardly *'Lord helps those who help themselves'*. He learned all he could and after a couple of weeks he was assigned to be among the night watch for the pilot.

Hobbs, the old pilot, who was also new from California, took a shine to Porter. "I never heard you cry out when the captain whipped you."

"Didn't want to give him the satisfaction. But my teeth sure hurt from clamping them so hard," Port answered, with a chuckle.

"Here's the trick, Porter. You got to enjoy the sea, enjoy that you are here. Soon enough the captain will forget his displeasure with you. You'll become one of the crew fully and someone else will be his whipping boy."

Porter snarled, "I don't live for someone else to be at the end of his whip."

The old man shrugged, "I'm just saying make the best of the situation. You can't change anything, so be happy with what you got. Learn from every heartache and bruise. Your time is gonna come. You are here for a reason. It's fate."

"I don't believe in fate, but I appreciate a friend."

Hobbs taught Porter to reckon the ships bearings by the stars and to use the compass. In time, Porter divined their course on his own and planned his escape into the busier sea lanes. He would find a way to return home.

Weeks passed and each day Hobbs taught Porter a little more, even giving him his old sextant. Being his only friend made the old man all the more precious to Porter. So when he didn't see the old pilot on the twenty eighth morning of the voyage, he went looking.

A crowd was gathered about the bunkhouse. Porter pressed in.

"Hobbs's is dead," someone said.

Captain Quinn smirked as he looked Porter in the eye. "The ruler of the deeps claims another soul. Eventually, all of us will be in his watery thrall."

Alone again, Porter went to the stern and contributed a single drop to the salt of the sea.

That night, Porter stood upon the heaving deck. Clouds roiling into a storm about to burst, seemed alive and malevolent. Darkness etched with lightning's like a chalkboard, seemed to write his destiny with undecipherable glyphs.

Then Porter realized he was not alone upon the forecastle.

A cloaked figure stood, oblivious to the rolling of the ship upon chaotic waves as light rains fell. Surely this was not one of the *Dagon's* sailors.

"Who are you?" Porter asked the darkly garbed figure.

"The god of the waters," came the ominous reply.

Furrowing his brow, Porter challenged, "What do you here upon this wicked ship?"

The cloaked man laughed, though Porter could not see his face. "Whose ship would this be, but mine if it is as wicked as you say?"

Unsure what the figure meant Porter inquired, "Are you . . .?"

"Perhaps," interrupted the cloaked man.

"What do you want then?"

He laughed again, "I speak through this vessel. I was told I will not be allowed to claim your soul. But I prefer to test my boundaries and sure enough, every time I do, they expand. So despite you're being a favored soul, I will take you here in the deepest parts of my dominion."

Porter wondered at who could have said he was favored? Who would say such at his current condition? Why would this bizarre being want him? "You are but a vessel?"

"You are confused, good. To have knowledge would give you no comfort, only terror. Know this, I take what I wish. This is my world, my dominion. You have skated the line for too long and I lay claim to your soul."

Lightning flashed and Porter thought he detected something

physically familiar about the cloaked man, his gait and build. "You!"

"Take him!" ordered the cloaked man, as he threw back his hood. Captain Quinn's cruel features became apparent, though there was glossy mad look to his eyes.

A score of blank-eyed crewman rushed from shadowy hiding places and struggled to take hold of Porter.

Porter grabbed the first thing at hand, Hobbs's old sextant. With a firm grip, Porter swung the device, smashing jawbones and breaking free of their onslaught. He pushed them back, holding them at the forecastle steps for a mad and bloody minute.

It seemed the entire crew was now in the fray and would soon overwhelm his blows. Roaring his fury, Porter jumped to the deck and made his way toward the shroud lines. His fists never stopped slamming the sextant into his tenacious doglike foes. He felt a man's skull crack as he punched and passed the skids reaching the shrouds. Porter leapt up the lines, but was pulled back before he made it more than three steps up.

Slammed to the deck, furious arms groped and prodded him whilst also punching, gouging and tearing him. Brought to his feet, the zombie like crew stretched Porters arms, binding him with taut ropes between the mizzen and main masts.

Captain Quinn in crazed devilish bravado shouted, "Rise! Rise up and claim from the clutches of Yahweh this misbegotten soul! Steal back this son of thunder!"

Porter gazed through bleary blackened eyes. Waves off the starboard side seemed to broil and part as tentacles darker than Gehenna's abyss rose, flailing against the surface.

"Behold, he comes!" shouted Quinn.

Porter now understood the meaning of Quinn calling himself a vessel. The demon god of the deeps, Dagon, held the minds of the crew in his tentacled grasp.

A dozen or more, sinewy long sucker laden fingers reached and took hold of the gunwales of the *Dagon*. The sailors in a trance stood by as the demon monster tilted the ship with its flabby bulk.

Stretched like Samson between dark temple pillars, Porter prayed as firmly as he ever had. He called for deliverance and strained against the lines holding him between the masts.

Captain Quinn, high priest to this dark god of the depths, intoned necrotic verse in wicked glee.

Dark abysmal eyes scanned the deck, locking on the bound man.

His titanic strength returning, Porter called, "Lord, allow me to take this demon to the deep! Never to return!"

The colossal squid faced demon reached. Slimy grips yanked Porter from the mizzenmast ropes and lurched him toward its beaklike maw.

Porter pulled away, futile as it was.

Snakelike appendages coiled over his body, caressing, squeezing, killing.

With a prayer still echoing through clenched teeth, Porter pulled, willing the temple to fall, even at his own peril. He did as much as he could do . . . on his own.

Ropes snapped and the Ruler of the deep took Porter from the ship. Saltwater, bitter as bad blood rushed into his retching mouth.

Death embraced him.

But prayers were heard and answered, even in the depths of the devil's realm.

The last moment before Porter hit the grim waters, he heard the grinding snap of breaking wood.

Following Porter and the deep demon like a drawn arrow, the mainmast cracked and tipped, plunging itself into the gelatinous mass of tentacles.

Underwater, Dagon screamed in forced breathless silence. Shooting out its tentacles in horrific constricted force, smashing through the hull of its namesake.

Porter rolled in the deep, casting off his bonds. He met the stricken eye of Dagon and kicked away as its beak snapped in tenuous despair. He broke the swelling surface.

The *Dagon* listed and took fire. Men awoken from their sorcerous trance, tried to fight the blaze, but either powder, opium or oil exploded.

In a fiery instant, Porter was the last man alive at sea.

Porter held to a broken piece of mast, rolling with the waves as the currents carried him into a sea lane. Weak as a babe, he laughed with joy as the good ship, *Brooklyn*, came into view.

Bound for San Francisco, Porter would soon enough be on land, where he belonged. Soon enough this son of thunder would pay his respects to a certain Mr. Kelly. And Porter swore he would never cut his hair again.

Tangle Crowned Devil

A black scorpion crawled ponderously up Porter's arm. His bowie knife sheared the stinger without knocking the creature off balance. He slid the blade back in its sheath, silent as sleeping death.

He flicked the crippled creature away and continued watching the rustlers camp from just below the spine of a shadowy crag. He wouldn't take the chance that even the dim web of stars might outline him.

Port was being extra-cautious as of late, quite a number of folks had been taking shots at him lately and he hadn't yet been able to identify them all. The likelihood that it was the rustlers themselves watching their back trail was the most likely explanation, but if that were the case we were they being so careless now?

When the moon dipped behind clouds, he felt his way down the jagged granite boulders and stalked toward the fading orange glow of the campfire. The floor of pine needles concealed his approach and the rustlers slept soundly. Even the watchman, a half-breed Lakota, called Red Cap was dozing against a tree.

The horses nickered at Porter's approach. He grunted softly to them and they quieted, still shying away. The scent of the predator was strong even with the cool wind whipping through the pines.

A horse neighed, waking Red Cap who peered blindly into the palpable darkness. The smoky dying fire gave stark shape to the night, each tree seemed a slender column of rough tiger striped orange and black.

Port knew that old Red Cap saw nothing but might feel his presence and wake the others, he had to move fast.

Red Cap glanced toward his companions, likely taking false comfort in their nearness. The tree he sat under ran sap across his homespun blanket. The stickiness threatened to trap his hands. He rubbed them furiously against his pants so they wouldn't mar his Sharps rifle.

A soft sound in the needles was all the warning Red Cap had before looking up in time to see Port's snub-nosed Navy Colt revolver trained on his chest.

"Put it down. Quietly," whispered Porter, harsh as steel trap. His long wild hair and beard made him look every bit the maniacal gunslinger-come-lawman. For good or evil, people knew him when they saw him. Legend had it that he had shot well over a hundred men, some called him the Destroying Angel.

"Porter, I didn't want any part of this. Honest," Red Cap said, putting down the rifle and rolling away from the tree. "Two-Toes, he said . . ."

"On your belly."

Port bound the Red Cap's hands with stout rope and then put the man's own dirty sock in his mouth to gag him. Porter then walked to the sleeping men and nudged the closest one with his boot. As the man rolled over angry, Port stuck the snub nosed barrel in his face.

"Shhh. Don't need to wake your friends up just yet."

Port repeated the process until three of the five rustlers were bound up like corn husk dolls. He kicked the last two awake. They yawned and exchanged horrified looks as they beheld the infamous gunman.

"Porter, you son of a—,"

"Save the sweet talk for the judge, Two-Toes," said Porter, tossing a length of rope at Two-Toes Turley, the leader of the gang. "One of you tie up the other. And if it ain't top notch, I'll be making you walk."

That prospect alone was enough to make the two men fight each other over who got to bind who. Once they finished Porter bound the last one and double checked the other.

"My hands, I can't feel 'em," whined Saw-Tooth Roberts.

"That's alright, you don't need 'em to ride anyway," said Porter, picking Saw-Tooth up by his belt and flinging him sideways upon a waiting horse.

With dawn's early light, Porter led the five rustlers and their herd of horses back out the box canyon and northwest toward Fort Kanab. Way out across the vale Port thought he saw a small light brown creature standing on its hind end watching them. It had antlers. He shook his head guessing a shrub must have been beside the creature granting it a tangled crown. He kept riding on, but it was a strange sight.

It wasn't yet noon when a boy of perhaps twelve or thirteen came riding from the east at a furious pace.

He was calling for Porter before he even hit earshot. "Mr. Rockwell! Mr. Rockwell! I found you! Right where Mr. Lee said you'd be."

"Easy son, give that horse a breather before she keel's over on you. What's got you so riled?"

The boy nodded and got off his horse, stroking the panting creatures neck. The affection he had for the animal was plain. "Mr. Rockwell, sir, I'm John Worrell, Hezekiah Deacon's nephew. My uncle has rich claim of a mining camp on the other side of Lee's ferry. We're down a box canyon that he discovered."

Porter listened and took a swig of Valley Tan whiskey from his dusters side pocket. "So?"

"We need help, something is a murdering at night."

"Claim jumpers? Ute's?" Porter took another swig.

The boy shook his head vigorously. "No sir. My Uncle could handle other men."

Porter squinted at the boy against the sunlight. "What are you saying?"

"It's a monster sir. Kills with its mouth and antlers."

The rustlers bound and uncomfortable as they were, chuckled at the boy.

The boy glared at the rustlers. "You tell them to keep their traps shut. I'm sorry, but this thing is real. It may sound like a story but tain't."

"Monster huh? How big? Big as a man?" asked Port. Holding his hand up to gauge height. "This high?" The boy shook his head. "This high?"

"No, it's a lot bigger."

"This high?"

"No, bigger."

Porter grinned, "Lot bigger huh?" He took another swig of his whiskey. "What are you all mining in this canyon your Uncle discovered? Pyrite? Mercury? Guano?"

"You don't believe me do you? Uncle says you're the only one that can help us. He said you've dealt with monsters before."

"Maybe I have, but I got a bounty I aim to collect on these rustlers. Its gonna pay twenty dollars a head. I don't have time for something that your Pa ought a shoot himself. Probably just a bear or panther."

"No it isn't. Its killed good men," protested the boy, wiping away a tear. "My Uncle said."

"My uncle said, my uncle said, look kid. I haven't got time. I'm riding to Fort Kanab."

"Uncle Hezekiah said you might say that. Said you might not remember him from the old days back in California, back in Murderer's Bar, but he remembers you. Said he knew what would motivate you." The kid reached into his saddlebag.

Porter, ever wary, kept a free hand near his gun.

The kid pulled something small enough to be concealed in his hand out of the saddlebag and tossed it to Porter. It glittered, capturing sunlight across its face. The rustlers saw it too, nudging each other in excitement.

Porter caught it and his eyes grew wide. A gold nugget bigger than any he had ever seen, even in the days of the gold rush no one had found one this big.

"There's more where that came from, if you will come."

"You could buy an army with this. Why's it need to be me?"

"Bullets can't kill this monster."

"Course not," said Porter. "What am I supposed to do? Grin it to death?"

"Everybody in these parts knows that Porter Rockwell can't be harmed by bullet nor blade. That a holy man blessed you like Samson of old. Your long hair and you lead a charmed life. You coming with me is our only hope of killing what can't be killed."

Port admired the nugget again asking, "Am I supposed to keep this for the job?"

The boy nodded. "It's to pay you to believe and have a little respect."

Port glanced at the rustlers behind. "Two-Toes, Red Cap, Saw-Tooth and you others, *if* I let you boys go—you leave the territory and I never want to see you again. Do we understand each other?"

The rustlers who knew they were facing a hanging, all nodded. Porter cut the bindings on the lead rustler and then the rest.

"You're gonna listen to this kid's tall tale and leave us out here? What about our horses?" grumbled Two-Toes.

Port wheeled. "You ain't got horses anymore. Get going 'fore I change my mind."

"You're a gonna abandon us without guns or horses? Why that's practically a death sentence."

"I could *use you up* right now, Turley," Port snarled, emphasizing the slang for killing.

"We ain't forgetting this." The rustlers shook their heads and begrudgingly started walking.

Whether they meant that in a positive or negative light Port no longer cared. The nugget was big enough to be worth twenty bounties and if Two-Toes and the others tried any more rustling, he would just snag them again for possibly a higher bounty. Things have a way of working themselves out.

Porter ushered the pack of horses after the kid down toward the southeast. They rode the better part of the day, all the while Porter asked the kid for more information.

"So why don't bullets work?"

"We've tried shooting it, cutting at it, nothing penetrates the skin. Uncle Hezekiah lit some bonfires a couple nights back. It stays away out from the fire but the box canyon don't have much wood left. And when the fires die down it comes back and feeds."

"Feeds?"

"It's a murderer, a cannibal, its eaten seven men and one woman," said the kid, looking away to wipe a tear. "A monster killed my pa!"

"Your pa?"

The kid nodded. "I wanna kill that bastard so bad, but there's nothing I can do . . . yet."

"Alright, answer me this. Why not just leave?"

"You saw the nugget. My uncle and the others won't leave. They keep pulling the gold out of a fissure the river must have cut open this last spring. Uncle says by next year the river may change and we'll never get back. He's rich and crazy as Midas. Me? I just want revenge on that murderer."

Port nodded, "Can't say I blame ya."

As Port watched his back trail he saw the little antlered creature away out in the distance and this time he was sure there was no brush or shrubs to give illusion to the diminutive abomination.

The kid looked back and grinned.

"You seen those before?" asked Port.

"Jackalopes? Yeah, some reckon they are lucky, others say an omen of death."

"What do you think?"

"I know they are."

They reached Lee's Ferry on the Colorado river by late afternoon. Porter arranged for his newly acquired herd of horses to stay there while he and the kid would be ferried to Deacon's camp across the river. Once across what was known as Pariah's Crossing, they followed a narrow trail upriver, half of the time in the river it seemed. Porter marveled at the stark canyon walls, they were carved deep red, streaked black and burning orange like fire in stone.

"I've been here before kid and there ain't no canyon like you're telling me."

"There is. You just have to know where to look. It's not far now."

Sure enough, just around a long bend in the river a wide wet sandbar opened up along the cliff face and tucked into the slanting golden shadows of this Grand Canyon was a slot canyon no wider than six feet. It reached up hundreds of feet to the mesa above. The closer Port looked, it didn't seem to be a force of erosion, instead it was a great crack in the high desert tableau; the birthing pains of an earthquake not long ago.

Beneath the musky scent of the river, Porter smelt the stink of death. This unhallowed natural hall reeked of grim loss and decay. The horses threatened to bolt and each rider was forced to dismount and lead.

At one-point Port looked back and saw the jackalope again. He guessed it had to be a different one because there was no way such an animal could have crossed the wild Colorado. He wasn't superstitious but he started to wonder about omens.

They walked through the serpentine canyon for only a few hundred yards when it opened up to the oblong size of a few square acres. Sunlight only touched down from the high canyon walls in a few spots. The ground was rock and sand. A variety of tents, makeshift huts and lean-tos were scattered throughout and a few mangy horses stood in a dilapidated corral made of rope and driftwood. The men looked worse. Haggard and hollow-eyed, like beaten dogs they watched Port fearfully.

Port's gut told him they were up to no good but considering few if any wore gun belts, he didn't figure they could be much danger.

A man with yellow hair fading to grey came forward to take his nephew in his burly arms. He then faced Porter. "I'm Hezekiah Deacon, I want to thank you for coming."

"'Lo, but I haven't done anything yet."

Deacon smiled saying, "But you came. I was telling the men about that incident in Murderer's Bar and I told 'em you were the only man who could take care of this."

Port looked shrewdly at Deacon. "How do you know about any of that?"

"Bloody Creek Mary told me, after you left following the incident with Boyd Stewart." He grinned at that, knowing full well it was more than just an incident. Porter narrowly escaped being hung following a thousand dollar shooting match—which he won.

"Don't tell me you're friends with that polecat Stewart."

"No, but Bloody Creek Mary said you killed some monsters. Scariest things she ever saw."

Port grimaced, recalling the event brought no pride or joy, just nightmares. "I was in the wrong place, wrong time. We were blessed to escape alive."

"I take it my nephew told you what we need here?"

Porter's eyes caressed the hollow, taking in every feature where something could hide. He had suspected a trap, but the broken look of the men and stink of death spoke that this was no trap for him.

"He told me enough. When can I see this thing for myself? Has it got a lair?"

"It must, but we've never seen it. Lives somewhere up the canyon, possibly up top, we don't really know. No one has dared follow the beast."

"So it's a dumb animal?"

Deacon's face went serious as the grave, "It ain't dumb, Lord no, this thing thinks and it hates and it relish's what it does. It's an evil spawn of Cain himself."

Porter rubbed a broad hand over his forehead and adjusted his hat. His hand instinctively felt for his pistol and the deadly comfort it gave. He had never heard of a beast that couldn't be harmed by flying lead, though the creatures in California were damn close. What could this be? "If I take care of this beast . . .?"

Deacon wrinkled his face. "Didn't the boy give you the nugget?"

"He did, but I wanna hear it from you."

"You're right, *if* the monster can be killed. You deserve more. We just ain't been able to mine more because of that thing."

Port folded his arms nodding, then pulled his Valley-Tan from his duster. "What makes you think I can take care of this?"

"You've got a charmed life, especially for a gunfighter and lawman. Word is no one can harm you with a bullet or blade, you're a modern-day Samson. If anybody can face this thing it'd be you."

"I been hearing that a lot lately, though I've had some folks trying to test that."

Deacon grunted and shook his head. "Straight up that wash, is where we think the beast is. Night will be the best time to try and trap it for you to kill . . . somehow. It only comes out at night"

"I only use the same tools as any man," said Port, gesturing to his Navy Colt and Bowie. "But sometimes you need a steady hand at the wheel."

"You certainly do."

"I am tuckered, wouldn't mind a bit of shut eye before twilight."

Deacon showed Port to his tent and said, "We'll holler when we're ready."

All of it made Port uneasy but he was dog tired from scoping out the rustlers all night and he truly wanted to make things right for the Worrell kid. Why did that name seem familiar? He drifted off to uneasy dreams and the heat seemed to climb making him sweat more than he should have this time of year. Jackalopes danced in his dreams, slapping their feet against the naked desert. A warning that something was coming?

Specters haunted his sleep and something stole over him until . . .

"Mr. Rockwell, its time."

Port roused himself and felt for his gun belt, it was gone! As was his Bowie.

Nothing to do but meet this challenge head on.

Stepping outside dusk washed blue black to the horizon that barely retained a shade of blood. Stars like serpent eyes blinked overhead and Port could swear that he didn't recognize the constellations for a brief moment.

A handful of small fires blazed in a wide circular pattern and Port wondered at the devious mannerisms of Deacon and his men. "What's all this?"

"We've called out the beast to take care of you."

Port furrowed his brow. "Did I hear you right?"

"You did murderer!" accused John Worrell, his voice almost cracking to splinters.

It was then Port looked at the ground and where the fires were placed. A great pentagram was drawn out on the ground surrounding him, alien glyphs written in blood were spaced between the dark star's points and Port was in the dead center. Alone.

"Now we've all heard the tales on how you cannot be harmed by bullet or blade. I never believed them myself, but hell we've been taking shots at you for three weeks now and haven't been able to hit you once," laughed Deacon, as if it were all in good fun.

"What'd I ever do to you?" asked Port, stalling for a moment as he eyed the canyon walls watching for a way out.

"You killed my Pa! Frank Worrell!"

Port rubbed his chin. "Yep. Got him right in the belt buckle. Thought your name was familiar."

Deacon continued, "And we can all see now you're unrepentant son of a bitch too. No remorse for your killing!"

Port chuckled, "I ain't never killed anyone who didn't need killing. Frank got what was coming to him. Everyone always does."

He might have taunted them further waiting for an opening to make good his escape when an unnatural chill fell on him like the mantle of winter itself. It was a cold cutting straight to the bone and it drained any love of life Port held. Only a dim recollection of what he cared for remained, drowning in a sea of emptiness and despair.

Then he saw the eyes.

Eyes crimson and full of hate, crowned with sharp tangled antlers.

From out of the ethereal abyss the demon jackalope stood before Porter with a wide twitching nose. His matted fur was a slain brown and long black claws hung from his paws. An orange aura hung over the demon looking like flames about ready to boil over in stark contrast to the overwhelming cold emanating from this forgotten specimen of hell.

"The Zuni's call him Átahsaia, and we decided that if you couldn't be killed by mortal means we would summon a demon to do it for us."

Porter grunted and spat. "Jackalope demon huh? That's diabolical."

"Indeed it is," confirmed Deacon. "I was able to summon and control him through this book of black magic I stole from a man name of Godbe. I reckon I'll get better use of it than that Brit."

"You make a deal with the devil you're gonna pay more in interest than you ever bargained."

"Don't lecture me murderer. We got you! And you're gonna be the one to pay!"

"Want your nugget back then?" Anything to buy some time, Port hoped even angering them might give him something to work with, but not this time.

"Átahsaia destroy him!"

The monster lunged and Port dodged, but the wicked claws still tore his jacket to shreds. Trying to roll away, Port was slammed to the ground, the air bursting from his lungs under the titanic pressure.

Port swept a leg out to trip the demon, but it merely hopped over his attack.

The treacherous men laughed at the spectacle calling out Átahsaia to slay their hated foe.

The Jackalope dropped down on all fours and tried to gore Porter with its hideous antlers, but Port grabbed the furthest one out and used the momentum against it, driving the monster into the ground.

Back legs kicked out sent Port reeling. Before he knew it Átahsaia was on top.

Turning blue from the pressure of a bear-sized creature on top of him, Port dazedly thought he saw a small typical enough jackalope slapping the ground with its big foot. No, it was scraping its foot along the ground, clearing a fresh trail of earth over the old. And Port understood.

Crushed down, Port's boot cut across a portion of the pentagram's circle. A whirlwind rushed through the gap and the monster sensed freedom turning its attention from Port to its unbidden masters outside, those foolish mortals who had dared try to command it.

"Now you boys messed up. I know the secret!" Port wiped clean a wide swath of the blood-soaked ground opening the door.

Like slick lightning Átahsaia was through the gap.

Taking a precious breather for the moment, Port marveled at the look of shock and fear wafting over Deacon and his men like palpable smoke.

The monster took one of Deacon's men by the neck and throttled him. Another was impaled by the antlers and flung away, jets of blood spraying the already tainted ground.

Gunshots fired, birthed in chaotic abandon, but nothing harmed the demon.

Porter scuttled out of the damnable pentagram toward the canyon wall where the little brown jackalope had been. It was gone, but Port sensed it had stood there for good reason. Sure enough his bowie knife, gun belt and cartridges were lying there.

He checked the revolver, loaded and prepared to take whatever presented itself.

But all was now silent and gone. Deacon, Worrell and their handful of haggard men were all on the ground, bleeding out from voracious wounds.

Átahsaia was nowhere to be seen, but that vile cold still filled the camp.

Shadows moved out in the gloom and Porter prepared to give it his all against the devil's jackrabbit.

Things swept in, surrounding. Chuckles and haunting whispers came and dread footfalls washed over the blood soaked sands. Voices crept in and the dying hellish flames only made Port blind to the encroaching mass. A figure moved into the half-light.

"Told you we wouldn't forget," said Two-Toes, with a jutting grin.

Port then saw Red Cap leveling his Sharps rifle and Saw-Tooth his scattergun, the others close behind. "I never doubted you, Turley."

"How'd you kill all these feller's? And where is that nugget I saw and more? Speak or Red Cap and Saw-Tooth are gonna open you up."

"You boys should run."

Two-Toes Turley gave a charity chuckle. "You ain't immortal. You can't *use us all up.*"

"No, but he can."

Átahsaia loomed behind Two-Toes and rammed his blood-red antlers into the rustlers back. Rearing up, it flung his body away into the night. Red Cap's Sharps rifle sang out once before he died but Saw-Tooth only screamed. The others full of terror ran gibbering a brutal moment before Átahsaia bound after them silencing them swiftly. The bone-crunching savagery lasted but a few seconds.

Porter held his ground, waiting for the demon to return, all went still and though the darkness was hard as obsidian, nothing materialized and the feverish cold vanished.

Looking down, Porter saw the little jackalope beside his leg, standing on its hind quarters. He reached down to its eye level and said, "Thanks."

The next day as Porter gathered his horses from the corrals at Lee's Ferry, old Lee called out, "Will you take a look at that?" He cocked his rifle and took aim at a jackalope standing out on the flats beside the river.

Port put his hand on the barrel. "Oh no, John. That's a friend that is and good luck to boot. Don't ever try and shoot one and that's God's own truth."

Fangs Of The Dragon

He who fights with monsters should take care to see that, in doing so, he doesn't turn into a monster himself. And when you take a long look into an abyss, the abyss looks back into you.

146., Beyond Good and Evil, Friedrich Wilhelm Nietzsche (Trans. by Wm Morris)

1.

The water lapped hungrily at the shore. Waves rippled across shadowy liquid, pushed by something stronger than the moon's dominion. Something splashed far out in the lake as the mournful melody of a flute carried and abruptly went silent.

An eerie green ball of fire raced across the night sky on the far side of the lake. It shot chaotically from side to side down the mountain as if chasing down prey, diving hard, it was gone.

A man driving his wagon approached the lake. "Look at that Ahab, who says there isn't even a lake monster to see around here?" said Phineas Cook, to the dog that sat beside him. "I see lots of things." He cracked the reins and forced the ox, Petunia, down to the lake-shore.

Bringing the wagon to the rim of the ebbing surf, he circled it around next to a massive gnarled stump.

Phineas didn't want to be on Bear Lake at night, but it couldn't be helped. Work at the mill had taken longer than expected and he still had to uphold the bargain with Brother Brigham. The rope was expensive and there wouldn't be a better time than now. Naysayers were asleep, as were curious onlookers.

Bleak stars hung overhead as Phineas removed a rowboat from the wagon and set it upon the lake-shore while Ahab chased his tail.

The ox eyed the water, snorted and threatened to depart.

He ran a hand across her flanks, "Easy, Petunia. I've work to do, nothing to be afraid of."

Ahab whined.

"Same for you. We capture this leviathan and we'll be able to take care of the Church's debts. Think of the good we can do."

Ahab buried his face with his paws.

Icy mist lingered over the lake as Phineas secured a thick hemp rope to the huge stump. He put a pair of buoys in the water, one larger than the other, next to the rowboat. From the buckboard he produced a flag, Old Glory, and attached it to the top of the larger buoy.

It was cold, steam flared from his nostrils as Ahab whined again. "You coward," he said, loading the buffalo gun and setting it within easy reach.

A mournful sound carried across the waters and Phineas watched a moment, discerning nothing in the gloom. He waited a minute longer and whispered a prayer with eyes open. "Lord, walk beside me."

He lanced raw mutton upon a great triangular hook. Ahab whined so he tossed a small piece of meat to Ahab, saying, "You wait here. Watch Petunia. I'll be back shortly." He attached the hook to the smaller of the two buoys by a twenty-foot chain.

Phineas pushed the rowboat into the lake, with the tethered buoys floating beside. He kept the baited hook in the boat with the buffalo gun. He waved to the pacing dog and rowed with soft sloshing sounds out into the lake. The rope slowly uncoiled from the stump into the frigid waters. It was fall but already frost danced across the valley.

Three hundred feet out and the larger flagged buoy jerked, held fast by the great stump. Phineas had another three hundred feet for the second buoy but with as late and cold as it was, he decided he needn't row that far. He pushed the smaller buoy to let it drift away.

The twenty-foot chain dragged from the boat. Phineas picked up the stout barbed hook and let it lightly into the water.

The smaller buoy shook as the weight of the chain pulled it taut. Phineas smiled. Nothing to do now but wait and let blessings come.

A tortured scream shot across the lake.

Phineas couldn't tell if it was human or animal nor from which direction it came. The boat rocked as he looked frantically in all directions. Picking up the buffalo gun, he was momentarily disoriented as the boat spun upon the dark mirrored water.

A horrifying roar echoed over the waters, terrible in its satanic majesty. Beastly divergent from the first cry, this was the sound of a bloodthirsty victor, not a victim.

If he had ever heard a monster, that was it. The sensation of that demonic call sickened him, inducing nausea worse than the time he fell into a swarm of pungent crickets. He'd never thought to feel that horrible again, but this enveloped him in thick dread.

Silhouetted against the hills, the greenish light of a fireball rose and floated across the lake some distance south, writhing worm-like in its flight. The color and speed were too strange for a lantern, the twisting trajectory maddening.

Phineas's eyes and rifle followed the thing as it moved away. He wondered briefly if he saw the eyes of a dragon, its colossal head lumbering back and forth as it swam the lake. If so, the brute would be far larger than he had anticipated, a behemoth for the ages.

The wicked firelight continued south, growing dim until it disappeared behind hills or sinking into the depths. Phineas couldn't be sure where it vanished in the dark. He pondered his predicament when a splash and knock against the rowboat made the blood in his veins freeze in piercing shards.

Something was alive in the water beside him.

Heart thawed and racing, he paused and looked over the side.

A thick wet tongue caressed his hand.

Cursing, he leveled the gun at Ahab's wet black face. "Ahab, you fool, I nearly killed ya." He pulled the dog into the boat and was promptly rewarded with its shaking dry. "As if I'm not cold enough," he growled, before rowing with all possible speed for land.

On shore, Phineas painstakingly loaded the rowboat into the wagon as the wind came down from the north. It whipped and gave him a chill as it cut sharply through his damp clothes.

"Let's go Ahab, we gotta get home."

The dog whined again as a loud creak caught Phineas attention. The rope to the first buoy was stretched rigid to the stump, water droplets catching moonlight before falling.

"The wind must be pulling her tight," said Phineas. "It's fine."

Creaking again, the stump lurched from the bank, exposing a few inches from the sandy shore.

Phineas frowned and stepped upon the stump.

"Wind must really be pulling, but this is too heavy to go any further," he said, stamping his foot to reassure himself.

Shuddering, both the man and the stump were suddenly heaved through the air and splashed into the lake, creating a white wake in dark churning waters as the monstrous unknown force pulled them away.

Screams were swallowed up by the cold water.

Ahab whined as his master was pulled out of sight.

2.

It had been a cold night on the mountain for Porter and he meant to stay indoors tonight if he could, but first he went looking for a drink. He was of medium size but broad shouldered and strong, a fighting man, a gunslinger. Dark hair beginning to pepper erupted from beneath his slouch hat and his beard was long and wild as the north wind. But the most disconcerting thing to the townsfolk that watched him ride in, what made them turn away, was his piercing pale blue eyes. The eyes of a killer.

Riding the full length of the town and back again, he was disappointed. No saloon and no inn. He cursed the luck that broke two bottles of Valley-Tan whiskey on the ride through the mountains.

The most promising sanctuary looked to be a general store. He tied his stallion to the hitching post, knocked grime from his worn duster and went inside. His heavy boots pounding the floorboards as the spurs chimed in.

The air inside was stuffy; sunbeams swirling dust graced through thin windowpanes. A thin clerk paused reading the latest edition of the Utah Magazine and smiled, "Morning sir, what can I help you with today? Name is Thomas."

"Got any whiskey? Valley-Tan?" asked the rider, looking about the sparse room.

Frowning, Thomas put down the paper and grabbed a broom. "No, 'fraid not."

"How about a room then?"

Tightening the broomstick, Thomas said, "No, sir, we don't. You ought to keep moving along if you're looking for such things."

The rider gave a lopsided grin and ran a hand over his long peppered beard. "How's about you direct me to Brother Cook then," he said staring through Thomas.

Thomas repeated, "Brother? You . . . you're Porter Rockwell?"

Port grunted, "You sure you ain't got anything to drink?"

"Yes, sir."

Pounding the counter-top, Port said, "I need a squar' drink!"

"Let me look again. Said you want to see Brother Cook? He's laid up in bed, had an accident last night, he did," said Thomas, as he rummaged through crates behind the counter. "Seems he fell into the lake, near froze to death afore he got home. Heard he blamed it on the lake monster."

"What's that?" replied Port, only half-listening as he squinted at a suspect case in the corner.

Straightening, Thomas proclaimed, "The eighth wonder of the world Brother Rich calls it. Right here in our own valley. You haven't heard of the Bear Lake Monster?"

"No," Port groaned, "What's in that case yonder?"

"It's for tinctures."

"Good enough, hand it over," he said, extending his broad palm.

Thomas paused.

Porter gestured with hands strong enough to break a bull's neck.

Reluctantly handing over a bottle, Thomas said, "You know the Good Lord doesn't want you to drink that."

Porter uncorked the bottle, sniffed it and took a swig. "Well, has *He* ever tried it with raspberries?"

Thomas curled his lips at that. "After last night I imagine Brother Cook needs all the help he can get. Soon enough President Young will have to address things too." He held up the latest issue of the

Utah Magazine to emphasize his point.

Porter looked at Thomas. "Don't know anything about that, I just need a place to sleep a couple nights. Give me four bottles."

"But you are here because of the monster?"

"Yup, a monster, sure" said Porter between gulps.

"You don't know much about it then do you?"

"Nope. I understand there's been some killings. Brother Brigham asked me to come take care of it. *If* there was anything to it."

"There is," Thomas said with conviction. "We need true authority to take care of the problem. You can wait for Brother Cook to be ready to talk, but understand this, he had a hook and chain tied to buoys and roped to a huge stump beside the lake."

"So?" said Port, quaffing another mouthful.

"This morning Brother Rich told me, he saw that stump in the lake heading north."

Port shrugged.

"Something pulled it up the lake, against the wind, the buoys were held down underwater. This thing may be too blessed big...even for you."

"I got my own blessings," responded Port. "Where is Cook?"

"Fine house, above the mill, just up the hill. Talk to Brother Cook, but he'll be no help. If I was you, I'd talk to one of the Lamanites," he said, gesturing south.

Port's gaze hardened at that remark; it didn't seem that long ago he met the Shoshone on the Bear River. Images of frozen blood and thunder washed over him. "Which one?"

"You'll want to find Ligaii-Maiitsoh. We call him Lehi; he likes that. Knows everything about the monster."

"That's no Shoshone name," said Port.

Thomas shook his head, "He's not Shoshone, they avoid him, not sure what tribe he is. But he's been good to us. He's nearly a convert."

"Where can I find him?"

3.

Stepping into the bright sunlight, Port stared eastward across the vast long lake. He stretched his back, which in turn let his brace of pistols leer from his person.

A young mother and her son took one look at the long-haired gunfighter and wheeled around.

Port grinned. Watchdogs are rarely appreciated.

He went down the steps whistling an old tune, but a sixth sense that always rode shotgun with him, whispered, look around.

Three men, dogged his trail. They followed on his right with the rising sun at their backs.

"Hey, Rockwell! Need a word with you," shouted the foremost of the three.

Porter pretended he couldn't hear them while watching them in his peripheral vision. He crossed the muddy street in long strides, so that he was on their right, with the sun and shimmering lake at his back.

"We're talking to you, Danite!"

Porter faced them where the alleyway between buildings flashed sunlight into their faces. He watched as townsfolk scurried off the street. All but a curious white haired old Indian, he just stared.

"Hey, Porter!" called the foremost man. "Heard, you can't be shot or cut."

Port spat, "You pukes need schoolin'?"

The first averted his eyes pulling his revolver saying, "Ain't you the funny man." A second with crooked teeth also drew a pistol, the third a shotgun. They kept their distance with guns trained on Port, who had yet to draw, but they respected the pistol handles sticking out of his coat.

"You want me to feed those to ya?" asked Port with a grin.

The three stood with guns pointed but still nervous. Crooked Teeth shook so that his pistol trembled.

"You boys think I've lasted this long to be gunned down by your sorry hides?"

The leader swaggered, "Maybe. You're getting old. Why not?"

Port prodded, "So why don't ya *try* already?"

Crooked teeth, whined, "Boss said we could just run him out of town."

"Huh-uh. He ain't gonna run. Are you Porter?"

Port shook his head.

The shot-gunner chuckled, "We got him."

Port winked.

Crooked teeth wiped his brow with his free hand, letting his aim go far afield.

Porter lunged sideways, drawing his two Navy revolvers. Shots blazed and echoed. Bone shattered as Port's lead was sown scarlet upon dirty white fields.

Bullets whizzed like mercurial hornets past Port's ears, but he was untouched. He was always untouched, but he also respected how close death stood, always over his shoulder.

The three lay upon the ground, alive but wounded, mewling.

"Quit you're caterwauling," Port ordered. He nudged their shattered elbows and forearms with his boot. "You pukes is lucky, I was aiming lower." Glancing about for onlookers, "Where is the Marshall?"

The only soul on the street was the old Indian.

"Chief, I need the Marshall or deputy, where're they?"

The Indian just stared.

The lead gunman stopped crying long enough to ask, "Arrrgh. Why don't ya just kill us?"

Grinding his boot heel into the bleeding arm, Port demanded, "Why'd you come gunning for me? Who put you up to it? How'd you know I'd be here?"

The man screamed as Port's heel pressed. The old Indian still watched impassive as ever.

"Well?"

A new voice called out, "Rockwell! You can't do that, it isn't legal." A smartly dressed man approached, followed by two deputies.

"You the sheriff?" Port extended a handshake.

"I am." The man declined to shake, instead pointing at the three wounded men. "I respect your reputation, but you cannot torture these men."

The deputies picked up the wounded and led them down the road.

Grimacing, Port said, "I suppose it's right for them to threaten me on the street?"

"Of course not, but times have changed. You're not the judge, jury and executioner. Not anymore," said the sheriff.

"I never was," answered Port.

The sheriff gave a sarcastic half-grin. "I could run you in for this."

Port glared.

"But I won't, I'll ask that you leave your guns with me while you're in town."

"Ha! *No*."

Paling, the sheriff blustered, "Fine, but any more trouble and you'll be locked up."

"Someone put them up to this, I've a right to find out who."

"We'll find out. When it goes before Judge Jenson, next week. They may counter-charge you, so if there were any witnesses, you may need their testimony."

"Got one saw the whole thing." Port looked for the Indian, but the old man had disappeared on the wide open street. "He was just here."

"I didn't see anyone when I walked up. This may turn into a case of your word against theirs," said the sheriff. "Maybe you better leave town before any of that happens, let Brigham protect you again."

Cocking an eyebrow, the old gunfighter spat on the sheriff's polished boots and walked away.

4.

Port rode to the house just up the hill. A black dog lounging on the porch watched him dismount. At the door it licked Port's hand.

"Hey, boy, what's your name," asked Port kneeling. He scratched its exposed neck before knocking.

A short blonde woman opened. "I'm so glad you're here. Come in," she said, beaming. "Ahab, stay outside."

Removing his hat, Port asked, "Really, ma'am?"

"Of course. I recognize you, Brother Rockwell. I'm Amanda Cook."

Realization dawned across his face. "Wheat! You're, Dave Savage's papoose, ain't ya?" Port said with a laugh.

"Mary, see that the eggs are collected." Ushering her daughter out to the hen house, Amanda smiled. "No one has called me my father's papoose in years. Phineas is going to be so glad to see you and get your help."

"My help, ma'am?"

DAVID J. WEST – COLD SLITHER

She turned her head, "With the monster," she said, raising her eyebrows. "That is why you're here isn't it?"

"I reckon so," said Port. "But everyone seems to know a trifle more than I do."

Amanda ushered Port into a side room where Phineas lay in bed. She tossed a chunk of kindling into the fire.

Heat made Port uncomfortable. He longed for a cool breeze.

"Sorry if I don't get up," sniffed Phineas, "but I got a terrible chill last night."

"What happened? Heard you fell into the lake because of a monster," said Port.

"I didn't fall, was pulled in. Maybe twenty, thirty feet before I jumped off the stump and made it to shore. I was afraid the monster would get me," added Phineas.

"You think so?"

"Yeah, folks have been seeing the monster for a spell. Lately it's been killing livestock and Indians. Figured if we could capture it, I'd solve some of our local problems and make some money to boot." Phineas paused to blow his nose.

"It's been killing then?"

Phineas looked surprised. "Yeah Porter, I thought that was why you were here. We all heard you were coming. I assumed Brother Brigham was sending you to help us deal. Have you throw down with it!"

Port scratched his beard. "Who told you?"

"That apostate writer Stenhouse. Been shooting his mouth off about how President Young is sending you, his avenging angel, up here to save face. Stenhouse has been up here the last few weeks writing up scandalous material for Godbe's rag. Keeps saying you'll fail, since Joseph's blessing for you weren't against tooth and claw. You read any of that trash?"

"Nope."

"You know how the Godbeites are don't you? The Utah Magazine?"

"Nope. Don't read much."

Phineas wrinkled his brow and Amanda restrained a giggle. "Well, they keep pushing for mining rights, trade with gentiles and abandoning sacred law. They're upset with Church doctrine and are

106

trying to change things. Think because they control the paper and wealth they have a right, I suppose. Things could get bad if they convince the government to seize church property. We're at a crossroads."

Amanda broke in, "They believe they can steady the ark and dictate the Lord's commandments, telling the Prophet *he* is the one out of order. They are Spiritualists, communicating with either ghosts or charlatans through séances."

Phineas nodded, "Personally, I think it's all their high falutin' British sensibilities, but I doubt any of that has to do with the monster itself."

Porter grinned. "Go on."

"This monster has been costing us livestock and even been killing folk on the south end. And Stenhouse is writing up articles, playing both sides, pressing for government regulation while also pleading sympathy from the Saints by saying if Brigham can't control a thing of the devil, how can he control Deseret."

"Brother Brigham," Amanda corrected.

"That's what I said. Now Stenhouse writes if Brother Brigham can't control Deseret, if he's not in touch with the Spirit, how can he lead the Church and be right about everything else," said Phineas. "Monsters should be easy, he says."

"His fault?" Port wrinkled his brow in disbelief.

Phineas shook his head. "It's not. It's ammunition, a distraction for something else. I don't know what yet. But they're sowing seeds of doubt and discontent, while something is murdering folks and livestock."

"Seems convenient," said Port.

Amanda nodded, "That's what I said."

Phineas pointed at the lake, "There is a connection somewhere, but one thing at a time. I already heard this morning from Brother Rich, that bodies were found in the Shoshoni area and I heard screams and saw weird fireballs last night. The monster got 'em."

"I'll go look around," said Port. "Is there anyone trustworthy who speaks Shoshoni to go along with me? I heard about some old Indian named Lehi?"

Amanda shook her head. "You don't need him. I can go with you and translate. Soon as Sister Ann-Eliza arrives to look after Phineas."

Port raised his eyebrows and looked to Phineas. "This could be ugly," said Port. "I've already got somebody gunning for me."

Looking up at the old gunfighter, Amanda replied, "You need someone trustworthy to go along with you. I can help get to the bottom of this better than anyone, and take a crack shot at the monster too, if need be."

"Not a monster I'm worried about."

Amanda answered. "Have no doubts Brother Rockwell, we do seek a monster. I've seen the slaughtered cattle and sheep. I don't think my Phineas realizes how lucky he is to still be alive."

Port raised his hands, "All right, little sister, we'll head out, soon as the relief arrives. Phineas, why didn't your fishing tackle work?"

Phineas sighed, "It did work. I had stout chains and rope, but my anchor was too weak. Monster tore the stump out. If you find it, I need that rope back, it was Brigham's."

"Brother Brigham's," said Amanda.

"That's what I said. The point is, Porter, this thing is big. I'm not sure anymore what it'll take to rein the beast in."

Port tipped his hat and said, "I'll keep an eye out."

5.

A skin-drum throbbed as Port and Amanda rode into the Shoshoni camp.

Port asked, "Why the drums?"

Amanda said, "They're letting everyone know we are here. Everyone is skittish after the Bear River massacre. The monster only increases the tension."

"I reckon so."

Crowds of people gathered, faces carved with somber expressions, hard and unfriendly. A tall, young man approached Amanda and greeted her in silence. She turned to Porter saying, "This is Many-Buffalo, he is Chief of this clan, Chief Sagwitch's son." She then told Many-Buffalo of Porter.

The Chief glared at Porter and revealed a scar on his breast.

Port intervened, "It doesn't have to be like this, we don't have to be friends, I just want to know about the trouble."

Many-Buffalo, gestured at his tribe and pointed at Porter.

"I'll get to that, but they aren't in a friendly mood," she said. "He says you were there, why should he speak to you?"

Rubbing a hand over his face, Port said, "I was there, but I've never killed an innocent man, tell him that."

"I will in not so many words," said Amanda. She translated to Many-Buffalo and pointed at the lake.

The talk from several of the tribe grew excited pointing at the lake, several made a ward against evil, but Many-Buffalo looked at the sky. He spoke quickly back and forth with Amanda, who pleaded Port's case.

Amanda finally revealed, "He wants proof that you are as good a man as I say you are, before he will discuss the monsters with you."

"Monsters? There's more than one?"

"First things first," said Amanda. "He wants proof."

"Like what?" asked Port, extending his hand to shake.

Many-Buffalo hesitated, and extended his hand to Port's, but with only two fingers out, the rest clenched back.

Port questioned, "What's that?"

"He doesn't trust you."

"Wheat! I knew that. What do I need to do to get him to talk?"

A mountain of a man stepped forward, creating a hush among the tribe. Thick and strong, he looked down on Porter scrutinizing him. "You are Mormonee?" he asked, bringing his bare chest to Port's nose.

Amanda said, "This is Big Bear."

"Yeah, I'm Mormonee," answered Port. "He is probably the second biggest Indian I've ever seen."

"Do you wear the sacred robes?" asked the grinning giant.

"Yes."

"Show me."

Port opened his shirt revealing the garments. "Satisfied?"

"The woman is Mormonee too?"

"Yes."

"She will show me?" He smirked.

Port shoved Big Bear, "That's enough. Can we talk or not, Many-Buffalo? Or do I have to teach some manners to your boy?"

Amanda shook her head.

109

Big Bear knocked Port's hat off.

"Tell him! I'm here to take care of things and if they don't help me, I can't help them!" shouted Port. "But I'm not here to play games."

Many-Buffalo stood impassive, then nodded to Big Bear.

The giant lunged, grasping Port in a bear hug, trapping his arms and lifting him off the ground. The gathering laughed as Many-Buffalo shouted in triumph.

Struggling to breath, let alone move, Port asked, "What'd he say?"

"He said, if you are the best the Brigham can offer, he doesn't need help," cried Amanda over the din.

Big Bear's laughter boomed into Port's face.

"Wheat! They ain't seen nothing yet."

Big Bear's hug cracked Port's back and grew tighter, forcing air from his lungs and still the big man laughed.

Looking Big Bear square in the eye, Port winked and slammed his thick forehead into Big Bear's nose repeatedly. The huge man blinded and bloodied, dropped Port, who landed on his feet. Porter slammed Big Bear an uppercut to the chin, dropping the man mountain. Rounding on Many-Buffalo, Port snarled, "Was he the best you got?"

Amanda translated.

Many-Buffalo frowned, but motioned for Port and Amanda to follow.

Amanda picked up Port's hat, and handed it to him saying, "You know, might doesn't always make right."

"Didn't *I* just prove that?"

6.

Though it was still afternoon on a warm day, Many-Buffalo kindled the fire inside his tepee. He took a powder and scattered about the perimeter of his dwelling, paying specific attention to the door-flap.

Sitting on buffalo skins, Port and Amanda waited, while Many-Buffalo sang a song of blessing and protection. Taking a seat opposite them, Many-Buffalo spoke quick, harsh-sounding words, staring deep at Port.

Amanda translated, "He said . . . to speak of such things as we ask . . . he must bless and purify his tepee. He will do it again . . . after we've gone. They've had problems . . . but he will not ask for help . . . since he was already denied."

"Tell him this. A proud man won't ask, but a proud man can answer. Tell him, I'm asking to know about these things, so I can help his people."

Many-Buffalo looked at Port as Amanda spoke. He nodded and went into a lengthy round of back and forth with Amanda, as she gave Port snippets.

"He says the lake monster . . . haunted the waters in the time of his ancestors. It has slept for many moons . . . and only awoke when . . . Mormons came. It eats sheep and cattle . . . perhaps even men . . . but it is not to be confused . . . with other curses that have befallen his people. Murders have come . . . the last few weeks . . . only. Sorcery has tainted the people. They fear the witch and skin-walker . . . more than they do . . . the lake monster. The reason . . . they have not moved yet . . . because these evil things follow them."

"What's that?"

Amanda shook her head, "I'm not sure but it has all of them afraid. He is reluctant to tell me more . . . because it invites . . . the evil thing into his tepee. They hoped Brother Brigham could help . . . but the . . . drawing man . . . told them Brigham . . . would not help."

"What's a drawing man?"

Amanda shrugged. "There is no word for it, I translated as best I could."

"What can he say about the lake monster? How big is it? Is there a way to kill it?"

She asked Many-Buffalo and he pondered a moment, before going into a number of hand gestures and excited speaking with a final disgusted look before throwing holy powder into the fire, that made it blaze brilliantly.

"He says they are related . . . that Mormons . . . brought the curse here . . . the monsters are linked to each other . . . yours and ours," said Amanda. "I'm not sure what yours and ours mean."

Port rubbed smoke from his eyes, "I thought we would get some answers here."

"I'm sorry. They're scared. This has touched them deeply," she said.

Many-Buffalo watched them and spoke again.

"He says their burial grounds . . . have been violated. Something steals from the dead. As for your questions . . . the lake monster . . . is long as four wagons . . . and its skin cannot be wounded . . . by a gun or knife."

"Kinda like me," said Port.

"He says . . . works of darkness . . . fill this land. We walk...the path of the . . . skin-walker. May the Great Spirit...protect us . . . on our quest. He will say no more."

Murmuring the drums outside beat again.

Amanda gasped, "Someone is here."

7.

A man on a rickety wagon pulled into the Shoshoni camp. Bearded and slight, he glowered at Port and Amanda as they exited Many-Buffalo's tepee.

"What's the matter Stenhouse? Upset I wasn't chased outta town by your blacklegs?" called Port, chuckling.

Stenhouse dropped off the wagon, tipped his hat to Amanda, "Mrs. Cook," and extended a hand to Port. "My apologies, the uneducated rascal's misunderstood my direction and inclination. I have not levied them out of jail and I directed the sheriff to let the lot of them stay a fortnight therein."

Port declined the handshake, as he tried not to smirk at Stenhouse's English pretentious accent.

Stenhouse continued, "Forgive my temper, I merely wished to meet with Chief Sagwitch's son myself, and worried that he already had guests, you see."

"Yeah, 'I see'," mocked Port, "you're upset we beat you here before you could spread more lies. How'd you know I was coming up to Bear Lake before I did?"

"Nothing of the sort, I came to speak with the Chief much the same as I imagine you did, as for knowing you would be here...whom else would Brigham send? Understanding his mentality, as I do, it was elementary, my dear Danite."

Port sniffed and spit.

"Regardless of what you may think of me, Porter, I am not the enemy. We may disagree fundamentally on authority, but our core is the same. The New Movement and I seek truth the same as you."

Amanda countered, "What was it Fanny wrote? To doubt one doctrine was to doubt all? Our core is not the same. You abandoned yours."

"Madam, I must protest."

But Amanda wasn't even close to being done, she reared up in the Englishman's face. Port stood back and smiled, this was gonna be good.

"You think we haven't all had hardships? You think we haven't all questioned the tests we have in life? Let me tell you something. You'll be caught in your own traps."

Stenhouse looked to Port for assistance from the feisty young woman, but the old gunfighter raised his hands, cocked his head and smirked.

"Don't you and the other Godbeites fool yourselves. This life isn't where you will be successful. It's in the eternities. Just because Brother Brigham might have given you some bad business advice or won't let you mine our mountains to ruin, doesn't mean you can become a law unto yourselves. If you lost faith in God, it's because you put your faith in the arm of flesh!" shouted Amanda. "Your lies and schemes will snap back upon you."

With that, she mounted her horse and cantered off.

Visibly disturbed at her words, Stenhouse slunk away.

Port followed after Amanda.

Big Bear, still cradling his broken nose, glared at Port.

Tipping his hat to the big man, Port gave his horse heels to catch up to Amanda.

She turned in the saddle, "I'm sorry about that, but I'm so tired of his lies."

"No problem, little sister."

"I did give him what-for, didn't I?"

"Yes, you did," Port laughed, deep and loud.

8.

Dusk rode in with Port, laying red like a mantle across the valley. With no clouds, it would be a cold night.

In the Cook home, Phineas gave his wife a warm hug before grilling Port. "So what'd you find out?"

"Whole lot of nothing. Many-Buffalo didn't have anything I can use and wouldn't tell us much of what's happened to his tribe."

Mary, the Cook's young daughter, offered Port a glass of water and hugged her mother's skirt.

"They're scared," said Amanda. "Something is happening. They feel powerless. And Stenhouse went out there after us."

"Really? What'd he want?" asked Phineas.

Port gulped down the glass of water and made a face, "Said he wanted to talk to Many-Buffalo. Don't know what for. Amanda gave him a good tongue lashing though."

Amanda blushed, "I did, I suppose." Phineas's beamed.

Port took off his hat and slumped into a chair. "Now, I need to find out why Stenhouse tried to get me outta town."

"He's afraid of you!"

"Well, he should've known his thugs couldn't do it. But why would he wanna talk to the Shoshoni? Can't imagine him getting any farther than I did."

"Nothing to do then but get some rest for the morrow," said Phineas. "Way past your bedtime, Mary."

"Goodnight, Papa," said Mary, hurrying to bed.

9.

The little girl rushed up the steps to the loft. The moon shone in her window like a finger of ice. Nestling in the covers, she said her personal prayers, closing her eyes as the lamp downstairs dimmed. She slept restless, dreaming of drowning.

She awoke with a start as a mystic green light passed her window. It wasn't the rising corn-yellow moon. Whatever it was lay outside her window. Sitting up, she gazed into the darkness and witnessed a pallid

114

form shamble through the trees.

From behind the closest tree, a taloned hand gripped bark and then a white face leered. It was wolf-like, with red eyes glowing like embers which burrowed into Mary's.

Fear petrified her, she couldn't look away from the thing loping closer. So frightened she couldn't speak, only shake. Did the monster smile at that? The hideous wolf-man looked from her to the front door.

It would come inside.

She shivered, too terrified to warn her parents. She heard father downstairs, talking with the strange long-haired man. Her lips trembled but no sound came.

The thing stood directly below her window. It seemed capable of leaping up and through the glass. Those eyes so blood-red and evil. She couldn't look away, what horrors did it have planned for her? Her parents? Her sleeping siblings? It would come inside and devour them.

The monster, with white talons smeared scarlet, motioned for her to come.

Compelled beyond fear and reason, Mary released the latch on the window.

Saliva dripped as its tongue lolled.

Mary pushed the window open.

The monster beckoned her to jump, its eyes hypnotizing.

Too afraid to move, to scream or even look away, Mary did the only thing left her, she cried a prayer deep inside for deliverance.

The wolf-thing beckoned for her to jump into its waiting arms.

Tears streaming, Mary lifted herself to the sill and precariously balanced, halfway in and out.

Licking its lips, it beckoned again as the moon illuminated its awful red matted fur.

Was there no relief? Did those who gave themselves to monsters deserve heaven?

Ahab the dog, bawled out loud in staccato.

The spell broken, Mary snapped back to self-control and dropped to the floor avoiding any possible eye contact. She heard Father and the long-haired stranger startle, each muttering as they stirred. The familiar cocking of guns told her they were prepared.

The wolf-thing snarled at Ahab, who cowered beneath the porch.

Praising the Lord for delivering her family from the evil of this thing Mary shut the window latch.

Raging, the beast summoned a ball of green fire in its left hand and cast it through her window. Flames erupted all about the bedroom as Mary screamed.

10.

"What the devil was that horrible sound?" shouted Port, drawing his pistols. He threw back the front door and looked into the gloom. Nothing.

Ghostly green-orange firelight blazed upstairs, licking the windowsill and rafters.

Phineas cried, "Porter, help! The house is on fire!"

Somewhere a child screamed an unholy fear.

Port replaced his pistols and stepped back through the doorway only to be grasped by the back of his coat and flung backward off the porch.

Stars reeled overhead as a black wind blew.

The breath knocked from his lungs, senses fled and only the fire above was visible. He struggled to sit up. Reaching for his pistols, his hands found empty holsters.

Forcibly lifted, someone slammed him to the ground. The most disturbing part to the Danite was the low rumbling chuckle the attacker let out. He couldn't see his enemy, but he heard him all right.

Port kicked and connected to thick shin bone.

The midnight assailant didn't chuckle anymore.

Rolling to his feet, Port snatched his Bowie, ready for anything.

As the enemy grabbed him again, Port's blade slashed across its chest. Blood and tufts of a white fur spiraled from the wound. Port trusted his honed senses to guide his hand. Listening intently, to his right a twig snapped. He barreled toward the sound, knife extended.

Port felt steel bite flesh, ripping the blade across what he hoped were vitals.

Howling in pain, an inhumanly strong hand took Port's shoulder, tearing cloth, and threw him to the earth.

116

Roaring, "Wheat in the mill!" Port launched up, renewed to fight his foe with blood-maddening vigor. He spun about, waving the Bowie, expecting another attack.

None came.

Dark blood along with flecks of white fur trailed into the gulf of night. Port raced back to the house to fight the fire.

Inside Phineas and Amanda held their daughter. The fire was out. Mary was shivering, wiping the last of her tears away. "You did it."

"I've never seen the like," gasped Phineas. "The room blazed like a furnace. You must have slain the thing because the witch-fire up and disappeared. Thank you."

"Yes, thank you," repeated Amanda, her own tears falling. "It's over."

Shaking his head, Port growled, "No, 'tain't. I didn't kill it."

11.

A long night brought morning headaches and breakfast questions.

"So what do you reckon it was?" asked Phineas.

Port chewed his mouthful, saying, "Probably that Shoshoni giant Big Bear. From what Mary said, sounds about the same size. Know I cut him bad, so he's probably gonna hole up in a sweat lodge for a while."

"What about the witch-fire?"

Stabbing another piece of venison, Port answered, "I've seen enough strange things in my time, to say anything is possible. Tricks is key to the sorcerer type. Probably a wolf-skin mask and bear-paw war-club."

"That was no mask," broke in Mary. "That was a monster."

Shaking her head, Amanda said, "That wasn't natural."

"Darkness can play tricks on you."

The little girl shook her head, "No, this was real bad. That thing is of the devil."

"Men can be monsters too," said Port, finishing his last bite. "Much obliged Brother Cook, Sister Cook." He looked to Mary and rubbed his broad hand over her head. "I'm gonna get to the bottom this, an' that's a promise."

Amanda threw down her dishrag, "And just what are you planning to do? Sounds like you're in denial of monsters."

Grinning, Port said, "No need to worry, ma'am. I think Stenhouse, the Godbeites and some of the Shoshoni are in cahoots. I need a few more answers and I'll get 'em."

Blocking the door, Amanda said, "None of that explains the lake monster, what we saw last night was something different, probably the same thing that has the Shoshoni frightened. There has to be more to this than Stenhouse and a few bribed Indians."

"I'm sure there is, but I can't take care of it, jawing 'bout it."

Amanda looked to Phineas, who nodded. "Then I'm coming with you. You need someone's help to translate and watch your back," she said.

Port shook his head, like a black-maned lion. "No, ma'am. I got an instinct about a few things I'd best check out on my own." Before she could protest, he added. "And I won't need a translator this time. Thanks for breakfast. Feel better Phineas." Port tipped his hat, adjusted his gun belt and went out into the cool morning.

As he made for the Cooks' stable, a hint of white moving in the trees caught his eye. It swayed with the light breeze at eye level. Port drew his trusty Navy revolver and approached with grim determination.

It looked like a tangled bunch of pale sticks strung in the pines facing the Cook homestead, but closer inspection revealed it was a curious cobble of interlaced bones, calico twine and a couple of dark feathers, about the size of his hand. It was some type of Indian fetish or charm. Then again it looked more like something a white man would make rather than a real Indian charm. The bones looked like chicken as opposed to eagle or crow. That and it smelt of coffee, not the succulent flowers of the field.

Port tore it down and put it in his pocket. He considered telling the Cook's what he found but decided against it, they were spooked enough.

12.

In town, a heated commotion carried over the streets. Men

shouted at one another and Port could feel the contentious spirit waxing. There appeared to be two opposing camps, one backed by Stenhouse, the sheriff, and their full gang of thugs; the other fronted by tall Joseph Rich, the local newspaperman, who was supported by a good number of townsfolk.

Port couldn't tell what started the argument.

Rich's strong baritone proclaimed, "I lost a horse to the monster. But that doesn't mean it needs to be destroyed!"

Stenhouse countered, "You're the beast's greatest advocate. It clears you of the secret gambling debts, you lost your mount to. It grants sensationalism and lurid stories for your amateur journalism, but you seem to forget the spiritual implications."

Men tried to shout him down, including Rich for the gambling crack, but Stenhouse persisted. "A duel is coming! The hour of struggle is at hand. If *infallible* Brigham," he said sarcastically, "can't cast out the devil, what good is he?"

A man swung at Stenhouse but was instead hit first across the mouth by one of the deputies.

Stenhouse continued, "If a man is to lead this people he has to be open to new revelation. We can change what doesn't belong. We can prosper with what the Lord grants us here in these mountains, there is gold and silver aplenty!"

Stenhouse had Port's full attention.

"My friends, Brigham is a good man but he has lost his way, don't you lose it alongside him, a new prophet will rise!"

"Yeah? Who?" squawked a man between Stenhouse and Rich.

"Why the very blood of the great prophet himself, Joseph the third."

A number of boos and catcalls came with the mention of Joseph Smith's eldest son. Port just shook his head.

"What about the monster?" shouted a man in the crowd.

Another cried, "It took my sheep."

"What can be done about it? It killed Big Bear and a half dozen braves last night."

Port's eyes grew. He struggled through the throng to get to the man who mentioned Big Bear.

The rebuttal from Rich was lost to Port's ears as he pushed and grabbed the man's shoulder.

"You! Who told you Big Bear is dead?"

The man spun trying to escape Port's grasp then breathed a sigh of relief, "It's you. You'll take care of this."

"What about Big Bear?"

"He's dead. Seen him myself yonder. Chief Many-Buffalo brought what's left of his body and the others into town a half hour ago."

"Was he cut up with a Bowie?"

The man blanched, "No! The monster took bites outta him. It's gruesome. Go see."

Port let go of the man's shoulder and drifted out of the crowd.

A familiar voice spoke, "Porter, what do you make of this?" It was Thomas, the shopkeeper. "You ever go talk to Lehi?"

Port shook his head, then spotted Many-Buffalo.

"You should, I'll bet he could explain things."

"Much obliged," said Port abruptly walking away.

13.

Many-Buffalo was surrounded by a dozen wailing women, the remains of his braves lay beneath a broad red blanket. He was speaking with local authority and Apostle Charles C. Rich.

"Brother Rich, can I take a look?" asked Port.

"Go ahead Brother Rockwell. Chief Many-Buffalo has just asked my help in blessing them for their journey."

Port nodded and looked to Many-Buffalo who still gave the unfriendly glare he had from the day before. Lifting the blanket's edge, Port looked upon the terrible visage of Big Bear. He expected to see evidence of his Bowie, but not this—carnage to rival the worst horror he had ever witnessed. Claw and bite wounds from something huge. The same atrocities had been dealt to three more men.

There went Port's personal theory for last night's incident. Big Bear could not possibly have been the enemy he fought in the darkness.

"Many-Buffalo tells me that you and Sister Cook visited him yesterday," said Charles.

"We did. So did Stenhouse."

"He said Stenhouse came wanting to know what could be done

about the monster, if there was anything he could do to help. He gave them some of the latest model of guns, repeating rifles and the like and yet, you see here what happened," said Charles.

Port squinted across the way at Stenhouse still fuming his 'New Movement' to the townsfolk. "Why try and get the Indian's to deal with this thing though? Why wouldn't he have that crooked sheriff and his blacklegs deal?"

"I couldn't begin to say."

Port threw back the blanket pointing at vicious wounds, "This gives more questions than answers. Seems worse than a bear attack."

Charles nodded, "These men could have handled a bear."

Narrowing his gaze, Port noticed Big Bear had a small bone fetish on his belt just like the one he found earlier. "Something is sending a message. But I can't read it, yet."

"Some messages can't be read," said the Apostle. "And when words can't cut the evil, it's time to use a sword."

Port grinned as he drew, spun and holstered his Navy Colts. "I find a six-gun is quicker."

14.

Port had a vague impression of where to find Lehi, the old Indian that supposedly knew so much about the monster. A whistle drew his attention.

It was Stenhouse, across the street. He beckoned for Port to come and speak with him in front of the sheriff's office.

Flexing his fingers, Port warily eyed the windows and hiding spots behind Stenhouse. He was ready to draw his Navy Colts like chain lightning if need be.

"What do you want?" he growled.

"Just to speak a moment, without the self-righteous she-cat beside you."

Porter grabbed Stenhouse's tie, yanking him closer, "You'll speak kindly about the lady."

"Hey! You'll keep your hands of Mr. Stenhouse," called the sheriff, from inside the office.

Port shoved the thin man away. "I've heard how you treat *your* women."

Stenhouse rankled at the insinuation. "I beg your pardon. We have had our differences, our run-ins, but I wanted to let you know that a new wind is blowing. Utah is changing, the railroad is here and new revelations come with it. You can be part of the old guard that is swept away and forgotten—or be a part of the reformation."

Port shook his head, "You really know nothing about me."

"I know this," said Stenhouse, his tone turning cruel and superior. "I spoke to Vice-President Colfax only a few short weeks ago, the government is tired of Brigham's unfriendly theocracy, his dictatorship of the territory, his dominion of Deseret."

"You always were too theatrical, Stenhouse."

"Oh no, not this time. This is real. They are going to invade, they are going to take our lands by force and destroy the Church if things aren't changed. We in the New Movement are working toward effecting that change before it's too late. We could use your help."

Port guffawed.

"Laugh," Stenhouse said coldly. "Evidence that Brigham is counterfeiting is being filed."

"That'll never stick," objected Port.

"Oh no? How about this. There are those who will testify that he ordered Mountain Meadows."

Port frowned, "That's a lie and you know it."

"Do I? Does it matter if the government gets hold of the evidence to destroy the Church? Our survival depends on change. Brigham is a fallen prophet. He has lost his way. He can't even repudiate a monster that threatens his own people—what about the monster that is the U.S. Army? The people must abandon Brigham and follow the New Movement."

Narrowing his steely gaze, Port rumbled, "What's your part in this? Who's gonna lose faith in the prophet over a monster?"

Stenhouse's tone changed again, "I'll tell you because I'm afraid. No one has put this together yet. Every night with a waxing moon, the body count doubles. The creature's blood lust cannot be sated. Brigham can't protect anyone. How many deaths have you prevented since you arrived? Yes, even the '*Destroying Angel*' is helpless against this monster."

"Then why doesn't the New Movement take care of it?"

"Things have to get worse before they can get better."

Port said, "Hogwash. You're all using this as an agenda. You make me sick."

"Say what you will, but shame is our only tool. To shame President Young into acknowledging us his spiritual betters. Only then will we step forward and alleviate this threat."

Port shook his head, "So, you will let men die to further gain your political ambitions? Out of my way I got things to do."

"You think so small. Better for a few men to die than for a people to perish in ignorance. We will bring balance to the Church," said Stenhouse. "New revelation has been given, the spirits have granted us release and wisdom. They have given us solution to our predicament."

Port rubbed a hand across his beard as if pondering.

"I offer you a place. Reject us and it will not be offered again and you will be swept away as so much chaff! The field is ripe. Where will you stand?"

Putting his nose inches from Stenhouse's, Port whispered, "That's the name of the game." He lightly patted the Englishman's cheek twice, then strode down the street to fetch his horse.

"What does that mean?"

"Figure it out," Port called.

A few minutes later, Port rode down the hill from the Cook's and came in behind the sheriff's office. He pulled the strange fetish of stick-like bones from his jacket pocket and tossed it upon the roof of the office. Chuckling, he rode on.

15.

Port rode with the wind at his back, watching the long lake and pondering. Why would the Lord allow these things to plague good people? What was the test? The lesson to be learned? What was his own part and responsibility?

All experiences are for our ultimate good, mused Port.

Sheep grazed in large swaths across the rounded landscape, most flocks were tended by young boys.

He trotted his stallion up to a tousle-headed boy and nodded,

"Afternoon, son. You out here a lot?"

"Every day, mister."

"Ever see anything strange?"

The boy smiled. "Besides you?"

Port chuckled, "Yeah, besides me. A monster maybe."

The boy went serious. "I thought I saw it once."

Port folded his arms, now he was getting somewhere.

"I was playing by the lake shore when I saw six or seven dark shapes out in the water. A big horse-like head with horns was coming out, right at me. I was so afraid. I couldn't hardly breathe, let alone move."

Port looked out at the lake again. "You saw it? Didn't it try to eat you?"

"No, it wasn't the monster," the boy smirked, "it was a herd of elk crossing the lake. The bull was in front, the cows behind. My fear made a monster."

"You don't believe in the monster?" questioned Port.

"I didn't say that. I'm just saying things aren't always what they seem."

"True," Port said. "Know where to find an old Indian, called Lehi?"

The boy pointed southwest, "Over those hills somewhere. No one lives near him."

"Much obliged," said Port, galloping away.

"No one lives near him," called the boy.

"I heard ya," shouted Port over his shoulder.

16.

Over rolling hillocks and past a few stands of trees Port saw a wisp of rising smoke, thin and gray, curling toward heaven through the light drizzle.

"Hello, the camp! Lehi?" Port called. Experience said you were better off letting folks know you were coming in.

Rounding the bend, a rotted tepee came into view. It looked smaller than the usual ten to twelve buffalo-hide tepees. It was made of perhaps eight skins.

Port's horse nickered at entering the clearing and tried to turn away. Glancing about for a possible predator, Port called again, "Lehi, you out here?"

"I am here," announced a ragged voice as the tepee flap peeled back and the very same elderly Indian from town the day before peered out. "Go away! What you want? Blood?"

Laughing, "You're the old man in town from yesterday!" Port dismounted the skittish horse. "You could've saved me the trip if you would've stuck around."

Exiting the tepee, Lehi frowned. "I have things to do."

"Take it easy. I just wanted to talk to you for a spell 'bout the monster. I'm Porter," he said, extending his hand.

Cocking his head, the old Indian stared with eyes hard and cold as the mountaintop. "I tell you as I told them. Monster comes to eat on clear night when moon grows like swelling belly." He stepped out of the tepee and stood uncomfortably close to Porter.

"They said you could tell me all about the monster."

Smirking, Lehi answered, "You want a story, you got to pay." He opened his hand, expecting.

The horse whinnied and backed away pulling the reins in Port's clenched fist. The ragged voice and unnerved horse put Port's guard up. He considered drawing his sawed-off Navy Colt.

Lehi grinned. "Forget it. I like you. We are the same, you and I."

Nerves calmed, Port said, "Anytime." He took one of the tincture bottles from his saddle bags and handed it to a pleased Lehi. "About last night, what do you know about the lake monster? What's it look like? Any weaknesses?"

Lehi nodded. "Trust in Great Spirit, but tie up your horse. Let us speak inside," he said, as he gestured to his faded buffalo-skin tepee.

A smell that Port attributed to the old man's lifestyle permeated the inside of the tepee, it was similar to wet dog but with a reptilian copper scent. Ratty old furs and skins made up the old man's bed. A handful of tools cluttered the far side of the tepee. A ring of stones held a few glowing coals in the center. Unexpected to Port, was a worn copy of the Book of Mormon.

"You read?"

"I feel it is truth," said Lehi, "but my reading is not yet bountiful."

Port grinned, "Me too."

Lehi sat cross-legged opposite Porter and pushed back his beaded breastwork, revealing massive scars along his chest and shoulder. The trauma displayed was so extensive Port wondered at how the old man survived.

Showing a missing finger and the stub next to it on his left hand, Lehi said, "This is where great serpent bit me, here and here." He pointed to his shoulder, chest and upheld his disfigured hand.

"When was this?"

"To my life . . . not long ago. Was first time I saw great serpent. I sang old songs calling for the Old Ones. But Great Serpent heard me and came. Him very angry with me," chuckled Lehi.

"Why is that?"

"Great Serpent not want to be wakened. He is lost and used."

Wrinkling his forehead Port asked, "Lost? Used? I don't follow you."

Wrapping himself in his cloak, Lehi said, "Great Serpent not meant to be here. He will not listen to me. But there is purpose in all things."

"How big is he? Can he be killed?"

Lehi lit a pipe before answering and stared into the smoldering center a long while. "I will tell you, because you are like me, a hunter of men. No gun of white man can kill Great Serpent. It is long as four wagons. It is a thing from old times."

"But why is it here?"

Lehi shrugged, "Why does sun rise? Moon set? It just is."

"Are you saying it can't be killed?"

Lehi smiled, revealing wicked teeth for an old man. "I say, do not even try. Monster will eat you."

Port didn't like his tone. "If it lives, it can be killed."

"You have brave heart. Perhaps there is a way."

Port rubbed his chin. "Go on."

"Would be dangerous. We would be risking our lives."

"That's my business. I've got a charmed life."

Lehi nodded and beckoned Port to follow. He stepped out of his tepee, and trotted out of the glade and into the thick brush. The speed of the old man amazed Port.

Lehi gathered a handful of pale roots. "We poison Great Serpent, tonight."

Port looked skeptical, "How come no one has tried this before?"

Lehi chuckled, "Who stupid enough to face Great Serpent?"

"Good point."

17.

Lehi had a wide raft that would take them out into the lake. It was slow going, but allowed for more fighting space in Port's mind. The raft seemed safer than a canoe which could be capsized, leaving them at the mercy of the lake monster.

Port left his stallion on shore with a good bit of tether. Considering Joseph Rich had already lost a horse to the monster, Port left his farther uphill. He brought his blessed Bowie knife, his two sawed-off Navy revolvers, and a 45-70 buffalo gun.

Lehi brought a deer-skin sack full of the poisonous roots, Port's gift of a tincture bottle, his flute, a tomahawk pipe, and a bit of firewood that he would use to make a fire on the raft over the top of a stone and mud section he had pre-arranged. A small burnt scar upon the raft denoted where he had done this in the past.

"Tell me again, how we're gonna get the monster to eat these roots," asked Port, regretting not having another bottle of Valley-Tan.

Lehi watched the gunfighter's eyes and gestured to the bottle.

"Much obliged."

Lehi nodded and said, "I will call Great Serpent. When he comes, his mouth wide to eat, throw in roots. But not until he right beside us. Very close."

"Could it sink us?"

"Sure. But I will sing our death song and chant old ways. You can shoot if you like, but it do no good. Roots work fast."

Port wasn't familiar with that many plants, but he never heard of a poisonous root such as this before, but maybe it was Indian magic.

Dusk came quick, casting red twilight over the valley. Somewhere a wolf howled and Port watched the shore. With the sun down, cold wrapped its arms about them. The cold sapphire waters did not look inviting.

Lehi lit his fire with a bow drill. He was amazingly quick. He blew on the shards of spark and they leapt into action as if commanded by the breath of the divine. The orange glow fought and won against the encroaching night. The old man lit his pipe and inhaled deep breaths, puffing them toward the west, to which he bowed.

Port expected him to do something more, perhaps something to the east but he didn't.

"We will let darkness grow a little stronger," said Lehi. "Then I will call Great Serpent out."

"How about another pull on that raspberry tincture then?"

Lehi handed Port the bottle.

An hour or two later their kindling was almost gone and Port dreaded the idea of being on the lake in the dark. "Well, is it time yet?"

Flute in hand, Lehi stood and played a melancholy and disturbing tune. The notes rose and fell in a jarring dirge that Port theorized was never meant to be heard by a white man. It was primal and savage, a true song of the wilds, full of wonder and midnight.

Something splashed out in the waters, forbidden to Port's sight.

"It comes," said Lehi.

"You sure?"

Lehi didn't answer, but blew a long note from his flute and went silent.

Port dropped the sack of poison roots at his own feet and readied the buffalo gun. If anything could penetrate the monsters hide, he reasoned it would be his 45-70. Glancing about, Port was ready, but no more splashing came.

Lehi broke into song, a sad and painful chant.

Port heard a splash like an oar hitting the water. The bright moon was just coming over Black Mountain to the east and Port thought he could see a canoe heading toward them. "Someone's out there Lehi, it ain't the monster."

The canoe glided closer and regardless of the dying fire, Lehi continued his chant. "Hey-yaw, taw hey-yaw. Zhoo' yea' Zhoo' yea'. Yana Glooshi, hey-yaw, taw hey yaw."

"Who's there?" asked Port of the darkness.

No answer came, or at least none he could hear above Lehi's chanting.

Port threw the last few chunks of fuel into the fire hoping to pierce the darkness a little better, absently wondering if whomever was about to meet them had seen anything up the lake.

The fire briefly flared and hid, perking up and down as it consumed its meager final meal.

Facing the incoming canoe, Port couldn't see anyone paddling it, just the form drifting closer. He strained to hear if anyone had fallen overboard or worse, if there was a struggle from someone becoming a monster's most recent meal.

"Hey-yaw, taw hey-yaw. Zhoo' yea' Zhoo' yea'. Yana Glooshi, hey-yaw, taw hey yaw. Oh yaw-hey! Oh yaw-hey! Yaw!" sang Lehi, powerful and deep.

The canoe was almost to the raft and Port puzzled over its missing pilot. He saw that the canoe was misshapen, strangely wider toward the rear. Was there a body slumped to the rear?

Gazing hard at the canoe, a wisp of flame from the firelight flared up for a fraction of a second and allowed Port to see two black eyes reflecting back the orange fire-light. Two massive eyes each set in the wider portion of what was not a canoe but the monster's head. Like a crocodile it had cruised upon them, drawn by the shaman's song.

The huge multi-fanged mouth sprang open.

Port braced himself, too stunned to shoot or grab the sack of poisoned roots.

Ferocious jaws came down, splintering the raft into kindling, snuffing the weak fire and coals.

Pitched into the air, Port was fell forward into the waiting jaws of the Bear Lake monster. He hit the giant tongue and was aware of a bright green light behind him as the cavernous mouth closed.

18.

Cold moonlight reached through the sheriff's office window, barely warded off by the wood stove. Eight men sat with greasy cards as the lamp guttered low. Stenhouse was the only man sitting out the card game, but his whiskey bottle was emptier than most as he wrote at a furious pace.

"Probably ought to call it a night," said the sheriff. "Just after midnight."

Stenhouse didn't bother looking at him from his crouched

position over the desk. "I'm not yet done recording the events of today. I have more."

The sheriff laughed obscenely and dealt the next hand.

A thunder rolled off the lake and even against the hugely waxing moon, a green-hued light approached, casting wicked intentions on the office floor like a dueling gauntlet.

Stenhouse visibly shuddered, saying, "It will keep going, it will keep going."

"You know what that is or something?" asked one of his hired gunmen.

"No . . . no, just unnerving is all."

Another hired gun added, "People been seeing 'em all week. Probably shootin' stars is all, boss."

From that remark the deputy told a crude joke causing riotous laughter.

Stenhouse turned from the desk glaring, "Be quiet, I am trying to work!"

A chorus of off-color laughter was interrupted by a loud thump upon the roof above their heads. Dust shook from the rafters coating the men in pale gray hues.

The card players looked up in wonder then terror as steps bounded across the roof. Stenhouse was halfway under his desk by the first thud.

"What is it?"

"Wha' could be so big?"

Frantic, Stenhouse ordered, "It doesn't matter, kill it, shoot, shoot!"

The sheriff looked unconvinced, "Shoot what? Sounds like whoever it was jumped off the roof. Slim, Roger, check it out." He beckoned toward the door.

Slim and Roger went to the front door, Slim gingerly opened as Roger covered him. With everything still as ice, they stepped out, pointing their guns in every which direction.

"Nothing out here, boss," said Slim.

A massive white hand reached from off the roof picking Slim up by the head, yanking him out of sight.

A chorus of gunfire followed, as Roger hit the deck. "Oh dear Lord, I saw it! Hideous!" As the shooting paused, he slammed the door shut and bolted it.

"Who was it?" demanded the sheriff. "Porter?"

"That was no man," wailed Roger.

A creaking across the roof was met with more lead, but no certainty. Something slammed against the door hard and final. Silence reigned as the sheriff stepped lightly to the side window to look. "Whoever it was threw Slim against the door. That's a strong man."

"I'm telling you that was no man."

"Shuddup Roger, he'll eat lead like anyone else."

Stenhouse beneath the desk looked about fearfully.

The deputy coughed and was glared at for his mistake.

The men waited for another sound. None came for the space of eight heartbeats.

Bursting through the window, a savage white shape roared as it rendered men too slow to defend themselves. Shots echoed from several pistols but the bone-pale attacker cast aside the lamp, blinding the men.

The crunch and splinter of bone and wood tore through the room that lead could not hope to stop.

Brief retorts from the echoing firearms illuminated the room, letting the terrified men see what they faced before the end came on black talons.

Roger ran to the jail cell and shut himself in behind the bars.

Unimpressed, the thing loped to the man cage, gripped the bars and tore the door from its hinges.

Roger didn't last as long as the door.

Almost mad with panic, Stenhouse raced for the front door, clutching his notebooks to his chest.

Three more shots rang out and the deputy, squealed.

Daring to look behind, Stenhouse saw green witch-fire engulf the office.

Stenhouse ran up the street in a panic and threw himself upon the threshold of what he prayed was refuge. He banged on the door crying.

Growling behind him, heavy loping steps drew near, but stopped cold.

Putting his arms over his face Stenhouse screamed.

The door opened.

Joseph Rich looked down at the gibbering mass of Stenhouse. "What the deuce?" Rich held his rifle at the ready and scanned the darkness as the hysterical crying man held fast to his knees.

"Bring him in," said Charles Rich, looking over his son's shoulder into the vacant gloom. "He needs a blessing."

19.

Porter had been baptized by water and by fire, now he was sure where the twain should meet. Hot fetid breath whirled about him like a hurricane as a monstrous tongue lashed, attempting to force him down a bottomless black gullet.

Closed inside the leviathan's mouth, Port gripped the top two rear fangs in the monster's maw, only they allowed purchase without shearing his hands off. The tongue, almost as long as he was tall, proved a formidable opponent. Kicking at the pink monstrosity, Port knew he could not hold out forever.

He despaired thinking of his holy blessing. Not cutting his hair would not help against being digested, no bullets or knives were needed to end his existence here. What of his children and Christine? What would they do without him?

Anger coiled up in him, like a serpent preparing to strike its deadly blow.

The tongue struck again, trying to fling him.

Roaring, Port launched himself at the tongue and grasped it as he would a greased pig. The air pressure changed and he knew there were at the surface. Twisting the tongue, the monsters mouth opened and Port let himself out, still grasping the end.

The monster wouldn't close its mouth for fear of severing itself.

Once outside of the teeth's way, Port noticed something stuck on the lower left jaw-line. A crude contraption of tiny interwoven bones and rawhide, similar to the bizarre fetish he had seen earlier.

The monster struggled, but Port kept a firm grasp with one hand on the slimy tongue. Try as he might he couldn't free the fetish with one hand.

A deep bass inside the monster reverberated out.

He let go of the tongue and yanked the interwoven mess from the bleeding gums.

It let out a rumbling purr, and Port could swear that the great eye went from a dull black to blue. Whatever wicked spirit had held the monster in thrall, was released.

Running a hand back and forth over the thick scaly hide, Port looked the monster in the eye. A thick eyelid closed in rhythm to his strokes.

It let out a rumbling purr yet again.

"What have I got to lose," he said, to the monster as much as himself. "Lemme up, Blue."

Port slid over the head of the calmed beast. He found he could grasp the folds of skin where the jaw ended. Port lightly kicked at its neck with his waterlogged boots and the beast started forward. He could even guide the direction of the monster as they cruised over the lake by pulling one way or the other just like a horse and its reins.

"Wheat!" Port called aloud. He had broken the wildest stallion ever.

The Bear Lake monster swam quickly through the water in a way that reminded Port of the seals he had seen in California. It was quick and he had to pull upwards a number of times to keep the creature from diving into the depths. It was exhilarating.

Piloting the monster to shore, Port finally realized how chilled he was. He needed warmth if he was to survive. Thinking of survivors...glancing over the waters there was no sign of Lehi. Old man must have drowned. Port bowed his head for some time.

The beast slumped its way onto shore using its shorter paddle like feet just as a seal would.

Port ran his hand along the monster's snout and ushered it away. He didn't want it getting any ideas about his horse nearby "Go on, Blue. Git. We'll be meeting up soon enough, I promise."

The monster seemed reluctant but finally went into the lake and disappeared beneath moon-stained waters.

It took some time to get a fire going, but once the blaze picked up, Port collapsed beside it. Who would believe it? Revenge could wait, he needed sleep after breaking Jonah's stallion.

Why had he named the monster Blue? He didn't know, but it made him laugh.

"Wheat," he chuckled as he fell asleep.

20.

Climbing off his horse, Port limped on account of his water-logged boots drying by the fire and shrinking to an uncomfortable size. He lost his 45-70 in the lake and one of his pistols and all of his ammunition.

Shuffling into the general store Port could only point at the ammunition.

"Morning Brother Rockwell. You weren't part of that mess last night were you?" asked Thomas the shop keep.

Port shrugged through bleary eyes.

"Did you drink all of those tinctures last night? No wonder you feel so terrible."

Port rubbed his face and responded, "No, just get me some cartridges."

"Anything else?"

"Cartridges!" hollered Port. "Wait, what mess last night? How'd you know?"

Thomas gave a patronizing smile. "Last night right across the street. The sheriff's office burnt down. Everyone who was staying there is dead, burnt up, except for Brother Stenhouse."

"Stenhouse? Where is that polecat?"

Sniffing, Thomas responded, "Brother Stenhouse is among the most respected men we have in the Church, he hardly deserves to be called a polecat."

"Cartridges and where is he?"

Thomas gulped, "I understand he is at Brother Rich's for the moment. He went there last night a crying and a hollering that something was out to get him. No doubt he was distressed about the fire that took so many lives."

Port paid for the ammunition and walked out, figuring he had almost all the pieces to the puzzle. Now to get the last one from the dog's own mouth.

21.

Stenhouse was shivering in the parlor, sipping warm milk. He started at Port's entrance, a dark avenging angel with the brilliance of the sun at his back. Charles Rich calmed him as Joseph shut the door and ushered the other family members out.

Joseph said, "He has been carrying on all night. Not a body in the house got a wink of sleep last night."

Stenhouse was still shaking, though the comfort of the Apostle had soothed him somewhat.

"Come and take a look at this," said Joseph, leading Port back outside.

On the ground in an obvious perimeter all about the Rich home, were big wolf-like tracks, as if a creature met an invisible barrier through which it could not pass.

"What do you make of that?" asked Port.

"What else? Father is here."

Port nodded and the two went back inside. Sitting across from Stenhouse, Port tipped his hat to Charles and said to Stenhouse, "Alright, don't feed me any cow pies. What is that thing? What do you know about it?"

Stenhouse looked at Port and quivered again, "It will find me."

"Are you talking about the Bear Lake monster?" asked Joseph.

"We got bigger fish to fry," said Port.

Confused, Joseph shot back, "No, we don't."

"Hold on son," said Charles. "There is a deeper conspiracy afoot."

Stenhouse stared at the wall and looked far away, remembering. "It was Harrison and Godbe. They started it. Sure, I was right there with them, along with Shearman, Kelsey, Tullidge and Lawrence among others but it was Harrison and Godbe that started it."

He took a sip of his warm milk. "I'm not mad. I have seen things. They discovered the answers when they went to New York and met the medium Charles Foster—he greeted them in Heber C. Kimball's voice! They knew it was Kimball communicating with them from beyond the grave. He told them our path was correct and Brigham was a fallen prophet, then others came and spoke the same; Joseph Smith, Alexander Humboldt, Solomon—even Christ spoke to them."

Joseph Rich snorted.

"Truly, they didn't see him, but he spoke to them and told what we wanted to hear. Our reformation path is correct and Brigham is wrong. He is not infallible."

Charles quieted Joseph. "He is speaking what he believes to be true."

"Of course I am. They brought back their ideas and wisdom. We have communed with spirits. Then Colfax came. The government wants to destroy Brigham and the Church along with it. We couldn't let that happen, we had to do something, reform the Church from within to save it. If we can show how we accept the world, they will accept us."

"What's all this up here then?"

"We tried to talk to Brigham, to make him see, but he was obstinate and cruel. We knew we had to make a stand but time was short. We met at the lodge, with the ferry on Bear River, Godbe's lodge. We held a séance. Harrison directed it. I remember it was cold no matter how we stoked the fire. A powerful force came to our room. It spoke from behind us, strong and vibrant. It surprised us. We all heard it but none of us could see it. It said to use an Indian shaman and the Bear Lake monster, to bring down Brigham. It said, His master wanted to bring down Brigham and would use his earthly servants to do it. We were all so thrilled to know the Lord was on our side."

Port rolled his eyes but remained silent.

"We were validated. I thought it odd to use a heathen for the Lord's work but we did as we were told. I found the shaman. He was staying just upriver from the lodge."

"What's his name?"

"Ligaii-Maiitsoh."

Joseph widened his eyes, "You mean Lehi? He's a friend."

Shaking his head, Stenhouse went on, "He is ancient as the mountains. He said he would call upon the Great Serpent to do our bidding. But something went wrong instead of just scaring people, the monster started killing people. I tried to help the Lamanites watch for the beast but it only made things worse."

"Ever wonder if you aren't on the side of angels, much as you think you are?" asked Port.

136

Stenhouse looked sharply at the suggestion. "There have been setbacks, but no, we are right."

"Then what was last night?"

Shuddering again Stenhouse said, "That wasn't right, I think it serves Ligaii-Maiitsoh. There has been a mistake. The fiend was supposed to be controllable, but it went blood-mad when it discovered the Shoshoni were in the valley. It has surely slain old Lehi. It will come for me next. I will never see Fanny again."

"That's enough crying. What is it about the Shoshoni?"

"The Shoshoni used to capture Navajo and sell them into slavery. All sorts of horrible things happened. I learned of this from Chief Many-Buffalo. The Navajo retaliated by sending witches out to destroy the Shoshoni, I believe Ligaii-Maiitsoh must be the last one."

Port rocked back in his chair, "I couldn't get him to tell me a darned thing and I even had a translator."

Stenhouse was surprised, "Why? He speaks perfectly good English. Oh yes—you were at the Bear River massacre; he was never going to tell you anything."

Port bristled as Stenhouse continued. "Many-Buffalo said his tribe was in the path of the skin-walker, and were under its doom. I wanted to help him but I knew there was nothing to be done when the crazy old man raved as he did over the Shoshoni enemies?"

"What about them fetish pieces I found? Collection of bones?"

"Some kind of curse is all I know. It lets the bloodthirsty creature focus where the shaman directs it," said Stenhouse trailing off as recognition washed over. "You! You put the fiend upon me!" screamed Stenhouse, rising from his chair for the first time.

"Just like it was put upon the Cooks and I couldn't have that."

"It wasn't for the Cooks—it was for you," snarled Stenhouse.

"I didn't know what it would do. I just followed my gut," answered Port.

Stenhouse still fumed. "You black-hearted murderer." He stood ready to fight bringing his fists up.

Port slammed him against the wall with ease. "This is what I do, boy," said Port, before letting him go. "And I never killed anyone who didn't need killing."

Stenhouse collapsed to the floor and wept.

Joseph asked, "What about the Bear Lake monster?"

"Smoke and mirrors," answered Port. "It was a decoy for the old shaman, I don't believe it will give you any more problems."

"You didn't kill it did you?"

"No, I made peace with it. It'll behave itself."

Charles Rich asked a question, "What will you do, Brother Rockwell?"

"We'll throw down with the shaman and his beast. I'll use 'em up."

22.

A posse was organized by mid-afternoon and rode out to old Lehi's camp. It was later than Port meant, but several of the men insisted on getting silver bullets cast. Fancy trays, silverware and jewelry that had crossed the plain as priceless family heirlooms was smelted and molded into balls for precious family insurance.

Port didn't worry about any of that for himself. There were twenty guns riding with him to fire those sacramental rounds. He had his Bowie knife that Brigham had blessed and already knew that it could harm the creature. If he needed to, he would cut the beast asunder.

When they were close, Port had them come in from two directions to triangulate their fire and trap the old man and his creature. He kicked himself for not trusting his, or his horse's instincts. The creature must have been nearby the whole time he visited with the old man. That would explain the wretched smell.

The tattered tepee was there in the glade but Lehi was nowhere to be found.

"There's nothing inside but this copy of the Book of Mormon that father gave him," said Joseph. "I don't understand. He has been here, living amongst us for weeks, he seemed like a good man. He quoted scripture. He said he knew it was true."

Port gave a lopsided grin, "Don'tcha think the devil knows it's true?"

23.

Thundering into town as dusk closed in around them, Port knew something wasn't right. Something whispered on the wind, and the scent of wet dog hung heavy in the air.

Amanda Cook raced her horse up to Port. She had been crying. "I thought you'd never return," she sobbed.

"Calm down, Amanda. What is it?"

"We were in the garden, gathering the last of the harvest, just Mary and I. That witch-fire wolf-man came back. Phineas heard our screams, he tried to shoot it and fight. It hurt him real bad. Apostle Rich is looking after him, but it took Mary. It tore her from my grasp. It spoke, like a demon from hell but it spoke, 'It said you and you alone had to come and get Mary at the lake shore past the camps.' What do we do?"

Port held Amanda close and looked her in the eye. "I will get her back."

"How? It will kill her."

"No, I'll take care of it. Rich, you very good with that Sharps rifle?" Joseph nodded. "Got a few silver slugs too."

"Keep to the tree line. If the right moment comes, take it. Everyone else stay put."

"I'm coming with you," broke in Amanda.

"No, you're not. Look after Phineas and trust me."

With that Port turned his stallion about and made for the lake shore past the Shoshoni camps, and the full moon glowed down like a dragons face.

24.

The Shoshonis had moved camp, but the markings of where tepees had sat along with cook-fire remnants still dotted the ground. The loss of Big Bear and the others would be a hard tax on the small tribe. He remembered his own people's exodus in the dead of winter. They'll be all right he told himself.

Fingers of ghostly clouds tried to shroud the moon, but still the cold light poked through, casting a long line across the lake. Where it ended upon the shore stood the white-haired old Indian, along with the little girl beside him. She was bound up like a trundle bed with a rag stuffed in her mouth.

Lehi, or Ligaii-Maiitsoh raised his hand in the common greeting, though the smirk on his face was mocking and cold. "I knew you would come Long-hair."

"My motivations aren't hard to understand, what are yours though?"

"I have blood of the Trickster in my veins. I am naked terror. I sow deceit and discord. I am your fatal error."

Port dismounted, "Well I am here. You gonna give me the girl?"

The tall old man smirked, and pointed a long spindly finger "She dies, but only after you."

Port drew his gun, "Where's your creature? Nowhere to hide down here next to the lake."

Lehi cocked his head and laughed inaudibly. "I have no creature."

"You're blood of the trickster, a natural-born liar. I know you have some kind of beast."

"My name is Ligaii-Maiitsoh, it means White Wolf in my people's tongue. If you knew anything about us, you would have known what kind of man wears skins of a predator."

"And I wear a dozen cow skins. Let the girl go."

Lehi didn't move.

Port sent a round nipping past the old man's ears, but he didn't flinch. "You got nerve, I'll give you that. Let the girl go or I'll shoot. I got no truck with kidnappers or rustlers."

"I know you. You don't know me," said Lehi. "A lifetime ago, I swore to serve the Trickster and his slave, the Master Mahan. They granted me powers beyond the white man's gun."

"Enough! Let the girl go, or I scalp you from the inside out."

Lehi grinned, revealing terribly big teeth, a jaw that jutted bristling with fangs. It grew wider and wider, impossibly huge and fearsome.

Port wasn't sure he was seeing correctly.

The old man's nose twitched and stretched. "You see what only the dead have seen."

Port sent a round through Lehi's chest. The old man flinched upon impact but no blood came, and his face stretched further. Port shot a second round and a third into the monster.

But the transformation wasn't complete. Fine white fur sprung from the old man's body, and beneath it muscles rippled. A howl came with the completion.

Port sent a fourth, fifth and sixth round into the beast, none of which produced so much as a drop of blood.

Grinning devilishly, Lehi tossed the bound girl into the lake behind him.

Amanda Cook screamed from farther up into the tree line, as she dashed downhill for her daughter.

"More to slay," growled Lehi, his transformation to skin-walker complete.

Port dove for the girl in the lake but the swift hand of the monster batted him aside.

His pistol knocked from his hand, Port strained for his Bowie. But already the beast took him by the coat and threw him.

The thunderclap of a Sharps rifle, boomed over the lake shore. A tuft of white fur flew, but still no blood came from the skin-walker's wound.

Amanda reached the water's edge and pulled Mary from the weak surf. The little girl took a deep breath, gasping from the cold water.

Then she was thrown back in the lake.

The skin-walker knocked Mary back into the waters while holding her mother like a rag doll. "Danite," it called, emphasizing the 'ite'. "Choose which to save, girl or woman."

Port had the Bowie out, despite how badly his body ached from the blow.

"Throw it away in the lake or I rip her apart, but choose," snarled the skin-walker.

Port knew Lehi was a liar, but he knew it could fulfill the threat. Even a silver slug from the Sharps did nothing against it. Only the Bowie knife Brigham had blessed in Nauvoo could harm it.

The girl was drowning; the choice must be made.

Amanda fumbled one-handed with something in her pocket.

The skin-walker stared cold-fire at Port relishing the Danites painful choice.

Somewhere above, Joseph Rich looked down the barrel of the Sharps, waiting to try another shot.

Mary sputtered in the cold lake water.

Port took the Bowie in hand and threw it true as he had ever thrown anything in his life, straight for the skin-walkers heart. "Lord, guide my hand," he prayed. "Help me end this creature."

The big knife flew end over end impossibly fast. And it seemed for a moment that Port's aim was true and he would skewer the fiend.

It caught the blade with the reflexes of diamondback's strike and sounded out in a cross between a dogs's bark and a man laughing. It arched to throw the knife back.

Port thought it would throw the heavy blade at him. He ran for the girl and drew her from the water like baby Moses. She gasped again her face turning blue.

Looking back, Port expected to be stabbed with his own knife, but the skin-walker reveling waited for Port to watch.

The blade went high and wide of Port, falling into the lake and disappearing in dark waters.

Port watched the trusty blade vanish in the inky darkness, glancing at the shivering girl, he had an idea. Facing the lake, he called, "Blue! Blue! Blue!"

The skin-walker taunted, "Calling for your knife's return?"

Amanda found what she had fished for, a small glass vial. She smashed it against the only part of the monster she could reach, its shoulder.

Consecrated oil dripped down the white fur, surprising the beast. Amanda tore free, running to her daughter.

The monster puzzled at her choice of attack. "What is this?"

Granting a thin reflective line down the monster, Joseph Rich took his shot, nailing dead center the shoulder where the holy oil covered.

Deep crimson flowed and the beast howled.

Bare-handed, Port tackled the fiendish beast, punching, kicking and clawing like the monster was the devil himself. The skin-walker resisted until Port jammed a finger in the wound, it let roll a string of wicked curses.

Groaning, it prevailed and sent the avenging angel flying into the cold surf.

Joseph ran down the hill hoping for another shot to present itself, but Porter was too thick in the fray and he dared no take another shot. "Do you have any more oil? It works!"

"I don't," cried Amanda, desperately trying to untie her daughter and run away.

The skin-walker raked at Porter with its claws, but try as it might it couldn't pierce his skin, the sharp edges could not gain access.

Yowling, it looked at the lake and dragged Port into the water.

Joseph took another shot, hitting the monster in the back, but missing the oil and nothing happened.

"If I cannot cut you, I will drown you," laughed the skin-walker, holding Port beneath the water.

Kicking, Port strained and fought but the monster was too strong, pushing him into the sandy bottom.

Underwater Port heard a strange set of clicks.

The shaggy white arms let go and Port sat up.

The skin-walker had stepped back away from the water. It beckoned angrily with its right arm, speaking a wolfish tongue.

Behind Port loomed the Bear Lake Monster.

"Blue, I need some help. Get him!" Port shouted, directing the lake dragon's gaze.

The skin-walker's chest began to turn a shade of pale green that was growing in intensity when Joseph shot it again, right where a stream of oil had touched along the ribs.

Wailing of pain and true terror, the skin-walkers glow faded.

"He won't bob off this time. Get 'em, Blue."

The Bear Lake monster lurched forward and swallowed the skin-walker, devouring the white horror entire.

"Chew him up, Blue! Chew him up!" shouted Port. "Wheat!"

An infernal, hollow cry sounded from within the beast, dimming and fading to silence.

Blue opened its cavernous maw and let its tongue loll out between titanic fangs.

Port patted the tremendous beast's snout and examined its handiwork. "No coming back from that," he said, picking random clumps of white fur that stuck in the monster's teeth. "You did good, Blue. Now back to the lake with ya, old friend."

The monster rumbled a colossal purr and turned to slide back into deep waters.

25.

Amanda watched in amazement, holding Mary close. "He is good?"

"Yes, ma'am. He just needed some help and understanding," said Port.

Joseph ran down the hillside shouting, "What a story to tell. I'll get this posted in all the papers across the country. People will come from all over the world to be a part of our valley and see the lake monster."

"No!" Port stuck a thick finger in the tall man's chest. "You're gonna tell everyone you made it up. No good will come of this tale being told for true."

Confused, Joseph looked at Port and the monster disappearing into the lake.

"You don't want what they'll bring to your valley. You don't want more trouble coming down on Brother Brigham. And you don't want 'em messing with the monster."

"I'll say I made it all up," said Joseph Rich, rubbing the sore spot where Porter had pushed. "I can't take back what has already been printed. But I can say now that it was all a wonderful first-class lie."

"Good. Some stories are better off that way."

Garden of Legion

The McHenry wagon train, bound for California, persevered through prairie fires, buffalo stampedes, Indian attacks, and even a bout of embarrassing dysentery, but their greatest struggle was when that flower of the prairie, nineteen-year-old Fannie Burton, became possessed.

Some recollected the pretty little blonde dabbled with an ensorcelled Ouija board stolen from a New Orleans juju man. Her mother claimed the girl was bewitched by a Navajo skin walker, and still others said she had taunted Satan himself late one night around the buffalo-chip campfire after refusing to say grace. Regardless of the sinister origin, something hideous held the girl in demonic thrall.

The once shy and reserved Fannie swiftly took a rough frontier situation from dreadful to dire and finally to disastrous. She ripped apart the Conestoga's, devoured the pitiful food supplies, guzzled or smashed their water caskets and, astonishingly, ate a pair of oxen...alive! The company attempted to subdue the normally weak girl many times, but even a dozen of their most able-bodied men were overpowered by the maiden with a newly developed voice that was deep as the pit of Gehenna.

She, or *It,* or *Them,* seemed determined to force the desperate McHenry party to die in the wastes, reveling in their cries of desperation and misery. Each day they grew weaker and she, *It,* or *Them* grew stronger. All hope seemed lost in the blossoming desert of the American southwest. Tormented by a devil in a black dress, it seemed the party's bones would soon bleach under a merciless sun.

145

Being good Christian folk, they prayed for deliverance and a man they later called the desert prophet materialized. He appeared to be of late middle-age, medium height and build, walking barefoot upon the scorching earth and, most important, he could exorcise little Fannie Burton of her demons.

Spying the holy man's approach, the girl cried aloud and wallowed in the powdered dirt, frothing, vainly trying to hide in a baptism of cinnamon-like soil.

The entire wagon train listened in hushed amazement as the desert prophet communed with the throng of evil spirits inside Fannie. "You don't belong here. You must leave. I command you in *His* name."

"Suffer us to enter into another set of the living," came the bottomless well of a voice from the convulsing waif. "Even, *He,*" it gnashed, "was so accommodating."

"You may enter into whatever lives on the other side of that nearest mountain," allowed the mysterious holy man.

A vile grin split the girl's face as her body shook one last time. An almost imperceptible mist spouted from her frame and flew like a swarm of ravenous locusts to the far side of the mountain.

Her own true voice restored, Fannie spoke hoarsely, "Thank you stranger, but who're you?"

"One of three who tarry," he answered, drawing her up from the baptism of fine powdered earth. "The demons shall not trouble you again. Go your way in righteousness."

Fannie ran to her waiting mother and father. As the rest of the McHenry caravan came out cheering from behind their wagons, a dust devil sprang up out of the dunes and the desert prophet vanished.

The McHenry party never caught his name, his tracks vanished into the shifting sands. Their problems were over, but two mountains away, the hell on earth was about to begin.

Port trotted to the top of the pass, the dust swirling about his horse's hooves like the phantoms of nipping dogs. The horse stamped at unseen ghosts and Port clicked his tongue softly to calm the beast. Grey clouds loomed on the horizon. Rain would strike the desert soon enough, drowning as much as quenching, and Port had no wish to get wet.

Port was a broad-shouldered man with long dark hair and a short beard. He wore a stained duster which canvassed the flanks of his dun horse. A brace of pistols jutted from his vest as he glanced back at his unwilling companion.

Lashed to the trailing mule's saddle was a scrawny, red-haired kid with a face so sun-burnt it almost matched his curly locks. A thousand bitter curses were written in his gaze.

Neither spoke. Port, a gunfighter turned lawman, had nothing to say to the horse thief. Likewise, the kid had nothing to say to his captor. At the top of the pass, each looked down into the canyon before them. A small reservoir collected precious runoff from the mountain peaks, while a town lay jumbled a little farther below like a half-shuffled deck of greasy cards that had been played too many times. A wretched sign designating the town leaned at Port's right. The name made Port crack a smile, it had to be someone's sick joke.

The ruinous sign read, *Eden*, pop - 37. The number had been crossed out many times. With each scratch, the population had decreased until there was no space left for the last few numbers. Someone had tacked an extra board on the side to accommodate the count.

The mountain looming on the south side was covered with as many pockmarks across its face as the ne'er do well horse thief. Tailing's from mine shafts spewed out discoloration and Port noticed few, if any, were working claims.

The town itself had two dozen buildings in various states of decay. There wasn't a single tree and no plants except a desiccated tumbleweed passing by in the ever-present wind. The only other sign of life was in the murky reservoir. Insects skeetered by, but not a single fish jumped.

Porter had seen less promising towns but not by much. This was a town of broken promises, failed dreams and dead hope. Still, maybe he could get a drink.

Riding in, the breeze seemed to pick up and whine at this desert oasis. Port thought he heard a fell voice on the wind but he paid it little mind. He rode straight for the faded yellow star, bleaching upon the front of a peace officer's shanty.

Port tied his horse and the mule to the rail, then dragged his prisoner inside, bringing a cloud of dust with him as he opened the door and shoved the kid through it.

"What can I do ya for?" asked a portly sheriff, startled from his late afternoon nap.

"I have a prisoner. I want to lock him up secure for the night. We'll be moving on in the morning to get before the territorial judge by tomorrow night. I have a badge; my name is—"

"I know who you are, Porter," the sheriff interrupted. "I suppose we can hold your prisoner."

Port removed the kid's bindings and pushed him to the sheriff, who put the kid in the tiny jail.

"What'd he do?"

Port stepped to the door, remarking over his shoulder, "Horse thief and murderer, he'll hang soon. Where can I get a square drink?"

"Lulu-belle's, it's the only place still open."

"Much obliged." Port shut the door in the face of the gale and strode across the cactus dry street.

Inside Lulu-belle's a hairy-knuckled barkeep wiped down unused glasses as an off-tune woman sang an off-color song. The carnival of patrons looked Port's way as he entered and then went back to their previous distractions. He went straight to the bar, thumping down two bits.

"What'll ya have?"

"Whiskey," Port said. "The wind ever stop blowing around here?"

"Not usually. The miners like it. Helps keep 'em cool. It's hot as hell most days."

Port's gaze tightened. "Wait, is this the cursed town I heard about?"

The barkeep smiled, "It is indeed. That's our claim to fame. The territorial governor cursed Eden as the wickedest city in the west and said we'd fade out, but were hanging on. We ain't hardly licked yet."

Port chuckled to himself. He doubted the town would last another year unless the miners struck something. Everywhere death and decay lurked, whitewash peeled leaving flakes like dandruff on the ground and a certain stink never left the air. It was a dead and bloated town, with inhabitants like fleas still clinging to the lifeless dog's warmth.

Something banged near the back of the saloon and distracted the barkeep. "Sadie, will you serve this gentleman?" he called, "I have to see what that was."

Port looked out the window as a single tumbleweed rolled by, helped by the ever present wind.

A homely saloon girl with a whiskey bottle and glass sidled up to Port, "Well howdy stranger, doesn't it get lonely on the trail all day?" She batted her eyes like a butterfly gathering nectar.

He gave her a dirty look. "I ain't looking for company, just a drink."

"Everybody likes company," she said through overly red lips.

Port grinned. "Maybe so, but not me." She offered Port the glass but he declined and took the bottle.

"You're funny," she said. "I'm Sadie."

"Howdy Ma'am, I'm Porter."

"You from nearby?"

"A bit up north." He noticed a pair of tumbleweeds ramble by on the street. He took another swig watching the sky turn azure as Venus appeared.

Sadie coaxed, "I hear it's nice."

"I expect you'd like California better," Port said offhand.

The barkeep hollered for Sadie again and she shrugged. "Anything else you need, just you holler."

Port gave a half charity smile and focused on his drink instead of the next tone-deaf song. Dusk was falling and the wind grew louder with a moan like a dying man's last gasp.

Port rubbed a broad hand over his face and pondered the ride in the morning. The kid would hang in another night. It bothered him. The kid was young. Still, that he deserved it couldn't be denied. What would the parents say when Port brought their son home? Wouldn't likely be thanks. Nope, not a lot of appreciation for his service out here. He took another long pull on the whiskey bottle.

The wind moaned again and the rapid sound of a boot heel kicking the boardwalk shook Port from drowning his troubles. He stood and stalked to the saloon doors, hand on his Navy Colt.

Not six feet from the swinging doors lay an old man with the blue face of one who'd been strangled.

Glancing around the corner, Port looked left and right. Not a soul was on the street, just those blasted tumbleweeds rolling in the wind.

"Someone give me a hand," he ordered.

The bartender and Port brought the dead man inside. His clothes were dirty and disheveled, food stained his shirt and jacket precisely where a napkin bib wouldn't cover. Tight red gouges across the neck revealed the cause of his murder.

"Who was he?"

The hairy-knuckled bartender answered, "Quinn Cleary, town lawyer."

Port gave the bartender the stink-eye.

The bartender gulped adding, "And town drunk. There hasn't been a lotta need for a town lawyer last few years."

"You don't say? Who'd want him dead?"

Shaking his head, the bartender said, "No one. He was harmless."

Wheeling, Port looked upon the rest of the motley group of patrons. "Anyone?"

No one volunteered anything. Most seemed in shock, but Sadie stepped forward, "He was liked by everyone, there weren't no bad debts or dissatisfied miners if that's what you mean?"

Port nodded, "I'll get the sheriff." He went out into the night, the dark wind whipping about him like a scorned lover. With the wary sense of a predator, Port kept an eye up and down the street and while a sense of dread filled him, he couldn't see another soul. He convinced himself the dread was merely the aura of the town in general. He struck a match to light his cigar but the wind blew it out.

A rather large tumbleweed rolled in front of him and stopped abruptly despite the wind.

Port looked at the noxious weed, rubbed his beard and gave it a kick, sending it flying into the darkness.

He continued across the street, looking over his shoulder several times. Lamplight flickered through the shuttered windows of the sheriff's office, and a hint of laughter filtered out against the moaning dirge of the wind. Port frowned, what could there possibly be worth laughing about in this stinking town?

The sheriff sat at the little wooden table playing cards with the kid. Each looked up in shock at Port.

Port barked, "This the kind of town you run sheriff? Granting the opportunity for a horse thieving murderer to escape?"

"It ain't like that. We was just playing cards."

"Yes, sir," the kid agreed, "jus' playing cards. I wasn't gonna try and escape...honest."

Port picked the kid up by the scruff and threw him into the jail cell. "He has killed three men already, for six dollars and a slow horse."

The sheriff looked indignant at Porter, as if he didn't believe him, while the kid gave his most innocent look.

"I suppose I can keep him locked up," muttered the lawman.

"You suppose? You got more problems. Someone strangled your town drunk, and *that* murderer is still on the loose." Port struck another match and lit his cigar.

"Cleary's dead?"

Port nodded, smoke flared from his nostrils. "Strangled with wire. We got him over in Lulu-belle's."

Putting on his gun belt, the sheriff wheezed and said, "I'll be over in a minute."

Not waiting any longer, Porter went out the door back into the blasting wind. More tumbleweeds rolled by. Several weeds were massed up against the open saloon doors. The wind extinguished his cigar, and he prepared to light another match. Port kicked the tumbleweeds aside and went in. The lamps were blown out.

Everyone was gone.

Port spun around wondering if it was some kind of joke, but the saloon was deserted. No one was behind the bar or on the low stage. Then it dawned on him that the dead man's body was gone too. Going up the stairs with his Navy Colt drawn, Port was ready for anything. A tumbleweed had been blown up to the landing. Port knocked it aside.

There were four small rooms. Two had doors cracked open. No lamps burned, but a hint of moonlight crept through the narrow windows.

No one in either room. Port opened the first closed door, standing as far back as he could reach and still turn the knob. He half expected a gunshot to explode through the door, but none came. Each room was empty as well, though the last had an open window with the wind whipping the sun bleached pink curtains like a banshee.

Port came back downstairs and puzzled. It had been at least five minutes. Where was that idiot sheriff?

He went back outside. Somewhere in the cold distance a horse screamed. Porter gave pause. The street was nearly covered with tumbleweeds, and his horse was gone too! "Wheat in the mill! That damn kid!" He waded through the sea of weeds that almost acted like they wanted to grab and hold him. He puffed on his cigar extra hard to keep it lit against the wind. The orange cherry flared and the weeds seemed to part a little. The door stood open. Expecting to see the incompetent fool dead, Port leveled his six-gun at the ready.

But the sheriff wasn't there.

The kid was. Hunched in his cell in the darkness, in a fetal position, he sobbed and jerked as Port entered.

"Where is he? What did you do to him?" Port demanded.

"I didn't...do anything. It was them . . ."

"Them who?"

"The weeds, they came to life. He opened the door and they rolled in. They took the sheriff. He screamed 'til he couldn't breathe no more."

"Horse chips!"

"They drug his body out the back. They tried to reach me but couldn't through the bars."

"You damn liar. Do you got friends trying to bust you out? Tell me or I am gonna shoot you here and now!"

"Better that than those things getting me."

Port wheeled and looked out the slit windows. The wind was forcing more tumbleweeds up against the door. Their scratching was unnerving. It almost looked like their myriad tiny branches were moving in a uniform, crawling chaos.

Port wrinkled his brow. The whiskey must be too strong here.

"They are trying to get in," moaned the kid.

Port puffed his cigar and said, "You're one defective bullet kid."

"It's true. Open the door and find out, you cold-hearted bastard."

"All right." Port opened the door, wary of gunmen on the street. He puffed on the cigar, looking with disdain at the weeds which fell back away from the door. "Yeah, kid, they're alive, either that or the wind moved them."

But the kid was as far back in his cell as he could be.

"Porter!" came a woman's voice.

Port looked and there on the roof of the saloon was Sadie and a handful of others.

"Run! Run! You've got to get away!"

Port looked each way down the street. "From what?"

"The weeds!"

He furrowed his brow again and the wind blew out his cigar.

The weeds closed in.

"Horse chips."

He leapt back into the sheriff's office, slamming the door as he did so, but the weeds clogged the threshold, keeping it open. So many rolled atop each other, that the pile was as tall as Port.

He did the first thing that came to mind. He shot the mass with his Navy revolver. Smoke belched from the six-gun but the weeds were unaffected beyond a moment's respite.

The kid screamed in his cell.

"Shut up!" Port kicked over the card table, which did nothing to the weeds. He then flung at chair at them. It crushed a few, but against the mass it was useless. Taking the other chair, Port smashed out the window behind him and dove through.

He landed hard on his elbows and knees, rolling to get up.

Weeds tumbled around each side of the office and then out the lip of the window.

Port was on his feet racing to the next building, a dilapidated Smithy's. Scrambling up a post, covered with tools, he managed to get several feet off the ground and above the weed's reach. Then he climbed up to the narrow slanted roof.

The weeds thrummed in unison and surrounded the tiny structure.

From his new vantage, Port could see thousands of weeds covering the town. Across the street, Sadie and a dozen others sat on the saloon's roof. The wind moaned and Port sat precariously for what he deemed one of the worst nights of his life. He chanced throwing matches at the weeds, but they rolled away until the matches died in the blustery night. Port knew there was no way he could burn the brush while they were so spread out.

Several times individual weeds attempted to climb the post after Port. One on one he could knock them away, but what about when sleep would eventually take him? He couldn't stay awake forever.

Dawn's light only revealed a greater nightmare. There were more weeds than Port had guessed. Not a single horse remained. There'd be no way to outrun the horde, and still the hurtling wind blew fierce as the devil.

He kicked another tumbler that clambered up. Sadie and the others above the saloon did the same with their climbing invaders. Port knew that eventually they would lose. He had to take the fight to the weeds. Looking across the lay of the land, the narrow sloping valley, the reservoir sat above the town. Port chewed his lip and hatched a plan. As much as he didn't like it, he would need help.

"Sadie," he called, "Are the miners still using their powder magazines? Do the mines go deep?"

"Yes. It's there past the east barn," she shouted, pointing to a lone shack at the far upper end of town. "But so what about the mines depth? The weeds can go anywhere a man can go."

"Much obliged."

She puzzled over his intentions and frowned, shielding her face.

Tearing off another, ascending tumbleweed, Porter then snagged a blacksmith's hammer from the post. He tossed it to the roof of the sheriff's office. Then he gauged the distance between the two buildings. It would be a long jump, especially since he didn't have much room to start with.

He didn't like heights, and while this wasn't that high, the weeds waited below, hungry as rabid dogs. They seemed to sense his intent and gathered thickly underneath him. It was now or never. More weeds were crawling up the post.

Port reached with all he was worth, whispering a prayer as he jumped.

His fingers grasped the lip of the sheriff's office as the wind was slammed from his lungs. Still, he didn't let go. He struggled over the lip of the flat adobe roof. Port lay on his back a few moments, breathing hard.

"Are you alright?" called Sadie.

"Yeah, never better," he panted.

Porter slammed the hammer at the roof of the jail cell. It was hard work and took longer than he would have liked. By the time Port burst through the ceiling, the kid below was screaming in terror.

"Shut up, it's only me."

Dumbfounded, the kid nodded and let Port pull him up to the roof.

Port whispered, "We got two things we can do. Nothing and die, or act and perhaps live."

The kid nodded.

"Now, I know you can run, so I got a job for you. I need a distraction. I need you to get the weeds' attention while I charge up to the powder box and blow the reservoir wide open. It'll wash this town clean."

The kid shook his head, "I'd rather wait here. Get someone else to do it."

"Look kid, I can't be yelling these plans across the street for the weeds to hear. I don't know how smart they are. Wheat! I don't even know how they are doing this. It's gotta be you."

"It could be you. I can run faster than you. Let me light the powder and blow the dam."

Port grimaced. He knew the kid was fast, he'd been awful hard to catch. "Here's my matches. There will be some powder kegs. Take one or two, whatever you can still move with. Get up to the reservoir put the keg next to the drainage channel, light it and get the hell away. Once a hole is knocked in that dam, it'll be like a river in flood. Get clear. You hearing me? These things will come tearing after you, so you gotta do it quick."

The kid nodded, "But what about after? I do this, you still gonna take me to get hung?"

Port narrowed his gaze. "No. But you're gonna head to Mexico."

"I don't wanna go to Mexico."

Port cocked his head and gave a wicked grin.

"I'll go to Mexico."

"Good lad. I'll lead the weeds south as best I can. You run north fast as the devil on your tail. Make sure this wind don't blow out your match."

Port dropped down to the slopping roof on the front of the office. He tore the sign from the rusted brackets and tossed it, smashing weeds beneath. He jumped down and ran serpentine through the streets of Eden. Weeds rolled after him like a pack of dogs.

The kid watched a moment then eased down the backside and

made for the powder magazine. On the ground he peered around the corner to determine if the weeds would even see him. They appeared taken with Porter and paid no attention to him or the others on the saloon.

Porter dodged the few weeds that rolled to intercept him and booted a few, but more came on until they were so thick on his heels that kicking would only waste his time. They lashed at his ankles and no amount of shooting or struggling would avail him.

The kid moved behind the ghost town shops to avoid being seen, but Sadie saw him. "Where are you going?" she shouted. "Help us!" He signaled her to be silent.

While they watched, weeds with a thousand tiny arms grabbed Port's heel and tripped him. He flailed and sent dozens spinning away, but for every one he threw a dozen more took its place. The weeds piled, reaching to strangle the human life they envied and hated.

Through some eldritch means, or from understanding Sadie's shouting, the weeds sensed the kid. A number of them, too far from reaching Porter, stopped and rolled north after the young blood.

The kid glanced from the edge of the hotel and saw them coming. He turned and ran for the powder magazine. He pulled matches from his pocket.

Port reared up, tearing weeds from his throat. He roared like a mad bull and swatted the balled weeds away. Like an infinite hydra they attacked from all sides.

The kid saw a hundred or more weeds rolling. He reached the powder magazine and threw back the door. Inside were a half dozen powder kegs. He picked up the nearest and ran for the reservoir. "This had better work," he muttered through clenched teeth. The weeds were gaining on him.

At the drainage ditch, the kid dropped the keg and fumbled with the matches. The wind blew out the first three—only two left. He looked over his shoulder. The weeds tumbled closer and closer. A light and the fuse went quick. He shielded the delicate blaze with his hands. The weeds rolled. There would be no time to escape and keep the fire alive. This would be his redemption.

"Sorry Mama," he whispered.

The keg exploded in raucous thunder. Black smoke, brown earth, and gray water spit in all directions.

The pursuing weeds stopped and backed away from the spilling reservoir.

An arm reached out from the mass of weeds, and Port was free for a moment before he was sucked back down by the malevolent force.

A torrent of water become a river, as chunks of the dam broke free in a mighty domino effect.

Porter knew he was turning blue from the vine's deadly grip on his neck. With eyes barely open, he fell to the dust. Torn in all directions, his tongue lolled in hot earth, then felt cool relief.

Water ran, slick and cold, as the weeds let go.

Porter struggled to his knees and saw the wave coming. He moved like a crippled locomotive and just managed to grasp a sturdy post as the river hit. Weeds were drowned and taken away past the corrals and abandoned bordello.

The tumbleweeds tried to hold to one another and again and again were washed downstream from the town.

Sadie and the others atop the saloon cheered and whooped. Port held to his post like a rod of iron, fearful of being carried away. When the water at last subsided to a few feet deep, he looked behind and saw a clumped mass of the drenched weeds.

They moved as one.

Forming together, they rose out of the ebbing waters, rounded like a head with hollow spots for colossal eyes and mouth. Shoulders appeared then arms, fingers, and a hideous weed-bodied torso. Thousands of wet tumbleweeds fused together to fashion a giant weed golem. The vines interlaced, wrapped and knotted about tenaciously. An inhuman cry echoed from the cavity of a mouth and the thing stood up, over three stories tall. It shook the wetness from itself and stepped forward with a ponderous gait.

Sadie screamed. The others ran for their lives to escape the colossus's awful gaze. Port shuddered, but still his mind sprang like a steel trap to find a way to defeat this demonic foe.

Coming closer, the awful giant stepped on the bordello, crushing it asunder. With the waters gone, the town was now just a mud track. Some of the structures had been knocked off their foundations and were laying haphazardly. The street in front of the saloon was the biggest clearing the town had left.

"Wheat! I'm a fool," Porter said to himself. "Now I got him."

"We have to get out of here," the barkeep shouted, tugging on Port's shoulder.

"You think you can outrun that?" Sadie asked.

"We just gotta outrun the others," the barkeep answered.

Port grasped his shoulder and swung the man around. "You wanna live? Get me a lamp! All of 'em! And be ready when I am! I gotta buy some time."

The barkeep stared at him like he was insane but dashed back inside.

The colossus was almost upon them and Port stepped into the muddy streets to face it.

"**PORTER**," it echoed.

"You know me, but I don't remember meeting you before."

"**WE ARE LEGION. OURS WILL BE A PLACE OF HONOR IN GEHENNA, WHEN WE DESTROY YOUR BODY,**" the voice came, deep as the pit.

"That's where we have our feud. I doubt I'll get anything for destroying yours."

The hollow eyes looked down on Porter, and an ominous sound that he believed was laughter echoed.

"**YOU HAVE NO POWER OVER US.**"

"That's where you're wrong. I do have power over your chosen body."

"**WE WERE TRICKED. BUT IT SERVES US WELL ENOUGH. WE CANNOT BE SHOT. WE CANNOT BE DROWNED. WE CANNOT BE BLOWN APART.**" It leaned in closer to Port. "**WE CANNOT BE KICKED, NOW.**"

"You forgot one," Port caught the oil lamp the barkeep tossed him. He threw it into Legion's mouth and shot.

Fire erupted and an inhuman cry rocked the town. The whipping wind gave the behemoth a tongue of flame, and it laughed again before shooting witch-fire back at Porter like a blast furnace. "**YOU**

HAVE ONLY GIVEN US MORE POWER TO DESTROY YOU! EMBRACE YOUR DOOM! Still sopping wet, the Legion thing was not burning.

The front of Lulu-belle's burst into flames, but the wily gunman dodged and ran about the slick street, taking cover behind the ruins of the blacksmith's.

The tongue of fire blasted again, igniting the forge and structure. Port crossed to a ramshackle house. Again the fire tore into the dry wood. Port faked left and went right, taking cover in the collapsed bordello. "You have to do better than that," he taunted.

The weed golem swung a colossal fist at Porter and shot its witch-fire tongue as he dodged yet again. Smoke obscured him, but as he chanced a look, the edges of the Legion's mouth blackened.

Sensing that its protection of wetness was wearing off, the golem brought up a hand and suffocated the fiery tongue. It cast its wicked gaze for Porter and realized too late it was surrounded by the flaming ruins of the town--a second sacrifice it never could have understood.

Sadie and the remaining others threw more oil, and the flames grew. Porter backed away through burning wreckage, choking on the smoke. The Legion thing was trapped, and its weed body sizzled and smoked as the wetness boiled off. Every path was blocked. It twisted and turned looking for escape, finding none.

"*WE WON'T FORGET THIS*," it roared, before dropping to the mud and writhing as dry weeds were burnt to skeletal ash. Dark things flickered amongst the smoke, and it seemed evil spirits, free of any mortal coil, fled up into the ether.

"The thing burned awful fast for being so wet," Sadie said.

"Yeah, it did," Port answered. "I'm glad at least one element was on our side."

A barefoot, middle-aged man of medium build stood beside them as if he had been there the whole time. "With every blessing comes a curse," he said. "And vice versa."

Port cocked an eyebrow and shrugged, "Horse chips."

Red Wolf Moon

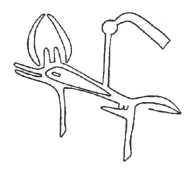

A rust tinged moon hung over the high desert like a lantern in God's own hand. In the swirling distance a wolf howled its respects. Cactus and sage cut ominous shapes amongst the stark landscape as stars above bled a weary cold light. Porter pulled back on the reins and listened through the whispering wind.

Knowing he was close behind the bandits made him more cautious with each mile. He took a long pull of Valley-Tan whiskey from his flask and listened again. Sound carried a long way on the eastbound wind. Porter scratched his beard and dismounted. The moon granted just enough pale light to be sure he was still on the trail.

The tracks abruptly disappeared a hundred yards back on a chink of bare rock, but Porter simply gave a soft laugh to himself. He knew full well that the Kofford gang had merely removed the mule's shoes to better hide their trail. It was a good trick, but wouldn't work on a tracker as experienced as Porter. There wasn't a predator alive as tenacious as the long haired gunfighter. He had but to scan a few yards on until he found an odoriferous sign.

Judging by the still wet and lukewarm horse pies, they couldn't be more than an hour or two ahead. If Porter pushed himself, like he always did, he should be able to get the drop on the Kofford gang while they slept. Experience played out that even the lookouts usually fell asleep by four in the morning. With any luck, he would have the lot of them captured and be riding back to Green River by sunrise.

He rode up out of a steep wash, wary not to silhouette himself against the horizon. A range of mountains attempted to conceal

160

themselves as clouds rolled in across the moon. These were the haunted Henry's, so named by Colonel Powell when he last passed through the area. Porter had heard some tales of eeriness associated here but nothing absolute. Jim Bridger himself said they were full of bad medicine. He passed through back before the Henry's had a name, always looking over his shoulder, just sure that something was eyeballing him. But he hadn't actually seen anything either. Porter mused that Old Jim sure did like telling his stories.

It grew darker the later it became. The mountains towered black nearly matching the sky, Porter only saw them because the stars abruptly stopped, outlined against the irregular peaks. Somewhere between the pitch-hued mountains, tiny firelight escaped one of the canyons. Porter mused that the Kofford gang must believe themselves free and clear. This was good, it would only make his job stalking them that much easier.

The wind shifted and Porter led his horse in a long circuit to stay downwind of the bandits. They might very well not smell a thing but Porter was cautious that their horses wouldn't either. His own mount was unfortunately in heat, but she had been the best available given the circumstances. She had endurance and was fast, fast as any horse alive, but right now?

"Blessings and curses." He reminded himself, thinking about the ridiculousness of it all.

He made his way to the north of the camp, to keep the wind in his face, figuring he would come up both beside and behind the bandits before dawn. Confident in his plan and the aid of night, he dismounted again, leading his horse amongst the shambling terrain.

Then from some unknown quarter of night, queer music whistled down the mountain.

Porter paused, wondering at what the fools were doing. But it only took a few more haunting notes for him to realize this was no white man's song. This was no melody from civilized lips. This hearkened to a primal need, it called from the depths of somethings soul.

A rising and descending piece, the ominous tone sounded like a warning to Porter's ears and he almost forgot that he was stalking the Kofford's.

Unable to tell what was happening, Porter led his mare on, cautious as a panther toward the camp. Twice the mare halted and dug its hooves uneasily at the ground.

"Easy darlin', we'll see what we'll see," Port whispered into her ears, calming the skittish animal. He wrapped the reins about a large sage. "I'll be right back."

The fluting stopped as abruptly as it had begun and a great wolf howl from across the canyon reared up against the black night.

Climbing to the top of a small ridge, Porter faintly made out the distant dancing fire and the rippling commotion beside it.

Men and horse screamed, each attacked by some savage dark force. A few wild gunshots reverberated across the gulf of darkness, but these did nothing to quell the raucous sound of slaughter.

Something was feeding.

A few more heartbeats passed and all was deathly still. Not a man, horse or gun left any retort against what had just happened.

The dancing flames died away and Porter wondered at the brutal massacre. True, the Kofford gang had been lying, murdering, horse thieves, but still he would have taken them before the hanging judge to be tried. Maybe they had done something to offend local Utes? That had to be the answer. Tomahawks made that awful crunching sound—not teeth.

A lone wolf howling, deep and guttural, broke the placid silence again.

That made no sense. Porter knew a wolf wouldn't linger around men, especially after that ruckus. Waves of eerie loathing washed across Porter and his wildest imagination threatened to roll over him like a flash flood in a slot canyon.

Rather than walk into what may be a trap, he decided to hunker down in the hollow with the mare and wait for daybreak. He fell asleep beside his horse, Navy Colt in one hand and Sharps rifle straddled across his chest. Dark dreams nestled upon his shoulders taunting. He shrugged them off. He knew why he was here. Justice for the Wagner clan. It tore him up that a small family homesteading out beyond Green River was murdered by that scum. Even if no one else ever knew about it, Porter would see justice served. It was a cold night and the wind pried at his hat and coat until daybreak.

Warm sunlight crept over the mountain peaks and slid in under his eyes. The mare nickered and seemed anxious to be away.

"Not yet. I gotta see what happened."

Porter watched the canyon and surrounding mountainsides for some time and never espied any movement beyond the wind whipping the tall grasses. He rode into the ruinous camp and was shocked at the brutal savagery. This was worse than anything he had seen back east.

The Kofford's had been torn apart, all six of them. One of the horses had been shredded down its side by what appeared to be four knife blades, the others were either gutted or had their throats torn out. Blood jelled in small pools all about the camp. Then the real curiosity dawned on Porter.

Nothing of value was missing.

That seemed unbelievable. Unless the attackers thought that it was cursed. Did the piping Utes, have a blood oath against these bandits and that was the reason they were so viciously killed?

Glancing about the gory details, a shine caught Porter's eye. He knelt and took a gleaming golden ingot from beside a dead man's hand.

Turning it over, Porter saw a Spanish crest stamped into the thin bar. Even superstitious Utes would not have left such a prize, they knew the value of the money rock. Strangely, the ingot had no blood upon it, despite it being held by a rendered dead hand. Almost like someone had placed the gold bar there on purpose after the fact. But who and why?

Searching for tracks as to who had done this, Porter saw only the wolf tracks. Big ones. He knelt closer to the ground looking for a light footed moccasin imprints, anything. But there were none.

Thinking he saw movement out of the corner of his eye, Porter spun with his Navy Colt revolver drawn. No one was there, but he could have sworn a pale woman had just been there. But there was only the lonely wind pushing the tall dry grasses.

He spent some time looking over the bodies but found no more gold or even any hint as to where the single ingot could have come from. With the exception of the meager sundries and horses they had stolen, the dead Kofford's had no valuables.

With a bad storm blowing in, Porter decided to cut short any more investigating and chalk it all up to vengeful Utes. The somber feeling of dread lingered about the gory camp and Porter wanted to be away almost as much as the horse. The mysteries could sit and the dead murdering bandit's bones could bleach in the sun too. If the Wagner's had any next of kin he would deliver them the ingot.

Or at least a share of it.

Beyond the Green River, Porter asked after any relatives of the Wagner's and was directed to a hermit on the fringe of the red desert named McKay. He was a dusky toned old timer who had lived there as long as anyone could remember.

"Yeah, I knew the Wagner's. Damn shame. I appreciate your going after their killer's and all but I'm not any blood to them," he said, gesturing with his crutch for Porter to take a seat on his front porch. "But I'd appreciate hearing the details. Bartering stories and such."

Sitting on the offered stump, Port asked, "You been here a long time? Any relation to the McKay's I know?"

"Probably, black Irish. Moved here in '49. Was gonna head to the gold fields in California but I fell in love with this valley and never went any farther west."

Glancing at the dry barrenness, Porter refrained from rolling his eyes. "How about south? Anything strange? In the Henry's?" he prodded.

McKay grinned, "I did a little prospecting in the Henry's if that's what you're driving at. That's where you found the Wagner's killers?"

"It is."

"You're direct. I like that. But I never found nothing. Sides, I wasn't panning. I was searching for the lost Ortiz treasure."

"Never heard of it."

"You wouldn't have. I only knew of it because the Paiute medicine man, name of Wash, told me about it when I got him real drunk. That old Indian told me that about two Wash ago, that's two of his lifetimes, Spanish were here forcing the Utes into slave labor. Digging for gold and silver. They struck a right purty vein and worked those slaves near to death gleaning all they could out of those cursed mountains."

Port rubbed his jaw line, "They do have a spooky feel about them."

"You bet they do, and this is why. The Spaniards would smelt the gold right there, molding ingots for easier transport. All spring and summer long they worked those poor souls. Finally, the Utes had enough, they rebelled. After what Wash said was a three-day battle, they killed all the Spanish but one. They took the men, gold and put it all back into the sacred mountain. They walled up the entrance, putting the decapitated Spanish bodies in there with it. The heads on the other hand, were taken across the valley to the dunes and left to rot."

Port nodded, adding, "I've heard of that being done before. So they would be twisted and crippled in the next world."

"Oh yeah, then the Utes took all the hooves off of the mules too. All of this was done so that the Spanish couldn't use the animals in the afterlife, not that they would be complete spirits without their heads either," laughed McKay. He offered a whiskey bottle which Porter gratefully accepted and took a pull from.

"You think any of that is true?" asked Porter, before taking another long swig.

"Sure is," McKay nodded. He got up and went into his cabin, emerging a moment later with a dull rusted conquistador helmet. "It happened. I found where they dumped the heads. Halfway to Goblin Valley. Found the mule hooves too, course that was in another spot right near the Henry's. The gold is there somewhere, but I don't think even the Utes even know or care where anymore. It's cursed and they won't touch it. But a man can dream."

Porter produced the gold ingot from his vest.

McKay eyes lit up like a struck match. "In all my days I never. Where?"

"Someone put it in a dead man's hand. Didn't make any sense. Like they wanted me to find it and poke around. I probably would have, but for that big storm."

"And the *wolf*."

"Wolf?"

McKay continued, "Big wolf. I never stuck around the Henry's after dark. Wash told me the wolf would get me. Said it has plagued his people for two Wash now. They won't hunt or camp within a couple hours ride of it."

Porter frowned. "Is it related to the uprising? Bad blood

unleashed?"

"That's what I asked Wash. He wouldn't say for sure, but I was able to piece together some from a few other Utes. Sounds like a sorcerer or some such thing cursed the mountains and the wolf that stalks the Henry's to this day is its terrible guardian. So don't go there or you will get ate."

Porter folded his arms with a disbelieving smirk across his face. "So where is Wash now?"

"Someone shot poor Wash a few years back when he came begging for food in winter. Anymore secrets he knew, the stubborn cuss, he took to a cold grave."

Port listened but must have had an unconvinced look upon his face. "So no one alive knows how to find the treasure?"

"Now hear me out. I ain't run you untrue yet has I? The secret to finding the treasure Wash said once; something about no peace until there is peace for the victims. And I don't know how that could ever happen. Whole lotta bad blood must have been spilt at these mines. No way for anyone to account for that now. Blood won't wash away blood."

Porter straightened, "I gotta tell ya, I didn't kill the Kofford gang. The wolf did."

McKay sat at attention. "You're plum full of surprises ain't ya? Can I ask why it left you alone?"

"I was still in the foothills, looking up into the camp the Kofford's had in the canyon. Too dark to actually see what happened, but Lord I heard it. A real slaughter from what I saw in the morning too. The Kofford's were murdering, lying, thieves; who deserved no better, but still . . . "

"So you found the ingot in the morning?"

"Yeah."

McKay lit his pipe and took a good long puff before answering, "My advice. Don't ever go back there. That wolf is baiting you. Maybe he knew he couldn't get you that night and did that to tempt you to come back. Don't. You get greedy or too curious and go poking around, something will happen. Your horse will throw a shoe or break a leg and you'll be stuck and the wolf will come down on you like a thunderhead of teeth."

"Why didn't it get you?" asked Porter.

McKay produced his crutch, "Let's just say I had an incident that made me reevaluate my priorities. I don't care to be food for wolves. I'd rather go out with a little comfort. Tragedy is the incompatibility of two good things."

Porter rubbed his bearded chin, adding, "Something else. When I found that ingot, I could swear from the corner of my eye, I saw a pale woman behind me. I turned, but she was gone. I think she was a spirit and crying. Any ideas about that?"

"Nope, you're on your own for that one."

The look in McKay's eye told Porter beyond a doubt that he knew something about the ghostly woman but wouldn't budge about that tidbit of information. Deciding in an instant that it was useless to pursue further Porter stood, "Much obliged for your help."

They shook hands. "No problem. Just remember what I said, don't go back there," said McKay, gesturing toward the Henry's with his crutch.

Porter nodded, mounted his horse and rode on.

Three times Porter was heading for home and three times he turned the mare around to head back to the Henry's. It tore at his craw that he honestly liked McKay yet knew the old man was lying. He had been free with information but had obviously held some things back, that and the use of the crutch was irregular.

He cursed himself, he had more wealth in that single Spanish ingot than he would likely see in a year's worth of monies made cow punching. He didn't need the hassle of trying to find more cursed gold or dealing with some kind of wolf thing in the haunted Henry's, so why was he turning around?

Porter hated to admit it, but at least in part, it had to be because McKay told him not to. He couldn't stand anyone telling him what he could or couldn't do. It also galled him that McKay was likely bee-lining it to the Henry's at this very moment to look over the bitter remains of the Kofford gang. Perhaps he knew some trick or other that would allow him to find the gold after the bloodshed. Maybe everything he had told McKay was key enough to take care of whatever that wolf thing was. If indeed there even was a monster wolf.

Port had seen a lot of strangeness in his time, weird things that crawled up out of the abyss or even just man's visceral inhumanity to man. Maybe that's all this was too. Just some deranged bloody-handed lunatic with a penchant for knives. Maybe several somebody's. The tracks had been indistinct and looked wolf-like but perhaps it was just a big scavenger and cautious Paiutes were the real culprits after all. It was still their land and who knows what offense the Kofford's had likely done to the tribes in recent history.

But none of that seemed the real answer in Port's heart. No, there was some darkness that lay over that mountain range. Something sick and twisted deep inside like an unnatural cancer. There was plenty of bad medicine there just like Bridger always said.

The storm moved on thru bringing a cold spell with it. Porter guessed it would be a bright clear night, with frost possible. Would tonight be the full moon? Or was it still waxing? He hated that he wasn't sure anymore. He felt for the Bowie at his side. It was always there but it was an encouraging reassurance to feel it again. He had the pistols and Sharps rifle fully loaded, but there was something about the big knife that granted a primal strength, an indomitable will in the struggle to come.

He pondered all these things watching an eagle soaring high on the updrafts while a murder of crows gathered and squawked a few ridges over. The difference struck him funny and he laughed a little. He wanted to laugh at life a little more than he did these days.

Darkness came sullen and quicker than expected. The orange on the horizon rapidly faded to violet before bruising indigo. Stars winked into existence, like pinpricks in the curtain of night and the cosmic serpent wheeled overhead.

Porter came from downwind again, intending to take the high ground above the Kofford massacre. Ever cautious, he dismounted and led his horse on foot the last mile or so in the dark. A bright moon began its arc over the Henry's just as he reached his desired overlook.

He watched with the patience of a chopping block and sure enough, something stirred down amongst the Kofford corpses. Port thought it was a coyote at first but then recognized the stooping gait. Inching down from his spot he carefully moved in on McKay.

To reach the no longer limping old man, Port had to cross a small dry gulch. He stepped careful, heel to toe to avoid loose shale when a stone gave way and he slid down on his rear, hitting his head.

Blinking, an Indian woman stood above him. Pale and sad eyed she extended a hand. Port reached for it, and his hand passed through hers. This only increased the forlorn look upon her face. She glanced back toward the mountain and silently vanished in a ghostly fade out.

Porter blinked again, sure he had seen her despite the bump on his head.

"Thought it might be you," said McKay, from the top of the gulch. His rifle was leveled at Port. "Gotta be careful sneaking round these parts."

Port started to stand.

"Not so fast. Take off that gun belt, slow and easy like."

Port undid the belt and tossed it a short distance from himself. "You ain't worried about the wolf?"

"Sure I am, but I know his schedule and weakness. You don't." Regardless of what he just said, McKay glanced about warily, as if expecting he could be wrong. "Now get over to the side," he said, beckoning with his rifle.

As the barrel was pointed away, Porter threw a flat piece of shale at McKay then lunged toward the old man. The flung piece of stone, slapped across McKay's hand and face. A shot rang out wild as McKay cried out in pain.

Porter slammed him to the ground, kicking the rifle away.

"Folks aim high in the dark old man," growled Porter.

"I wasn't gonna do you no harm. Honest. I just wanted to get my share."

Porter grunted at that and twisted the man about, then bound McKay's hands with a thin piece of rawhide.

"You can't do this Porter. Pick up that gun and be ready for what comes. I got silver bullets in there. You don't know!" McKay was urgent and legitimately frightened. Porter picked up McKay's repeating rifle. It was a fine piece.

"That wolf is gonna come, I swear it."

Watching, listening, smelling, Porter caught nothing his rational senses could touch. But his heart said otherwise. The more he thought about it, the more he was sure that the ghostly Indian maiden was trying to warn him.

"Speak the truth McKay, or I'm gonna leave you here as wolf bait," growled Porter, as he shoved McKay up over the rise.

"You wouldn't do that. You can't!"

Port laughed and pushed the man down on the ground, before picking him up by the belt. "You wanna try my patience?"

"The wolf won't come out til after midnight. That's gotta be soon. I got them six silver bullets and a double load of silver shot in the scatter gun yonder. Might not be enough."

"You still ain't really told me anything," said Porter.

McKay looked Porter over, swallowed and said, "I've been hunting for that gold for twenty years. I earned it. I always knew it was near this canyon, where I found the mule hooves, and the slag from the smelters. It's got to be right near here, but I could never find it and that damned wolf. He's killed three of my partners already. And he'll get us too, if you don't let me get the shotgun and we ride!"

Porter pulled a flask from his coat pocket and took a swig, all the while keeping the rifle and an eye trained on McKay. "You are a sorry liar. There is something, but you ain't told me anything but a line of half-truths. What do you know about the ghosts?"

"Nothing."

Porter scrutinized McKay and spit. "I'm gonna leave you here and come back at dawn, if I don't start hearing some truth."

"Alright, I'll tell you what Wash told me and what I learned after I shot him."

Porter cocked an eyebrow at the mention of the old Indian being shot, though he wasn't surprised by anything but the admission of guilt.

"When the Utes rose up against the Spanish, started stoning and knifing them, a few Spaniards managed to hole up in a cavern for shelter. They took squaws as hostages, thinking it would preserve them against the braves. Thing is, the braves could not be turned aside even for their women. Ortiz killed the women one by one hoping to put the fear of God into them. Wash said a medicine man lay a curse on the Spaniards by the power of some heathen god. Now anyone hunting for gold at night is bound by magic to this mountain, as are the ghosts of the maidens Ortiz slew. Neither can leave."

Porter grunted at that but said nothing as he watched the darkness.

"That's how I know its gotta be around here somewhere. The ghosts are here and can't leave. It's close. That's why I didn't want to tell you about it. It should be mine. I earned it."

Port stifled a laugh.

A wolf howled from deep in the night.

McKay struggled frantically at his rawhide bonds. He tried to stand but Porter pushed him to his knees again.

"That's the wolf coming for blood. He is bound to this mountain same as the Indian maidens and can't leave until—"

"Until what?"

"Until someone breaks the curse. And you can't break a curse on the dead."

A ghostly witch light appeared on the mountain side, swinging back and forth, beckoning to Porter. Again he heard the flute and wondered at the gloomy tune. It was hard to suppress chasing after the light and music.

"What is that?" he asked, McKay without even bothering to look at the man on the ground.

"Witches," McKay spat, "witches that want to curse you and eat your spleen. They must serve the wolf."

"I've had about enough of that attitude."

"What you gonna do about it? You need me."

"The hell I do," snarled Port, pushing McKay over as he strode toward the mysterious fire light.

"You can't leave me like this."

Porter turned and drew his bowie knife. McKay winced as Porter cut the rawhide. "Get your scatter gun and keep watch. You try anything—"

McKay nodded, "I'll keep watch, but don't go toward the witch light."

"I have to see."

Porter was halfway between the witch light and McKay when he could finally make out the figures holding the light and the players of the flute, a trio of ghostly Indian maidens.

They were at once both beautiful and sad, proud and broken. They gestured to the mountainside which warped and revealed a

171

cavernous doorway where Porter would never have believed such a thing could exist. Dried branches and twigs filled the cavern so that no one could get past.

Porter heard McKay scrambling away in the darkness, then the quick hoof beats of the old man retreating on horseback but the maidens had his full attention. They pulled at the straw and sticks clearing a path so Porter could get into the mountain.

A howl and a scream echoed across the valley.

Porter paused, wondering if the old man's death was his fault.

But there was no time. Silent, yet urgent, the maidens formed a path through the rotten brambles into the belly of the mountain and Porter squeezed through.

Clear blue light emanated from the ghostly maidens illuminating the ancient mineshaft. Port strode over the bones and armor of conquistadors scattered over the cavern floor. They were pin-cushioned with arrows and hatchet dents. Among them were the skeletons of innumerable Paiute children. There was no wondering at the maiden's sorrow.

Behind a venomous growl tore into the somber peace. A massive wolf yearned to launch through the passage. Striving forward its red rimmed jaws snapped and a negative shadow light of blackness leered from its empty eye sockets.

Porter reached for his Navy Colt and emptied the six shots into the monstrous beast. None had effect. He cursed himself for a fool, he had left the Sharps rifle with the silver slugs outside as he entered the mountain.

Only the monstrous bulk of the wolf slowed it from being upon Porter already. Its matted grisly fur twisted as it inched through the brambles. An aura of fear wafted off the monster like stink on a festering corpse.

Porter willed himself the courage to not avert his gaze—a gaze into the madness of the abyss-like eyes. He backed away, farther into the mineshaft come tomb. Rusted sword hilts and broken flintlocks littered the floor. Porter knew that none of these relics would avail him.

The hideous wolf smashed through the final decayed branches. Desiccated haunches readied to latch onto Porter.

"Conquistadoro?"

The monster paused. "Que?"

"I thought so. No reason for a Paiute curse to attack Paiutes. No reason for them to keep away, but from you . . . yes. You would have an ax to grind."

Port edged backward and glanced over the pile of bones. One final pile of empty royal looking armor lay in a heap, surrounded by three piles of smaller fragile looking bones.

"They called your bluff didn't they and sealed you in here."

"Soy una Brujo. Sé que la oscuridad arts," came a voice like a death rattle.

"Yeah, I'll bet you do. Some men have an awful will that can transcend even death. But all things must come an end."

What could only sound like laughter wheezed from the maw of the wolf. "Lo que ya está muerta no puede morir."

"I'm sure you'd like to keep thinking that."

Porter bet everything on the hint that he knew of the Spanish legends—that and that the ghostly Paiute maidens had led him here in the first place, the one place where the curse could be undone.

"But I know your name . . . *Ortiz.*"

The monster turned each way looking for escape but the tunnel had become a round chamber without exit. Only Porter, the three ghostly maidens and the wolf Ortiz remained.

"Me pueden quedar atrapados, pero todavía puedo matarte."

Porter beckoned, arms wide open for the assault. "Let's tangle!"

The wolf Ortiz leapt, jaws agape, dark claws glinting.

Knocked to the ground, Porter saw the hollow throat begging to receive him. Fangs gnashed in desperation to destroy the one man who knew the true identity of the cursed beast.

Taking hold of the jaw, Porter spread the monster's mouth open until it snapped. He lifted the crippled monster above his head and slammed it down.

Ortiz tried to limp away but Porter's bull hands grabbed the cursed werewolves tail and yanked him backward. In a suicidal last ditch effort, Ortiz dove for Porters throat.

But one last knock to the monster's skull and it forgot its drive momentarily. Insulted, it leapt a final time.

A heap of dry bones hit Porter and fell to dust at his feet.

What remained of Ortiz was no more, the curse lifted and the way

173

out of the tunnel appeared once again?

Porter stepped forward and then the gleam of gold bars, piled one atop another called to him. He stopped, taking the glorious wealth in with his eyes like a starving man at a feast. There was gold enough to buy the territory, gold enough to become a king. He reached out.

The ghost maiden stood before him and shook her head, she pointed at the bones of the children, then at her own and those of her sisters.

"I'm sorry Ma'am." Porter pulled the original gold ingot from his pocket and tossed it on the pile of others. "My apologies. Rest in peace. You've earned it."

He exited the mouth of the tunnel and it closed up behind him like a hunger was finally satisfied. Porter knew he could never find it again. He also knew he would never try.

Killer Instinct

Deep in the ages before old men repeated the stories they were told as children, the last thunder lizard haunted the valley between the Twin Mountains. The valley was his and the red man knew not to disturb him . . . but the white man didn't.

Cattle baron H. Roth Garfield laid claim to the big valley and homesteaded the Hero-T ranch. It was named for his deceased son. Ranging over thousands of acres consumed a lot of men and Garfield housed them all at the magnificent Hero-T. It was an ideal location, wide long meadows fenced in by stout pine forests and snow clad mountains. Situated halfway between the Oregon and Santa Fe trails, Garfield sold cattle in all directions.

At least he did, until the thunder lizard, called Unktehi by the red man, awoke.

Having made a fantastic sale of a few thousand head of cattle to the army at Fort Union, Garfield declared a celebration. He gave each hand a generous bonus and brought in a grand piano and mariachi band for the big night. Barrels of beer and casks of whiskey were divvied out freely and even the red-lantern girls from San Isadora came. They all banged the drum and sang the songs of life, lust and laughter. And they reveled as loudly throughout the valley as had never been heard since the dawn of time when Unktehi was spawned.

So, rudely awoken from his long slumber, the stalking demon despised the raucous melodies and blaring horns, the giggling women and carousing men. Waiting until dark, the monster watched and when even the horned moon hid behind veiled cloud, he struck.

Tramping into the carnival square with the speed of a ravening wolf, Unktehi rendered man and beast. Horses screamed as they were torn apart and men cried out for their mothers as they died. The lizard's mighty jaws clamped down and those that could, ran and hid in deep shadows. He crushed horns and sombreros, and swallowed drunken snoring fools slumbering upon card tables. Some brave souls tried to shoot the demon, but nothing could penetrate his thick scaly hide. The thunderous repeat of rifles only further upset the monster and these men merely died next.

Unktehi slew some thirty souls, and by dawn's early light the nightmare vanished back into the slot canyons. His great three toed tracks left a wake of such awful destruction upon the Hero-T that men whispered afterward across the territories when mentioning the doomed ranch.

Gunfighters and hunters came and gunfighters and hunters died as no bullet nor blade could harm the beast. Too wise for poison or traps, Unktehi or Render, as the white men called him became a blight upon a once fair land. Shaman's from the five nations were consulted and all said the same, the land was Unktehi's. Leave or die.

In the weeks to come, the monster returned chaotically, feeding upon whatever it found whether man or beast. The Hero-T soon had more ghosts than men to run the ranch and it was said bad luck covered the house of Garfield like flies on a corpse.

Garfield's golden hall of dreams became a sad and somber place full of grim despair, until Porter came a riding.

Rain fell like angel tears as Porter rode through the Hero-T ranch's broken gates and was challenged by a scrawny buck-toothed watchman.

"Who're you?" asked the watchman, with fear only slightly hidden by disdain. He saw a broad shouldered man with long dark hair and a full black beard. Pistols jutted from Porter's vest and his wide brimmed slouch hat did not conceal his penetrating gaze. His hands were strong and his voice burned like hot hammered iron.

"Name's Porter. I'm here to see Garfield," he answered, riding on past the slack jawed watchman.

"You're Porter? Sorry, I reckon."

"Uh huh." Porter stopped at the stables, unsaddled his dun horse. He tossed a nickel to the stable boy to groom, feed and water the horse. Porter then strode to the Manor house.

The foreman, Uncle Ferdie, held the door open. Port passed through and addressed Garfield who lay stewing in his misery at the dinner table. "'Lo, H."

Garfield blinked and wiped his bloodshot eyes. "Porter?"

"It's me."

"I haven't seen you since California. What are you doing here?"

Port grinned like the devil. "You know why." He tipped his hat to a handful of women who eavesdropped from the parlor.

"I'm thankful, I really am, but there isn't a thing any man can do. I'm ruined and had best leave this cursed valley before all my people are dead. This Render, a demon beast of hell . . . he took four men in the bunkhouse night before last. I cannot ask anymore of anyone."

"You ain't asking, I'm offering. I heard this . . . *Render?* Can't be shot, poisoned or cut." Porter sat down across from Garfield and scratched his beard.

"You heard right. Nothing more can be done. You best head on out. I know you've been considered a destroying angel to whole lot of men, but that's men. This is different. This thing is a satanic curse. There isn't anyone alive who knows how to kill such a demon."

Port pulled a flask from his vest and took a long pull before answering, "Killing's an instinct for good or bad. One of the only talents I got. I'll find a way."

"Can't be done," Uncle Ferdie taunted, as he came out of the gloomy hallway. "Porter, you may have quite a reputation as a blood thirsty killer, but I gots no doubt most of those was in the back. I heard 'bout you in California. You and a Brown had a saloon in Murderers Bar, and look what happened to Brown?"

Garfield grumbled, "Enough Ferdie."

"Naw, it's alright," said Porter. "Go on since you know the story so well, *friend*."

Ferdie wiped his thin beard, answering, "I will. You had a partner, Brown, running your saloon and hotel during the gold rush days upriver of Sutter's Mill."

Port nodded.

"Then one night, Brown was horribly murdered. Seems just a day or so later, you up and disappeared. Pretty suspicious. I believe I heard most of the folks there in Murderers Bar was looking to lynch you. You think that was bad, let me tell something . . . this here . . . is gonna be a whole lot worse." He gestured all around to drive home the point.

"You talk a lot of rot for a drunk. I took bloody handed vengeance on those that murdered Brown. They're dead and buried like anyone else that ever crossed me and all of 'em have holes in the front. Everyone knows I took care of those *things* that rolled into Eden City, the wolf-man in the haunted Henry Mountains, the Finnegan gang and the skin walker of Bear Lake. And there's still plenty of tales I ain't never told anybody. But I don't recall *ever* hearing any such tales about you around the campfire, except maybe the one about why you're still alive but none of your cowhands are, *friend*."

Ferdie frowned and slunk away amidst the giggling of the women folk.

"You might've been too hard on him," said Garfield. "He's a good foreman."

"Sometimes yapping dogs need a kick."

Garfield nodded but said nothing as he lit his pipe. Outside the rain pelted the windows with an incessant rapping and the trees swayed against the wind. Porter sensed a dark aura hung over the Hero-T ranch that leeched the will power from its inhabitants.

"Tell me a little more about the *Render*."

Garfield puffed on his pipe, sending smoke rings over his head like dirty halos. "It's big. Big as an elephant. Pear shaped body. Walks on two legs, large as tree trunks, has a mighty tail that swings around like a thunderbolt. The arms are tiny, have claws but they are not to be feared. It's the mouth. A long snake-like head with a maw full of bristling teeth like buffalo horns. Could swallow a man whole if it wanted, but usually it tears them apart first. It's gruesome I tell you. It does most of its killing with its mouth, some with the feet, but it's usually that awful fang sprouted mouth."

Porter listened and took another pull on his flask. "Sounds like a dragon."

"I suppose it does. But while dragons are reptiles and have scaly skin like it does, they're reptiles. Reptiles are dumb but this monster is too smart for traps or poison. *Render* isn't any reptile. It looks reptilian for sure, but it's warm blooded."

Porter cocked an eyebrow. "Thought you said no bullet or blade can pierce it."

"None I've ever seen. But I felt the thing once. That first night while it ate thirty of my men and a couple gals from San Isadora, it pinned me against a dead horse and the barn. It was gulping down on some poor bastard and I felt its huge leg and it was warm. That tough scaly leg was warm! So, it's no dragon. It's a warm blooded demon."

Port sketched a charcoal picture on a sheepskin and showed it to Garfield who had him shrink the arms even more.

"The arms are even smaller. No bigger than a man's."

"How fast is it?"

"I think that's part of what makes it so dangerous, is that it's warm blooded. I've been in the south and seen alligators moving slow when it's cold in the morning. *Render* don't mind, he's been seen hunting at night and in the snow. No reptile could do that. So he's fast, can run fast as any horse. Hell, if he's chasing a horse, he gets them, they're dead."

Port adjusted his drawing and Garfield nodded. "You got it about right now."

"How about its senses? Eyes and ears, nose?" asked Porter.

"Big eyes and nostrils, can't say I ever saw its ears but it sure ain't deaf. It doesn't like the sound of rifles even if they can't hurt it."

"Anything else you can tell me about it?"

"It roars, makes the most hideous sound you ever heard, like a hundred bears coming out of one cavernous mouth. It is the devil's mouthpiece."

Porter pondered a moment longer and looked out the window toward the high desert wilderness. "Every creature beds down sometime. Any ideas where *Render* might?"

"Johnny Martin and that Tabeshaw kid tracked it to the marshes against the north face. Said they figured it went through the swamp to the canyons and caves on the other side. But . . .,"

"But what?"

"They told us about it and the next morning they headed out after it with some buffalo guns and powder kegs. We found what was left of them the next afternoon. Hardly a grease spot, but Ferdie, he recognized the Tabeshaw kids hand and Martin's mangled lower torso halfway to the marsh. Some hooves were left behind too. We never went out that way again. We buried the hand and torso right there because of the worms."

Port growled, "You ain't giving me too terribly much to go on, H."

Garfield guffawed bitterly, "You know why? There isn't anything else to tell you. This demon spawn defies God with its very existence. This thing should not be. It's an abomination. I talked with the medicine man of the Dakotah's, Walking Bear, and he said Unktehi, he called it, has been here since they came into this world. He said the demon owned this valley and that we were the ones trespassing. He said we should just quit, just leave. He said it would take a greater killer than the demon itself to win back this valley."

Porter put his feet up on the table.

Garfield got up and looked out the window at his broken creation. "What can be done? We have sent more lead at that thing than we did at Santa Anna when I was young. Heaven doesn't love me."

Port grinned answering, "You say guns don't work? Guns have never worked against me either in a manner of speaking. Maybe I'll meet this monster head on without any guns or knives. Just so's its square with the Big Man."

Garfield spun on Porter glaring, "The medicine man said we should walk away. I cursed him for his advice. Walk away from all I built up? I thought he was insane and we hung on. But no one will come work for me anymore; the odds aren't in their favor. Over a hundred men have been slain these last twelve weeks. Bounties only brought death to more men and here you are proclaiming a weaponless plan?"

"Wheat! H., I am the weapon."

"You're as insane as the monster. But maybe it takes a monster to kill a monster."

Port raised his flask and took another pull. "Maybe it do, H. Maybe it do."

The rain stopped, but a curling fog clung to the landscape like a death shroud. Somewhere in the distance an owl hooted and the wind whipped off the pines sending needles spiraling. Up on the mountain peaks, snow pushed off the frozen stone like a comet's tail.

If the grim aura didn't drape itself over the place, Porter would have thought it all beautiful. But before the sun set he wanted to have a personal understanding of the lay of the land. He asked the dozen ranch hands crowding around the false comfort of the fire ring.

"Anyone willing to show me the way to the marsh?"

The cowboys looked at him with barely concealed disgust.

"That's where the demon lives," said one, spitting a wad of tobacco.

"Render is on the other side o' the swamp. You ought to go back where you came from, if'n you know what's good for ya, cricket cruncher," said another chortling.

Porter exhaled loudly saying, "I want to see it. Someone just tell me the way."

A fat hand with red sideburns rumbled, "You durn fool, we just told ya. You're asking for a pine box."

"No, he's asking to be dinner," another cackled.

Porter wiped his beard saying, "Just point me in the right direction. I don't need your concern."

"No!" shouted the first, spitting again. "You can't ride in here acting the hero. We all done our best and there ain't no such thing as hero's anymore. No one faces that rending demon and lives. You get on your sorry dun horse and git! We don't need you."

Porter cocked his head at the ranch hand. "Now, that's just unfriendly."

The man spat his mouthful of black juice at Porter's boots and grinned.

The hammer-like fist of Port hit the man square in the jaw, unhinging it. "Chew with your mouth closed."

The men gave a wide berth to Porter as he stepped over the unconscious tobacco chewer on his way to the stables. The boy he had paid a nickel waited out front of the swinging stable doors.

"I can show you the way."

Port looked back at the cow hands who would no longer meet his gaze. The chewer struggled to get off the ground. "That alright with your pa?"

The kid steeled himself before answering, "The Render done ate my pa a fortnight ago." He then turned his face to brush away a tear.

"Sorry kid. You sure you wanna do this?"

Eyes blazing like dark burning embers, the kid answered, "Yes sir. I wanna see that monster fry in hell."

"Well saddle up and I'll see what I can do."

"We only got a couple hours of daylight left kid. This ain't gonna be too far is it?"

The kid trotted his horse closer to Port's. "No sir, I reckon not. I've only been to the marsh one time but it wasn't far. Just over these hills and past those trees."

"Tell me kid, can you hear this Render coming?"

"Sometimes yes, sometimes no. It can be sneaky. But it will growl and roar at times, so you have fair warning."

Port looked at him nodding, "You're a brave kid."

They passed through a stand of aspens that grew close enough together they had to ride single file. The horses snorted and Port kept a vigilant eye out on either side of the trees though it was difficult to see more than fifty feet.

"They smell something," said the kid.

"I do too," grunted Port. "The rot of the swamp and peat bog." Porter dismounted and led his horse, through the last of the trees to the grassy meadow that extended a hundred feet before hitting the swaying cattails.

Fog wafted over the clearing and murky waters beyond. Behind the swamp loomed titanic granite mountains. A cleft in the rock disappeared like a passageway into a mountainous tomb.

The boy shivered upon the back of his horse and pointed, "That is where the Render lives."

Port handed the kid his reins and walked closer to marsh. His boots sunk into the mud somewhat as he neared the staggered shoreline and he knew the horses would be worse than himself. But what about a creature the size of what he had been told? Sure enough a dozen paces to the south there was a cow path of sorts leading to a break in the reeds.

Except it wasn't a cow path.

Alternating each direction were tracks. There was no getting over the size of them. Massive three toed prints with a stride the length of horse between them. They embedded several inches into the soft earth and were full of marsh water. Porter looked closely and saw that the water was clean and still. These had to be at least a day old by his calculations. Each toe ended in a point, claws as big as his hand. Port looked toward the slot canyon in the mountain. He didn't hear anything but couldn't get over the feeling of being watched.

The mist had closed in some and the red glow of dusk stole over the mountains to the west, turning them black against the horizon.

"Maybe we ought to get back. We don't want to be caught out here after dark," said the kid softly.

Port nodded, watching the deep canyon across the marsh. "You're right, nothing more to learn here on our own."

The crack of lightning and subsequent thunder spooked the horses. The kid startled too and almost lost his grip on Port's reins.

"Easy, we're leaving. That was close."

But the boy's eyes were frozen staring at the crest of the meadow to the south. He pointed, but while his mouth opened, nothing came out. Something moved through the fog. Shadowy and vague, it slipped between cascading banks of gray. A phantom just beyond recognition.

The hairs prickled and stood up on Ports forearms as he caressed the pistol at his side.

It came closer, slow and steady.

Port narrowed his gaze. The shape wasn't right. It was too short, too chaotic.

Parting through the mists revealed an old Indian shaman. His gray hair was fashioned in a braid and a few feathers clung, splayed down. He held a crutch like staff and silently lifted it toward Port.

"Walking Bear? Ain't coming to count coup on me are ya?"

The ancient Indian gave what might either be a grimace or a smile. It was hard to tell because of his many wrinkles and lines. Walking Bear looked old as anyone living, his deep mahogany skin almost matched his buckskins. He also looked to the cleft and then ambled toward Porter and the boy. "Not wise to be here now," he said, slowly.

"Wheat. You're here."

Walking Bear grunted. "I came to warn you. Let us get back to the ranch." He tugged on Port's reins and swung his head in a demanding fashion.

"Take it easy old man. We were about to head back anyhow."

The old man grunted again.

"Kid, let him get on with you."

The boy fidgeted in his saddle and slid back a hand's breath.

Walking Bear shrugged and said, "I can walk as fast as you can trot."

"Suit yourself. Let's get back into the trees and be on our way."

They slipped through the aspens but not before all looked to the jagged cleft one last time. The stillness seemed to echo and the foreboding was palpable.

"It is not safe to be near Unktehi 's lair," repeated Walking Bear, after they were beyond the aspens.

"Didn't figure it was, but I wanted to learn all I could for myself. I saw his tracks, he's a big 'un," said Port, as he bit the end of a cigar and fumbled for a match.

"He is large, but he is not yet full grown."

Port's eyebrows raised and he neglected to light his cigar, letting the match burn out. "Not full grown?" He muttered through his teeth clenching the cigar. "Whad'ya mean? How do you know that?"

"Unktehi dwelt with his mother once and she was greater still."

"You mean there is two of 'em?"

The old shaman nodded. "I saw them hunting the buffalo many moons past, before the white cattle men came, when I was a boy. They and the thunderbirds dwelt here, but like all things they change and return to the earth."

"But those two are still here?"

"Perhaps, but perhaps the mother has gone the way of all things and sleeps forever in the earth."

"You almost sound disappointed."

He moved his hand across the horizon and down. "I am sorry to see any creature's time pass. My time comes soon as well. It is as the Great Spirit moves in all things. There is a season for all."

"Even these monsters?" asked Port, indignant as he lit another match.

"They had their place. But as the white man encroaches a deadly struggle comes. The other white men do not know how to kill Unktehi, but you are blessed by the Great Spirit. You have the blessing way of doom, the instinct of killing and will surely find a way."

"Thanks, I suppose. You don't have any more direct pointers though do ya?"

The old man took Port's cigar and puffed a moment before answering, "Look and you will find. The way of the gun is not the way to succeed. As you made a boast, you shall be tested. Trust not in the arm of flesh but have faith in yourself and the Great Spirit's guidance."

Frowning, Port mumbled, "You can keep the cigar. Something tells me, I ain't gonna be able relax yet."

"No, you won't," agreed Walking Bear, with a wry grin.

"With all you just told me, did you really come all the way out here just to warn me off?"

Walking Bear shrugged, grinning, "I also wanted the cigar."

Night fell black as coal and ten times as hard. The last of the ranch hands threw a few cords of wood beside what was now Porter's bonfire, then they too disappeared to whatever shelter they could find for the night. Only the kid and Walking Bear remained beside the long-haired gunman.

Garfield made a brief appearance. "I'm offering my sincere thanks Porter. If you can take care of this, I'll be forever in your debt."

"I know," Porter said, tossing a log on the fire. "How about a drink?"

Garfield nodded and went back inside the manor house.

Port heard the bolt slam down and shook his head. "You two can get some sleep or whatever you want. Sure don't gotta stay by me."

The kid nodded to Port, but pointed at a barrel beside the manor house. "I'll be in there."

"Why not? It'll give a good view. Now, Walking Bear, I'd rather not wait all night. Anything we can do to get Render to come sooner than later?"

The old man produced a skin kettle drum from his deerskin bag. "Unktehi does not like the noise the white man make. This drum will annoy and draw him near in anger. And in anger you can perhaps defeat him as he shall make mistakes, for he is clever but anger clouds the mind of all creatures it touches."

Port said, "I'll take you at your word for that." He sat on a stump facing out and away from the fire so he wouldn't be night-blind. He loaded his three pistols and checked his Sharps buffalo gun.

Walking Bear sat in the dirt before the fire, heedless of the danger that would surely creep up from behind.

The kid sat slumped over the rim of the barrel, with a dirty blanket across his shoulders. He crunched into an apple and Port signaled that he wanted one too. The kid however wouldn't leave his barrel and threw the apple to Port, who narrowly caught it before it landed in the roaring fire.

Walking Bear began drumming and chanting a song of his people, an old song that called out in the night, noble and fierce. His voice was clear and proud, timed to the steady throb of the drum, calling out the demon, Unktehi.

"Waiting is always the hard part," Port lamented to himself. "But being hungry makes the food taste that much better."

The drums beat echoed and they were answered. An awful roar like angry cracking thunder swung out of the night and made the ranch dogs yip and bark in fear.

Walking Bear continued his steady primal beat. To Porter it matched his heart. Upon hearing the terrible roar his heart thumped, boom, boom, boom, boom, fast as it could.

The Render, Unktehi, was coming.

Porter felt the bowie knife at his side; the blessed blade gave him cold comfort. He watched the clouds clearing out as the storm moved on south east. The bleak stars appeared and twinkled. They seemed unfeeling and cold, their light frail.

Walking Bear never relaxed and perhaps even drummed a half-beat faster.

Port stared at the open range toward the cleft, though he could only see a hundred yards at best. A cat or raccoon stole through the edge of the corrals. A night hawk swooped low, briefly illuminated by the firelight. The smell of the pines off the mountain was stronger now after the rain and the light tremble of every fourth beat rocked Port upon his stump. Every fourth beat was stronger, shaking the ground harder.

Every fourth beat?

The kid screamed.

Port swung around to see colossal darkness looming behind. It blocked the stars from view and coalesced into a twenty foot, mottled grey tooth ridden horror.

Jaws agape, its massive head tilted slightly as it snapped at Porter who narrowly dodged and rolled away.

On his back, Porter drew two Navy Colt thirty-six caliber pistols and emptied them into the monster's underbelly as it passed over him. The bullets ricocheted off the scaly hide. The monster hardly acknowledged the attack at all, giving its lightest roar yet.

Port rolled again as the swampy tail thrashed where he had just lain. It sent the heavy stump Porter had been sitting on sailing across the yard like a skipping stone.

Grabbing his Sharps rifle, Port attempted to get a bead on the monster's eye or failing that, a nostril. But the behemoth swung around with such speed, Port's one shot was a glancing mark to the monster's impervious jaw line.

The great taloned feet slammed down and Port felt the rifle torn from his grasp. He heard the crack of wood and twisted steel as the monster's step destroyed the Sharps.

The heavy step crashed behind Porter. The snapping of the titanic maw gave such fear as he had ever known. He weaved as he ran, dropping near a water trough for cover.

The drumming, if not the chant of Walking Bear continued and Port reeled at the thought of the old man still singing what could only be his death song.

Was it a distraction? The monster nudged at the trough, as if to coax Porter into revealing himself to be run down and eaten. But the drumming worked. The monster having lost sight of Porter, wheeled to go after Walking Bear.

Unktehi cleared half the distance as Port rose and drew his final pistol. Aiming at the back of its head, he emptied the thirty-six caliber balls at the base of the monster's skull and as close to its predatory eyes as he could.

Walking Bear drummed and chanted without fear.

The monster hesitated looking at both men. Walking Bear retreated a few paces, still banging the drum and giving his loud throaty chant. Porter attempted to reload the cap and ball pistol, cursing at the loss of the Sharps.

Port was struck at how tiny the monster's arms were. It was as Garfield had told him. It killed with its mouth or feet, the arms were virtually useless. For as large as Unktehi was, the arms were no bigger than Port's.

The killer instinct within Porter awoke. The red ballad of death sang and Port knew the tune. Whether it was helped along by the Great Spirit mattered not, because the man in his struggle against death answered the call.

As the monster threatened Walking Bear, Porter dropped his useless pistol and charged bare handed at the brute. "Wheat!" he roared like a madman.

The drum beat louder as Unktehi salivated.

Porter leapt up the monster's knee and grasped the left arm. He twisted it back against the monster itself.

For the first time ever, Unktehi knew fear. This man, this insect was hurting it. He snapped at the man but could not even come close to grasping the tenacious foe.

Porter swung back and taking hold at the monster's elbow, slammed it backward until the bone cracked and Unktehi screamed.

The monster panicked, considering trying to fall over on the man, but feared what would happen if it was on the ground and unable to get up. Instead it swung its massive body in circles hoping to toss or shake the man aside like a dog scratching fleas.

Port hung on for dear life as he was dizzied by the spinning monster. Like the bull of the gods, Porter rode the demon, shouting, "Wheat!"

Unktehi jerked and twisted, snorting til blood foamed pink at his nostrils and still the bear of a man would not let go.

Bracing himself, Porter used the momentum to wrench the arm back at the shoulder and break it.

Unktehi screamed again and vomited in terror. Never had anything caused such dire pain. And the drum beat on.

Porter took the limp arm and twisted it and flexed against the steely scales until a spur of jagged bone from the inside, bit through. Port worked the tear until he could turn the arm about again and again. He tore as Unktehi raged. Muscle and sinew gave way as the hard scales flexed and buckled, revealing soft flesh. Hot blood flowed freely cascading in rivulets down Ports straining arms.

One last twist and pull.

The arm came loose and Porter fell to the ground still clutching the scaly arm and two finger like claws.

Deep scarlet splashed across Porter's face as Unktehi ran into the darkness, bawling more like a crippled goat rather than the thunder lizard he was.

Porter held the bloody clawed arm aloft and shouted the primal barbaric cry of victory. This time it was his voice that rocked the night and made the beasts fall silent.

Walking Bear ceased his drumming and the ranch folk stepped out from their shadows and hidey holes. Garfield came out marveling at the gory sight.

"Get my horse," ordered Porter. "Things got a blood trail like the Colorado. We need to finish this tonight."

"You heard him," shouted Garfield, "Mount up!"

A dozen men rode into the darkness after the monster following the blood trail across the meadows and through the aspens all the way to the marsh. Even upon the inky waters, crimson swirled toward the cleft.

"Maybe we should wait to the break of day," suggested Ferdie.

Port's eyes flashed and the instinct was on him too strong to wait, too strong to let things go. It was too strong to deny. He walked into the waters alone until he was swimming through the murk, his feet unable to touch bottom. He trudged out of the cool waters and still the blood trail beckoned him on into the darkness like the promise of a cooing lover.

The cleft wound around through a copse of trees and finally into a sheltering overhang of rock where the bones of monstrous generations rotted and the last of its kind came to die.

Render, or Unktehi as the Dakotah named him, lay upon its belly, snorting blood as it breathed heavily. Its great amber eyes blinked. The wound of its stolen arm spurt jets of blood in time with its dying heartbeat. Porter ran his hand across the face of the monster and felt pity for a thing that knew nothing but how to kill. Was he the same? He told himself he wasn't, while still wondering in his own primal beating heart.

Porter put the muzzle of his Navy Colt to the great amber eye and said, "You're done killing."

Unktehi snorted in response, as if resigned to his fate.

"But I ain't."

The shot echoed off the canyon walls and the beast was still. Morning's light washed over the mountains and the others finally dared to venture inside the cleft.

Porter had fallen asleep beside his grim prize. It took four strong men to lift Unktehi's gory head and they marveled at the last of the thunder lizards. They spoke of the wealth such a find could bring and stories they could tell in the taverns on lonely cold nights.

Garfield patted Porter on the back, "What can I possibly do to thank you? You're a hero, like those legends of old. How can I repay you?"

Porter stretched, took stock of his bloody garments, broken guns shook his head and answered, "I still need that drink."

Right Hand Man

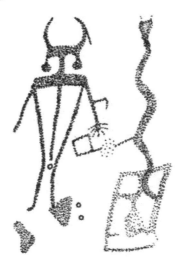

Account written by George D. Watt in January of 1870 and left in the possession of Daniel Bonelli in St. Thomas, Nevada.

We had only been in St. Thomas proper for but a few hours and already Brother Brigham's de facto and oft times drunken bodyguard, Orrin Porter Rockwell, was embroiled in the middle of quite a ruckus with the local red natives.

It seems that the Paiutes, who camp alongside the 'Big Ditch' – a canal that flows through St. Thomas to irrigate the fields therein, began to have a dispute over a woman. Supposedly one man decided to claim the wife of another man and the two began to scrap over her and gradually a large number of the restless braves took sides.

They did have the civility to lay aside their weapons and duel using only their bodies until one alone could claim victory and thus gain the woman. But of other such barbarities in the fight they had many, especially in the way they treated the squaw during the conflict.

She, unfortunately had no say in the matter, but such is the way of the savage. The two sides did beat each other furiously wrestling and boxing one another after a fashion and it did sway each way in an undefinable manner as far as I could perceive.

When they weren't beating each other over the head, they would then grab the woman by the arms and pull her each way in a veritable tug of war virtually killing the poor creature.

Now some of the Saints did try to intervene and thus save the woman but they were largely beat back by the strong willed natives whose blood was up in the heat of the moment. And of course Brother Rockwell's intervention was especially misconstrued as he has all the subtlety of a pair of brass knuckles.

He approached them when they were pulling hard on the young squaw and he admonished them to let her go and settle the dispute without harming her. They however took it to mean that he was saying he wished to join in the fight and he, being a white man, was the instant focus of their wild aggressions.

Rockwell suddenly had some twenty braves assaulting him and while for a moment one might have thought that the bearded gunslinger would be overwhelmed, Rockwell who has always been a hard man to handle, proved himself to be the meanest, toughest man I have ever seen.

I should add that at this point in the evening, Mr. Rockwell had already had a fair amount of drink in him and could not nearly have been at his full wits and capabilities.

At one point the braves had all taken hold of Rockwell by his arms and legs, picking up fully off of the ground and having him stretched out like a Christmas goose, but he ferociously kicked his legs until they were forced to drop him and he struck them with his fists until all tumbled down and then all at once he was punching them into submission. He whipped the lot of them and they did concede and allow him full access to the squaw. She herself was more than resigned to such a grim fate as that.

The braves having fully accepted that he was the victor, now cheered that the conflict was resolved and that he was the 'wyno' Mormon. I was amused as though 'wyno' means good in Paiute the double entendre for our alcoholic Brother could not be missed.

Rockwell then did try and turn her over to that man whom he believed had the legitimate claim to her, but she did refuse such saying that he [Rockwell] was the man who had fairly won her hand and that she did belong with him now.

This put Rockwell in more of a fix that he had anticipated even facing off against twenty men. He told her he was already married and she only brought up the LDS custom of plural wives. Rockwell said that he did not wish to take her from her people and upset her family and that she should stay with her first husband.

To this she reluctantly agreed, though she said she was still truly his squaw and would only stay with her first husband on Rockwell's permission and that when he should desire her, she should come to him by and by.

She did also give him a small beaded medicine pouch she said she had made and placed sacred items inside. She said it was enchanted and would protect him from the great evil and ghosts he would soon encounter in this red country. Rockwell reluctantly put it around his neck, wearing it with apparent chagrin. But I must add that he did never take it off so long as we were in the Muddy Mission.

And so ended our first night in St. Thomas, which I must say ended up being the lightest of the conflicts of the visit to the Muddy Mission.

Now Brother Brigham had asked Bishop Leithead to have a flat boat large enough for a wagon and team, prepared for the sake of going down river to do some exploring of the region. This was accomplished shortly before we arrived but upon inspection Brother Brigham seemed to have changed his mind and declined to float the river. This was obviously disheartening for those who had worked so hard on the project as timber was hard to come by here. But he did encourage the Saints there to remain and work hard in the region even if they should remain there forever.

That last particular remark is on account of the restructuring of the territory boundaries and that as of now the Federal government had moved the markers now making St. Thomas within the state of Nevada instead of the Utah territory, and as such the inhabitants were now a full three years behind the exceedingly high state tax commissions of Nevada. This did constitute quite a financial burden upon the folk as making a living in that arid land was already difficult enough.

These incredible hardships of living in this desolate land did make quite a few of the Saints wonder on their place in the kingdom and I can't say that I blame them.

I did have a long talk with Brother Daniel Bonelli on my own tribulations within the kingdom and with my recent reconnection after having been disfellowshipped on account of my adherence to the counsel of William Godbe. I cannot as yet say that I was wrong, but at this time neither will I say that I was absolutely right. The fate of the Godbeite reformation remains to be seen.

The flat boat did however see its use. The matter began on the next morning, when one of the Paiutes came to our camp and did call specifically for the help of Brother's Brigham and Rockwell.

Apparently the squaw Rockwell had rescued the night before had been taken by a bitter shaman by the name of Toohoo-emmi who was reputed to be quite evil and always working mischief in the area. He had slain the woman's husband and made some incredible demands that we all knew by no means would Brother Brigham abide by. This Toohoo-emmi was lord of a place known as Kai'Enepi or 'Demon Mountain'. The other Lamanites came to express several similar grievances and soon enough the chiefs delivered their pleas to Brother Brigham for help in dealing with the wicked shaman who was so vexing their lands and peoples.

At first it seemed that Brother Brigham would not hear their pleas as he had said that they should sort this thing out themselves but this only caused confusion and much grumblings. It looked like things were going to get out of control and in an attempt to normalize relations with area bands, we did convene a meeting with Tut-se-gavits, chief of Santa Clara band; To-ish-obe, principal chief of the Muddy band; William, chief of the Colorado band; Farmer, chief of St. Thomas band; Frank, chief of Simondsville band; Rufus, chief of the Muddy Springs band above the California Road; and Thomas, chief of the band at the Narrows of the Muddy. Sixty-four braves from the seven bands accompanied the chiefs to the meeting. And this was one of the few times I saw Brother Brigham smoke the peace pipe with the Lamanites.

To the overall request for assistance Brother Brigham replied that he would do what he could while also saying that they should still take care of their own problems. To-ish-be replied that while he agreed there should be a separation and such that this was a spiritual matter that was beyond his people's abilities and that we [meaning the

Mormon brethren, who said we had the Great Spirits blessings in all things] should be obligated to do something about this wicked man who could consort with devils. This made Brother Brigham smile in a way he knew he had been caught with words. He agreed to send one who he called his right hand man for just such a situation, Orrin Porter Rockwell. Brother Brigham said he would have Rockwell go out and resolve the matter—if the Paiute would also put forward a squad of their own best men for the job and in this they very specifically volunteered a young medicine man whom the local saints called Chief John as well as five of their stoutest braves. Chief John was somewhat reluctant to accept this charge and I did understand that for some reason he was looked down upon, but until later I had no idea as to why.

And here is where I was also roped into accompanying this venture as Brother Brigham decided that I should go along and record their doings. It would be fair to wonder if he wasn't punishing me for the whole of the Godbeite debacle and I did wonder if this wasn't a surreptitious way of simply being rid of me should some unfortunate accident happen along the way. It is unkind of me to write or even think such things but this wretched land and heat has played with my very reason.

It was agreed that we should depart in the morning and that evening as I shared dinner with the Bonelli family I was told of some of the more sinister happenings in the area that were attributed to this Toohoo-emmi. Brother Bonelli told me that the goings on in St. Thomas have been eerie as of late. That it is not meet to go out at night as strange things have been seen in the hills at night and some folk have been known to disappear. He said that the call of wolves has been terrible close and that he and others have taken to melting down silverware for the sake of keeping the pure metal as bullets close at hand. Brother Bonelli did give me a handful of the precious cartridges should I need them on this adventure.

We did have the good fortune of Chief John speaking good English as he would be our translator if needed along the way. Neither Rockwell nor I speaking Paiute with any proficiency. We took the afore mentioned flat boat down the river to gain entrance to Toohoo-emmi's abode. It was said he ruled from an ancient cliff palace that sat atop Kai'Enepi, the Demon Mountain. Our respective leaders bid that we should float downriver until we arrived at the trail leading to his mountain; take the fight to him and force a resolution of some kind.

It was a pleasant enough trip down the river and Chief John did tell us a number of things about our antagonist. It seemed that this Toohoo-emmi, whose name meant 'The Black Hand', had once been the chief medicine man for the Paiutes but had rather recently been deposed since he began dabbling in black magic and being far too removed from the Great Spirit. He had been seen going into trances with his eyes only showing their whites and talking with unseen forces. All of this may very well have been fine except that firstly some animals [horses] had gone missing and then finally people started to go missing and it was assumed that Toohoo-emmi was sacrificing them after the manner of the Old Ones.

Chief John was the one who had exposed these horrible crimes and he was then made medicine man for the tribes. This was a dubious honor because he had not been trying to take that position but merely right the wrongs that had been done. He had at first expected to exonerate Toohoo-emmi of the wild rumors and accusations but instead found indisputable evidence to condemn him. This certainly put a strain on things as I understood they had been quite close at some time.

Rockwell was rather indifferent toward all of this, spending a lot of his time using his saddle as a pillow and drinking Valley-Tan, letting his hand trail lazily in the warm river. He expressed no interest in Chief John's tale and I felt it would be up to me to make peace once we found Toohoo-emmi and had the maiden returned and other wrongs righted. I hoped that by expressing Brother Brigham's annoyance at this behavior we could peaceably conclude the matter. I should have recognized Chief John's worry earlier on but I was ignorant of such things then.

It is true that sometimes we become blind to our own world outlook and standing, we can become complacent and forget outside views and I have stood in that place far too many times.

We had travelled some distance downriver when Chef John pointed out we were being followed and I was horrified to find out by whom or what he meant.

A trio of great black snakes swam in the river pursuing us. They dipped their heads every now and again and when they did I saw their scaly tails twist in the water a good ten paces behind where their head had been, I estimated these reptiles to be in excess of twenty feet long!

I woke Rockwell and asked him to look and be wary. He casually took a drink of his whiskey and blinking, answered that it was but beavers, and true these heads were near as large as or even larger than a beaver's head, but I assure you, they were indeed snakes of enormous size.

Chief John explained these serpents were servants of the Toohoo-emmi and would protect his domain from the likes of us. I took hold of a paddle as I had no gun and I again urged Rockwell to take up arms against this impending threat. He laughed and said there were no such snakes so large nor in this part of the desert. Granted, he did use much more colorful language than I shall repeat here.

The other five braves were in a panic, crying out "Nooyooadu!" But they did utilize their bows and rifles to prepare for the coming assault.

The serpents made a swift reconnoiter of us aboard the flat boat and did strike almost simultaneously panicking the horses into breaking their tethers and flinging themselves off the flat boat and into the river and very nearly cap-sizing us in the process. I regret that it took such dire action to bring Rockwell's attention to our situation.

Rockwell was up in a flash and had his snub-nosed Navy Colts firing like the devil's own cannons, and I must admit I did wonder about a house divided against itself. It seemed that for now the devil did protect his own as the snakes dodged his bullets and ducked back under the waters no harm done to them but we had lost all of our horses and one of the braves already.

Then the snakes did launch themselves at us once again. I did batter one of them with a paddle, dazing it, I suspect for it dropped back down into the murky waters but it certainly was not yet deceased.

One brave shot a pair of arrows into a serpent and it remained sluggish though it did not halt its attack. Another brave was knocked off the flat boat but Chief John managed to sink his tomahawk into the sluggish one's head slaying it, though in its convulsion it hit him in the chest and fell back into the river.

Rockwell watched swinging his pistols whichever direction he did look and it saved him, as one snake reared from the waters suddenly and was met with both barrels full into the mouth. This blasted beast also slid back into the river with a splash of gore across the flat boat. I tried to remain steadfast in the face of such horrific violence and felt it was near beyond me.

With but one serpent left, we all kept vigil and also did rescue the one brave who had been knocked into the waters. We had absolutely lost the horses as they did not rise from the surface and we did suspect the serpents had grabbed their legs and drowned them along with the first brave who was knocked overboard.

There was some swirling in the murky brown waters but nothing came of it but our own fears.

When the final serpent did not attack, Chief John said he suspected that it had been Toohoo-emmi himself and that without help the wicked shaman would not attack as fierce a foe as we few again by himself, and that Toohoo-emmi had many other resources to fight and wear us down including other black magic's that did bring much fear into the braves though I am quite sure that it was not his intent to worry them.

Chief John said we were floating nearer to the abode of Toohoo-emmi and bid us be watchful.

We floated to a spot in the river where a small canyon opened giving us but a very narrow view like unto a doorway to another realm. Beyond the cliff walls we saw in the distance some verdant greenery while a small reddish stream flowed into the Virgin River. I expressed some surprise that this stream and canyon were not on the maps that had been supplied me by either George Brimhall or Anson Call but then neither did they mark a map with any place known as Kai'Enepi either. As near as I could understand Chief John's explanation, he seemed to be trying to find the English words to tell us there was a 'glamour' over this place and that what was once a sacred place of the Paiutes was now polluted and held in thrall by this Toohoo-emmi and his wicked band.

Rockwell guided the flat boat into the sandy beach area of the canyon and we did ground the vessel and pull it as far onto shore as we could muster now lacking the horses. We staked and roped it to some boulders though it would be no small feat for someone else to come along and dislodge it, even perhaps a large wake of the river could do the deed, but we were resolved to continue on despite the potential loss. None of us thought leaving a lone man behind to guard the flat boat was a worthwhile venture in this dangerous country.

We had not gone far beyond the shoreline when we found two dead men. One had his head blasted away by gunshots and the other had no head, as if cleaved by a tomahawk. Two arrow wounds were also in his backside. It took my getting some used to the idea but Chief John insisted these two men had been changelings or shape shifters and were in actuality the serpents we had so recently encountered. This was the wildest explanation I had ever heard but I could not deny the bloody truth at my feet as much as I truly wished I could.

Porter was silent at this revelation, but neither did he say it was as impossible as I had first pronounced.

We hiked along the narrow cliff walls always with an eye to the sky above which gave us but a sliver of light in this dark canyon. Thrice rocks tumbled from somewhere far above nearly braining us in the process. Chief John said this was the work of the Nimerigar, or little people. He said they were cannibals and allied with Toohoo-emmi. Again I scoffed but felt a grim fear well up in my breast as I thought I saw some dark child dash behind a boulder. Sure that my eyes were playing tricks on me or that perhaps I had seen a child rather than a tiny man I expressed as much to Chief John who bid we prepare for an attack.

Rockwell spit out a curse and I told him to remember who we were and what we represented and he looked at me with those deep killers' eyes and I found myself unable to continue speaking.

A shrill high-pitched cry echoed from the cliffs and the sharp twanging of bows announced the attack of the vicious Nimerigar. Tiny arrows filled the clearing before us and the miniscule shafts caught one of our braves in the knee. He had time but to shout in terrible searing pain and then he passed away while convulsing and foaming at the mouth like a mad beast.

Poison! A treachery most foul! Chief John warned us to avoid even a scratch from the deadly missiles. The tiny needle like armaments bounced and ricocheted from the boulders about us and soon enough it was clear that the diminutive assassins were flanking us as our cover from this storm diminished.

Porter cursed again and said something to the effect of having enough and he would test his mettle here and now.

He stepped out into the barrage and yet, none of the cursed darts struck him, it was as if he bore the wake of a great airship before him and the missiles did swirl out and around him on a peculiar breeze, such could not be said of his bullets though—as he took aim at the Nimerigar and shot a score of them before they fled in terror.

Rockwell even captured one, who was no larger than a babe in arms, though fully grown according to Chief John. The little man had an ugly head that was quite large by comparison though all of his tools, clothing and moccasins and the like were similar in fashion to the Paiutes, though just the size for a doll. I should add that he had wretched teeth and did spit and hiss furiously as Rockwell held him by the nape of the neck.

Chief John was quite taken aback but did proceed to try and question the Nimerigar, who as Chief John later told us had never before been captured by any man, let alone a white man to whom they were usually invisible.

Bitter though he was, the Nimerigar, whose name he said was Pu'wihi, said he and his war party were to defend against the enemies of Toohoo-emmi, as he was now their true Lord and master.

I sensed that I was witness to the dying of a race that would soon be no more, as I understood some small amount of the exchange between Chief John and Pu'wihi that there were no longer any women left to the Nimerigar and that it made Chief John sad though they were his ancestral enemies. I felt I was uniquely disposed to feel that pain, as that very loss and decay is a part of my own religion and belief.

Bargaining with Pu'wihi seemed to make little headway but finally we were able to work an exchange of the tiny man showing us the traps his people had left on the trail balanced upon our word that we should no more harm his folk if they too left us alone. To this he agreed and he then did call out a sharp cat-like cry and yipping that was met some miles down the canyon and we saw no more of the tiny people. We did however keep Pu'wihi a prisoner accorded good treatment. His curious presence was unnerving to me.

We made camp for the night against an overhang in the rock, that would not allow any enemy to sneak up behind us and even gave good cover should enemies try and shoot at us.

Rockwell said he did not like the place but it was getting dark and there was no way to get the braves to continue on with us in the gloom.

Not that I wanted to myself as this was a truly dark and frightful place. Strange calls filled the night and even Pu'wihi said he did not know all the creatures that made such awful cries.

Chief John blessed our spot and bid we always keep two men on vigil all night to ward against any evil dreams that might befall us.

I found it a hard place to go to sleep as the sandstone was both hard and cold and the eerie feeling of doom hung upon me thicker than my wet blanket. But sleep I did for some time in the early hours Rockwell shook me awake saying to hold onto something solid and try to get to the highest point beneath the overhang.

I was confused and groggy with sleep but I heard an awful roaring that filled me with such terror, I wondered at what wretched demon was tearing down the canyon toward us with the speed of a locomotive. It must have been a giant for I heard the snapping and twisting tree trunks shattered at its very passage and I wondered aloud how we could possibly fight this devil.

Rockwell answered there was no fighting it, we should simply weather it out in the high ground.

I did not understand, but he had been so very nonchalant about all of our trials and now as a giant was thundering toward us he simply moved to the upper edge of the hollow and grabbed hold of a boulder. I shouted at him over the approaching din, that perhaps no bullet or blade could harm him but what was I to do against this new foe and who I asked was it?

Flash flood was his taciturn reply, and then a mowing demon of crunching twisted roots, brambles and tree branches' turned end over end pushed by deep brown waters. We were all huddled up against the far side of the overlook as the scraping hands of the wood and water monster pawed at us, spit in our faces and took hold.

One of the braves was stuck through the gut and carried away into the morass, churned, chewed and swallowed before he could even scream. Pu'wihi had leapt onto Chief John's shoulders and was the highest among us, not that it was entirely safe. Brambles crashed among us and clawed deep gouges in the stone and our flesh.

Then it got worse. I heard an even deeper sound of cracking stone as hairline fractures above our very heads spread like black lightning.

"This is Toohoo-emmi's black magic at work," shouted Chief John.

What could we do? Be crushed by a hundred tons of rock above us or eaten alive by the flash flood below?

"You a praying man?" asked Rockwell, "better pray now," he said, over the thunder.

We all did pray in whatever tongue was ours at birth. The cracks in the stone above our heads grew in size and the flood did not cease in intensity. I was praying with all my might and yet I did doubt that I would come thru this crushing predicament.

The waters were still churning like a death roll but what should fling itself at us but a massive log. Rockwell and Chief John each instantly seized hold of the upturned thing and jammed it against our roof.

The other braves helped and we all did hold it steady against the great load bearing down upon our collective heads.

The grating force of thundering doom did not cease but the mighty trunk held but a few moments longer.

Pu'wihi cried aloud saying the waters were receding and in truth they were. Rockwell cried that we all had to dive into the waters despite the torrent and make for just upstream as he gauged the cliff above us would fall the other direction. It meant trying to go against the current but that would be our only escape.

We dived into the dark muddy waters and I instantly felt dragged away. It took all my strength to simply stop being pulled downstream. I caught a hand and felt myself yanked toward the far side. One of the braves had a handhold in stone and was pulling me toward him.

Rockwell was the last to jump away just as the trunk was snapped like a match stick against the stupendous crumbling cliff face. I couldn't see for the splashing water and freed dust behind. I thought him surely dead.

Chief John and Pu'wihi had made it to the upper edge and called for the rest of us to make it to them.

The brave and I struggled but made it to waters only a couple feet deep and we trudged on, albeit on the opposite side of the torrent. It was then I realized I had lost every single possession I had brought with me. Even my shoes were stolen by the river in flood.

Calling out, we found that we had only lost that gutted brave and Rockwell. We gathered about a small rocky knob and tried to start a fire. There were now only Chief John, Pu'wihi, myself and three braves. I wanted to be happy I had lived but given the circumstances I was now hit with incredible despair. Surely this wicked man Toohoo-emmi would come for us now that we were beaten, disheveled and largely unarmed in his canyon. The wave of fear and anxious trepidation was staggering.

Then Rockwell burst from the waters like the Kraken himself. His eyes glowed fiercely and I did not doubt any longer that he meant to kill this Toohoo-emmi and he was surely the man to do it.

Rockwell still had one of his pistols although he said his ammunition was soaked and may or may not be any good. He also had his bowie knife. One of the braves still had a spear, another a bow with a few arrows and Chief John had a knife. It was a pitiful armory for what we meant to do but there was no turning back now.

Chief John explained that the sudden wave of despair I felt was more of Toohoo-emmi's black magic and that I should resolve to will it away the next time it came. I wanted to believe that as strange as it may sound to those of a rational thought process, as I did not wish to admit that I could be responsible for my own melancholy arrest, but alas I did think it was likely my own self and not some black magician casting it at me from the great beyond. Too often that blanket of misery has rested upon my shoulders and caused sleepless night and gloomy days. I should overcome such but it is a road one must walk alone.

By the time the weak fire had almost dried us, it was near morning. Faint glows gathered in the crack of sky above and we felt as if we might have a moment of peace. But Chief John said he thought that Toohoo-emmi would send men down the canyon after us in an effort to sweep thru after the flash flood in the likelihood we would be weak and disoriented. I asked that if he had sent that wave of despair out like a cloud over us, did he not know we yet lived?

He said yes, he knows at least a few of us live but how many he could not be sure. He also said that Rockwell's life force may have given the impression that we had greater numbers than we truly had and we should be wary of a great force coming.

Rockwell laughed at that and said he liked those odds.

I was not amused and took to finding stones I might use in a sling, which I fashioned myself from a torn shirt sleeve.

The other unarmed brave also hunted for something he might use as a weapon while Pu'wihi said he knew where a cache of weapons was though they were not for our size. We said we should gladly take them all the same.

He had us follow him upriver just a short quarter mile until we came to a small side canyon, we could not fit thru the entrance but Pu'wihi quickly disappeared thru it. I did doubt we would see the diminutive big-headed man again but he did return with a few of his peoples spears which were almost the size of regular man's atlatl. I gladly accepted three of them as well as a tiny obsidian knife. The other braves received the same as I, but Rockwell was not interested in such primitive weapons. He took to rolling his ammunition in his hand hoping the powder was dry and complaining that he had lost his whiskey while I had no shoes!

The day had broken and we heard forces echoing down the canyon walls. Chief John said it sounded like at least a dozen men, surely the shock troops of this terrible magician. We made as ready as we could in a fork, where we thought it would be best to ambush them and strike first, hard and fast. It was not gentlemanly by any means what we planned to do but these are desperate seasons.

It was more than a dozen men, perhaps two dozen. And as I steeled myself to cast one of the atlatls in my hand, Chief John cried out, not in outrage or the call of the warrior but in joy. These were his friends and compatriot tribesman from further afield come to join us in the good fight.

They spoke quickly but with some enthusiasm. It seemed that some brave rafting downriver soon after us came across the dead snakes and went back and spoke of our victory. This so heartened the chiefs that braves were eager to join our cause whereas earlier the few who had come were indeed brave souls fully expecting to be killed in the struggle. There were some words I could not follow for the sake of the two men who had died, Two-Sheep and Antler Head. But now we had a veritable army to bring Toohoo-emmi to task.

Rockwell was also quite pleased as they gave him some of their stores of ammunition and one of the braves had an extra pair of moccasins for me which meant the world in the sandy rocky ground.

We forged ahead up the canyon, I couldn't help but hum my favorite tune by Sabine Baring-Gould upon our march. This was indeed a glorious day and we would triumph I was sure of it now!

We did not have to go more than a few miles to where the canyon widened somewhat allowing a fuller view of the sky. Here the canyon walls were incredibly high as black things circled far above.

Chief John pointed out Kai'Enepi and the cliff palace of Toohoo-emmi above and we did marvel at its ominous face. It was near the top of a sheer mesa, small black windows stood out from the angled towers of red gold stone and I found myself thinking that it looked like the eyes of a three headed predatory raptor. In all my wildest dreams I never saw such a cruel edifice and did wonder again at the circumstances of my place here.

Rockwell alone was undaunted, spouting such raw words of American courage as I did doubt the Paiutes save Chief John even understood though they did acknowledge the spirit of his good intent and were ready to follow him up the spine of sharp rock to the terrible cliff palace.

Here Pu'wihi said he must leave us for he could not engage in this open rebellion of his Lord's people, but he did whisper that he hoped for our success and that if we should survive, he would be grateful as it would mean the dark lord's mastery over his people must be ended. He seemed to express some trepidation in such being possible.

Rockwell urged him to tell his people to join us and fight back against this common foe, but the Paiutes were indeed skittish at this suggestion having always regarded the Nimerigar as their sworn racial enemy. I could readily tell that the diminutive man regarded them in the same light.

Pu'wihi said he would speak with his elders but to expect no such help from his broken people that they were few in number and he did not know if even he might be shunned for his association now.

Fair enough, said Rockwell.

High above we could see dark shapes of men moving about the citadel and we did wonder at their numbers and resolve. Surely there must be more of us, but it would be a far climb to the summit and even then we should be wearied and worn. The angle up looked to be quite steep and had just enough slant that a man might walk or crawl with his hands, but should he slip or tumble I did not think anything would stop him until he should hit the ground, and of that end, I am sure that man would be no more.

We prayed as a group and some of the Paiutes did sing their death song. Some smeared colored mud upon their bodies and hair and in so doing they looked positively monstrous, appearing more like golems of mud and clay than men of flesh.

We all drank our fill of water and did fill our skins. Rockwell and Chief John did set us to go up the cliff face but to have some small amount of distance between the men so that if one should be shot with arrows and fall and roll he should not force the rest of us to tumble after. Also they had it in mind that a wave of our fighters might be able to loose arrows while one group advanced, then the other would cover them while the other climbed higher. In such a way we might minimize our possible casualties and save lives. I must say I was surprised at both Rockwell and the savage's tactical sense. It was wholly unexpected.

Rockwell led the foremost group while Chief John should lead the second. I was with the second as I had no gun nor was I of any real experience with a bow or spear. I just hoped to find a useful means of assistance somewhere along the way.

Rockwell became the point of the spear going forward and did find his way about some jagged boulders and did warn others coming behind of loose stone and what he perceived might be traps or purposeful rock slide spots.

The long haired gunfighter of a saint had gone past a few of these hoolies when a catamount leapt upon a man right behind him, tearing the poor brave to pieces before Rockwell and the others shot it to death.

It was indeed suspicious and quite unnerving to the men. It was also curious that the beast had not attacked Rockwell who should have been the first to disturb it, passing within only a few feet of its now visible bone strewn lair.

That was when Chief John pointed out Rockwell's medicine pouch that he still wore given him by the squaw he had won. She had said it would protect him and now it seemed that it assuredly had come to pass. I now wondered after his previous encounters with the great serpents, the Nimerigar, the flash flood and now the mad catamount.

Rockwell laughed it off, but neither would he remove the enchanted piece of leather and bead work either. He urged us on to the cliff palace, though to be wary of more traps.

206

We were perhaps half way up the summit and in an area where there were no more large boulders for anything to hide behind, nor for us to receive any cover should the still absent enemies above shoot at us. As I came to this realization is when their missiles did fly toward us.

Both stones and arrows came now from some height above us within the cliff palace, though I rarely caught a glimpse of our assailants for I was oft dodging the threat.

A rock the size of a man's head took the head off a brave beside me and his body went tumbling after.

Rockwell shouted that we should charge their placements as best we could be keeping a steady stream of fire to keep their heads down and aim off.

This was exceedingly difficult for both the terrain which was almost sheer, the lack of rifles and the perilous assault from above.

I could not hope to cast one of my atlatls at this range and had to trust to the others to keep such a retaliation strong. I saw Rockwell hit several of the men at the top of the parapet and city, for I saw them fall from its front and land upon some flat surface at the base of the cliff palace's walls.

From somewhere yet farther on within the cliff palace, we all heard a strange dirging horn blast thrice and almost all of the Paiutes now shook with terror for the sound was indeed answered by cries from some infernal beasts farther upon the slopes. The Paiutes cried aloud saying that it was the Eaters from the Sky and even Chief John was unnerved at this terrible revelation.

Rockwell however had closed a good distance to the cliff palace and was well ahead of any other man. He still fired his guns in rapid succession and every few shots I saw another one of the defenders fall or cry out. If it were not for his reckless stalwart behavior I do not believe any of us would have left that mountain alive. This at least renewed the Paiutes courage enough that they did heed Chief John and rush up the slanting face despite their fears, which were not unwarranted.

The strange cries echoed from the canyon walls and I heard such an awful report as I hope to never hear again. It bounced from the cliff face behind, above and below. It was disorienting and I could not tell from which direction the monstrous call began.

Then they were upon us.

Hideous monster birds of a greater size than I would have ever thought possible. Like denizens of some lost world these reptile looking avian's swooped and clawed and grasped at us and only now was I grateful for the atlatl spear for it saved me twice from their awful clutches. Others were not so lucky. I saw a brave grasped about the shoulders by those sharp talons and carried high above only to be dropped and dashed against the rocks. The foul monster birds then dove and took chunks of his flesh squawking at one another only to take flight again and try the same upon another poor soul.

We now faced two fronts, the tumbling rocks and arrows from the cliff palace above and the monster birds that swooped at our exposed backsides.

I managed to look up at the cliff palace in time to see Rockwell ascending the first level and shooting men who came at him with clubs and spears. At least the barrage from above vanished.

The trumpeting enemy blew upon the horn again and I heard his cry as Rockwell sent him spilling over the side of the palace walls to crush his skull amongst the jagged stone.

Chief John shot one of the monster birds and this seemed to allay the fears of the Paiutes who fought back with renewed vigor and more of the monster birds wheeled from the skies with mortal wounds until there were no more.

We dashed up the face to reach the pinnacle city all the while ready to clash with our assailants. Oh, how my blood pumped through my veins at this wild cataclysmic battle. Never in all my dreams had such a confrontation occurred as when we met the savage painted men that awaited us at the top.

I relate herein that some of this was a bloody daze to me as I was struck once with a glancing blow on the head from a war-club but I did feel my spear pierce the foe and I know I drove the weapons point home in his breast until he expired. Men died all around me whether my comrades or the dark painted enemy I could not fully tell for the din was so very loud and the blood, oh the blood that washed over this fell tower! Sounds of Rockwell's guns blazed somewhere above and I made my way toward the sharp serenade of black powder.

Then Chief John was at my side and bid me follow him as he had a rifle and we went up ladders from one level to another. Cyclopean stone towers met us at every turn and in some few were dark things waited, relics of a bygone eras when wicked men held sway over this land and always the trail of blood from Rockwell's fearsome talent was left apparent at his recent passage.

I began to fully understand and appreciate Brother Brigham's words that Rockwell was indeed his 'Right Hand Man' in such matters as these, though I would not believe it if I were not living them myself.

In our journey through the cliff palace we did find a chamber of slaves that had been stashed away by their foul masters. These poor souls were gaunt, sick and feeble; they were afraid that we meant them harm, but Chief John assured them we were there to help and he did enquire of them the whereabouts of Toohoo-emmi and his most powerful acolytes.

They told us that the above mesa had a terrible kiva and that entrance was forbidden to only but the most trusted men of Toohoo-emmi. Were the slaves to dare approach, they were pitched off the cliff. The slave then said that if we had attacked the cliff palace then surely Toohoo-emmi and his men had retreated above to their sorcerous refuge.

Out upon the level stage overlooking the whole of the canyon, I could just make out a veritable ladder of a path with handholds cut into the living rock and as I scanned all the way to the top I saw Rockwell disappear over the edge. I told Chief John and we did prepare ourselves to follow.

Chief John called to the Paiute braves and three of them joined us on the ascension. I was last in line as I held less skill in the climb and was the slowest amongst us. Halfway up the dizzying height and I realized I bore no weapons either but I would not stop now.

Clinging to the holds I made my way over the edge to look upon the horror of the kiva's entrance. I was aware of the existence of these underground chambers and their sacred use to Indian rituals and practice, but I had never yet beheld one for myself and this was not what I had expected. A dark rectangular entrance loomed ahead and I could not help but notice the resemblance to a skull's mouth, as the mound loomed up and two dark, what would could only be described as eyeholes, were spaced evenly farther up. The aura coming from it gave me chills and though it was full daylight, all seemed dark and foreboding here.

I wondered that I should be so alarmed, as this was the longest space yet where I had not heard Rockwell's guns and I wondered if he yet lived.

Chief John leveled his rifle and bid the three braves accompany him forward into the entrance. I was close behind and as I took a step inside, cold wind met my face and a terrible smell of stale blood and offal met my senses threatening to catapult my morning's nourishment free. Chief John and the braves went down the ladder and I followed.

Pillars of light from the skull's eyeholes above pierced the dark but the rest was lost in shadow.

We are not alone, whispered Chief John.

Nothing was in sight and I moved forward a step but was quickly pulled back by Chief John as something struck right where I had been. I felt the air and heard the thump.

We surely disappointed the ambush by not perishing.

I saw the quick movement of black on black only because of the sheen of sweat glinting faintly upon the muscular giant who charged me.

Then the flash of guns lit the gloom and a cry of shock and pain revealed we had lost a man. Framed against the gunshots I saw big shadows of men charge and soon I was struck across the mouth by a broad hand and taken to the dirt floor. Chief John's rifle blasted a man and I felt a body fall against me on the ground. I struck back against who I know not. And then just as suddenly it was over.

Breathing heavily, I was picked up and brushed off. Chief John's voice said we had slain the men who meant to ambush us and that we should go outside to the cliff behind the kiva where he believed Toohoo-emmi and Rockwell had gone as everything inside the kiva had been but a trap or distraction.

I was dazed and bleeding from a scalp wound but I followed and realized we had lost two of the braves who had come with us but Chief John was resolved to hurry and deal with this wicked threat.

Outside and behind the skull like mound of the kiva stood Rockwell, facing a tall man covered in black paint who held a woman to his chest with an obsidian dagger to her throat. He called out in broken English for us to surrender to him and he would spare the woman.

Rockwell answered, Like Hell. He had his pistol trained on the man but did not pull the trigger as he did not wish for the man to pitch her over the side if he was hit. Let her go! Rockwell ordered.

Toohoo-emmi knew he was in a desperate situation, his men were all dead and we had conquered his sacred city. He had nothing left but a hostage and a glass knife. His terrible eyes swept back and forth at us and he muttered some wicked verse low under his breath.

What foul powers of darkness can be contained in but mere words I know not, but I was a witness that they do take hold and demand to be reckoned with. The Paiute brave who had followed us all the way up the slopes and fought beside us suddenly went mad and tackled Rockwell sending them both off the precipice.

Toohoo-emmi threw the woman at Chief John and lunged with his knife. I was in shock but grasped the woman and pulled her from between them. She was either in shock or drugged as she went limp in my arms and went to the ground.

Chief John grappled with Toohoo-emmi and I went to assist him when I heard Rockwell's cry for help.

He was not dead?

Clinging to the edge of the cliff with both hands, the long haired gunfighter had the possessed brave holding at his left foot and growling like a mad dog.

"I'm trying to shake him loose but I can't do that and climb up," shouted Rockwell.

I looked behind me and Toohoo-emmi and Chief John were in a terrible tussle. I looked to Rockwell and he shouted, "Hurry up and do something!"

I picked up a stone the size a fist and looked from Toohoo-emmi to Rockwell and his assailant.

Rockwell saw what was on my mind and said, "Don't miss!"

The mad brave was trying to bite Rockwell's slipping boot and I carefully released the stone and hit the poor deranged man square in the face. He swatted at the missile and came loose of Rockwell and plummeted the hundreds of feet to the ground below, all the while clawing at the air as if he might suddenly take flight.

I extended a hand to help Rockwell up when I felt someone tugging at my shoulders to send me over the brink!

Toohoo-emmi had knocked Chief John senseless and was striving to eliminate me! The last of his foes still at the summit.

I pushed back in vain, Toohoo-emmi was much the stronger and I had no traction.

"Watt! Duck!"

I looked just in time to see Rockwell training his pistol right at me. I ducked and I felt the heat, powder and air cascade as the bullet went right past my ear. I was deaf in it for days. But Rockwell had sent a slug right into Toohoo-emmi's face. Yet the wicked shaman was not dead!

He gargled and grasped at his face as blood poured over his black-painted body, his cheek and ear were ruined but he was not yet even close to dead. He turned and ran from us as I pulled Rockwell up and over the edge.

Chief John had been sorely struck but was still alive as well. The woman remained catatonic but appeared otherwise undamaged.

I helped Chief John to his feet and senses as Rockwell went in pursuit of the foe.

Toohoo-emmi had run to back side of the mesa and to another ladder and further down a relative back way to Kai'Enepi. As near as I could tell, from this high place you could climb down into another slot canyon and eventually make your way back to the Virgin River.

Rockwell was already halfway down when Toohoo-emmi reached the bottom and began kicking and knocking away at the long ladder in an effort to knock Rockwell loose.

He succeeded in knocking the ladder loose and it started to fall over to the left and into an awful gorge. Rockwell leapt free and caught a jutting pinnacle of stone.

Toohoo-emmi then disappeared into the crags and we saw him no more. It took Rockwell sometime to be able to climb back to our position.

We would camp in the cliff palace that night and care for our dead and wounded. Chief John led us all in prayer to cleanse this place and among the purifications that were done, we did burn some of the towers and the great skull kiva at the summit. It was a bonfire for the ages and finally by morning did the thing collapse upon itself and release what evil spirits it held.

The next day we began the long arduous journey back to St. Thomas and Rockwell did grumble exceedingly about, "The one that got away."

Chief John reminded him that we should see Toohoo-emmi again soon enough and though it was a bitter defeat for him, the black magic medicine man would not leave us alone for long. He would have to be challenged again.

We reached St. Thomas a day later and I did then begin to relate the events to President Young and herein record them for myself alone as it was not recommended that we share such foul sorcery with the body of the Saints.

The last night we remained in St. Thomas, there was a dance and gathering of the Saints. President Young did advise them to be sober minded and such but it did not dampen the festivities much. I was discussing some of the recent political maneuverings with you [Mr. Bonelli] and as you may recall I was called away by a Brother Sorenson.

Now I shall relate the rest of the evening to you and leave this full recollection in your care as I cannot take it back to Salt Lake and further scrutiny.

I was told that on the southernmost edge of St. Thomas there was a ruckus of some kind. Some said that it was not unlike the one the first night we had arrived and that it was involving the Paiutes. Still I was advised to go as I had some doings with them in the days previous and it was thought that perhaps I could help in calming things down.

I arrived to discover that Brother Rockwell was already there and was facing off with a rather large Paiute. Who to my astonished eyes turned out to be Toohoo-emmi himself. He spoke in an angry broken English, calling down blood and fire upon Rockwell for the destruction of his city and his acolytes. That he did blame both Rockwell and Chief John for the desecration of his sacred priesthood and he was there for terrible revenge and through the power of Xuthaloggua [his toad-like idol] he would conquer.

Chief John had not been found as yet but Rockwell did not seem worried. He said to the big Paiute, "Throw down and do your worst."

Toohoo-emmi then raised his hand which held the curious idol and crying aloud the earth rumbled and rose at his very feet.

I was aghast at the sight of it.

In a circle of some twenty feet round, the ground churned and pitched as if boiling and then a blast of lightning went from his hand that held the idol of Xuthaloggua, to Rockwell, centering upon the medicine pouch from the Paiute maiden that he still wore.

While the lightning from the toad did seem intense it was swallowed whole by the medicine pouch and no harm came to Rockwell.

Whatever force there was blasting from the vile shaman, it was taken and held by that maiden's magical pouch. Rockwell looked askance at the blackened pouch and then to Toohoo-emmi and he said dryly, "My Turn." He drew his snub-nosed Navy Colts and emptied both barrels he into the dark shaman.

Yet here was no discernable effect at the impact of those slugs! The dark man smiled mockingly and proclaimed the power of Xuthaloggua and I could see that even Rockwell was worried a moment.

But as Toohoo-emmi went to attempt a second blast from his idol, the Paiute squaw who Rockwell had rescued twice over, struck the toad-like deity Xuthaloggua, with a broad stick.

The wicked shaman did wince in fear as the broken clay god crumbled in his hands from the sundering. He then grabbed the squaw and stabbed her with his dagger.

Rockwell shot again and this time blood flew from the shaman's chest.

I counted at least nine direct hits in the big man's torso as he shook with the force of them who then fell over dead with a look of astonishment upon his face and pieces of the broken idol in his dead hand.

The maiden was dead and for her Rockwell did mourn.

But those who had gathered cheered and swept over to Rockwell and then some cast stones at Toohoo-emmi's corpse and even his destroyed idol. Before I could say anything, Rockwell admonished them to stop and bury the wicked man's body right where it lay, especially since the ground was already broken up and made for easy diggings.

After this was done, Chief John arrived and asked about what had happened. He looked to the medicine pouch Rockwell had and proclaimed that it had done what it was intended and was now used up. That seemed to strike Rockwell fine and he cast it off.

Chief John was also rather concerned on where Toohoo-emmi was buried and he was shown approximately where that was. But because the ground had been thrown up in such force it was difficult to tell exactly where the body lay so a guess was ventured forth to tell Chief John and he then went and fetched a small sapling of a sacred palm tree which he did plant on the spot that most agreed was correct.

I thought it a strange custom but he assured me that it was necessary. He said that unless great care was taken it would be possible for as powerful a sorcerer as Toohoo-emmi to rise again from the clutch of death unless his dark spirit was contained by the sacred tree.

I had seen the broken shattered body full of bullet wounds and my rational mind thought that his diabolical resurrection impossible yet, I had seen many terrible wonders that week previous including the lightning from Xuthaloggua and upheaval of the earth at his command so I cannot be sure how many more dark and mysterious wonders are in our world, hidden away in some terrible corner of the globe, defying, Nay! Even mocking our imagination and comfort in the world at what is both right and sane.

Rockwell and Chief John and I did take the maiden's body farther out into the desert and did give her a sacred funeral pyre, which we alone did witness.

I leave this record with you my friend, that in case such information is ever needed again it will be at your fingertips to be put to good use.

Until then, farewell.

Striding Through Darkness
Or
An Episode of Chapel History

The ground on which we stand is sacred ground. It is the dust and blood of our ancestors. — **Chief Plenty Coups**

It was late spring in the high Uintah's. The golden dawn looked warm against the high mountain tops as the sunlight caked the distant snowy caps a brilliant pink hue. The air itself however was chilled and save for the trotting of Porter's horse, there wasn't a sound. It seemed like everything was frozen in midair. Even the ever-present wind was absent here.

Porter had been up plenty early to watch the sunrise as he had barely slept a wink. Cruel dreams taunted his sleep and the cold nibbled at his toes too. He had his horse step over or around the occasional sagebrush growing here and there. This road didn't get a lot of traffic, it being well off the beaten path to most anywhere else. On the positive side he mused, it didn't have hardly any ruts.

He crested the peak overlooking the town of Wallaceburg. A scattering of pines and willows dotted the town between two dozen various homes and barns. The largest building was the whitewashed church in the center of the town square. The steeple stood prominent and tall like the mast of a wayward and lonely ship. A swift brook snaked its way across the fields, winding here and there through the town before finally meandering on its way down the valley. Surrounding fields stretched out and away from the settlement along with a handful of outlying farms and ranch houses complete with crisscrossing pasture fences.

As Porter rode slow and easy down the slope, a young tow-headed boy in a checked shirt ran toward him, with his hat flying behind his neck yet held in place against his shoulders by the thong across the neck.

"Hello sir. Where are you from?" asked the boy, with a bright smile.

"I'm Orrin Porter Rockwell, out of Salt Lake. I've come to take a look around these parts," he said, from the saddle without having his horse slow down its jaunty pace at all. The boy ran alongside undeterred.

"Will you stay long? We don't get visitors here too often."

"Don'tcha? Not sure how long I'll stay yet. How many visitors do you get, Son?"

"Maybe just a couple a year."

Porter stopped his horse with a gentle, "Whoa." He looked closely at the boy. "You know the visitors? They still here?"

"Yes, sir. No, sir. They moved on a month ago or more. Real sudden."

Porter rubbed at his salt and pepper beard. "Did you see them leave?"

The boy vigorously shook his head. "No sir. No one did. My Ma and Pa said they must have had enough of some the trouble here and left in the night."

"Your Ma and Pa said that?" grunted Porter. "Is there a place to stay here in Wallaceburg?"

The boy nodded. "My Pa has an extra room over the barn. There's an extra stall too."

"Sounds good. Which place is your Pa's?"

"That corner lot. With the stone wall around my Ma's garden box."

Porter tipped his hat and tossed the boy a golden coin of Deseret. "Much obliged. What's your name?"

"I'm Timothy Ward. My Pa is Truman Ward."

Porter started his horse moving again. "I'll be by in a bit. Where is your town's mayor?"

"Bishop Palmer is our mayor. He lives in that white washed house across the street from the church."

"Thanks Timothy. We'll talk again," said Porter, with a nod, he then kicked his spurs to his horse to hurry it ahead of the boy and get to the mayor's house unaccompanied.

The handful of folk walking about Wallaceburg watched Porter's sudden appearance with some surprise and wonder. The women folk whispering one to another like hens clucking while the men brooded quiet but with concerned looks to each other.

Porter's horse reared and panicked as he entered the town square as if something was terribly wrong, but he couldn't see anything that should spook it so bad. People moved in normal enough fashion and Porter steadied the animal until he was able to dismount and tie her up. It shied closer to the Mayor's home then turned facing toward the church as if watching for a catamount that was about to strike.

"What's your problem?" Porter asked, trying to watch and see what could possibly be the matter. Sensing nothing more himself and seeing the townsfolk watching him but otherwise acting perfectly normal, Porter went up the steps to the Mayors front door and rapped loudly. It was a solid thump. This was a very secure door. Porter heard a thick bolt being thrown back before it could be opened.

An older man with grey mutton chops opened the door with a "Yes? Can I help you?" He was obviously surprised to see Porter. "Aren't you Rockwell?"

"I am."

With a questioning look on his face Palmer asked, "Isn't there anyone else with you?"

"Nope."

"Well. Come in, come in," he said. "I'm Mayor Palmer, I'm also the Bishop." He ushered Porter inside while also looking fearfully about the town square. "I'm not sure which title I signed when I sent the letter."

"You know why I'm here?" asked Porter, finding a comfortable chair and removing his hat.

"Of course. As I was saying, I'm the one who sent to Salt Lake for help. We've had troubles, mysterious events for some time now that we had chalked up to just plain bad luck, coincidence and what not. But it's only gotten worse lately."

"Well lay it all out for me," said Porter, talking his hat off and letting his long salt and pepper hair unfurl about his shoulders like the snows melting off a mountain. He pulled a flask from his coat pocket and Bishop Palmer looked at it curiously.

"Is that holy oil for blessings?"

"Not exactly," said Porter, as he pulled the stop and took a long pull.

"I never go anywhere without blessing oil, but I can see your reputation precedes you. We've all heard the stories—"

Porter held a hand up cutting Palmer off. "We ain't here to jaw about my stories. You go on and tell me yours."

"I was just going to say that while I respect your work for the brethren on many points. A gunman isn't what I was expecting to aid our community. We need prayers and faith driven fortitude. We need a holy man."

Porter chuckled. "I've done an awful lot more than just use my guns."

"Yes, well I was hoping perhaps one of the Twelve might come and set things a'right. Perhaps a prayer circle on our behalf at the very least."

"The Lord helps those that help themselves," grunted Porter, already bored with the conversation but doing his damndest to remain patient.

"Do you think we might wait and see if someone else with more authority might arrive soon? I—"

"Whoa, nobody else is riding to your one horse town but me. I'm here because I'm a problem solver. Plain and simple."

"Yes, well. You should know we aren't dealing with a human adversary here. There is a wasting sickness upon our town. Even now my wife has succumbed and I fear she may not last the week. Most of the town is ill. This is something we need a higher power's help with."

Porter again raised his hand, halting Palmer. "Look, I've tangled with near anything you can think of a time or two and I've heard all about the wasting disease."

"This isn't something we can just fight. We're sick."

"But did you send riders to check out your water supply?"

Palmer was exasperated and raised his voice a little. "Of course I did. It's pure water. Besides, I don't believe this wasting disease is natural. We've drank the water here off the mountains for years. No, this is something like a plague brought down on us and I don't know how to fix this and I'm sorry but I have my doubts that a gunman, even one so blessed as yourself, can do anything about it either."

"It's good to have opinions," drawled Porter, as he stood up and put his hat back on, "but it's even better to know what you're talking about first. I'm gonna stick around and see what I can put together about all of this. I've already arranged a place to stay on awhile. You let me know if there is anything or anyone I ought to take a look at further." With that, he saw himself out.

In the bright sunlight, Porter glanced around the town square. None would meet his gaze and most of the folk outside hurried away. Across the street sat the church, rather large for such a small town. It had white washed stucco siding, just like the mayor's home. Six steps from the ground led to big double doors stained deep maroon with ox-blood and further accentuated with aged copper rivets along the inside trim. A high vaulted roof gave it an imposing stature while a dark vented steeple reached farther into the heavens than anything this side of Provo. A dark bronze bell hung inside catching a bit of sunlight while the weathervane above looked like an angel lying prone with a trumpet at his lips. Those prize relics doubtless came from another church back east ages past; they would have been lugged across the plains and finally utilized here. Countless days and hours of work had gone into the massive structure, especially considering the size of the town. Someone must have hoped that this place would blossom like a rose in the wilderness and it never had.

Porter's horse was still awful skittish; its eyes leered huge at the edifice and it was then that Porter noticed there were no other horses, cats or dogs anywhere near the town square. Odd for such a town, there should have been at least a few riders with horses and what town didn't have cats and dogs roaming all over its borders?

Porter tipped his hat at a few ladies walking but received nary a look or reply to his face. There's no pleasing some people he mused. Probably didn't help that his horse was still so spooked that it looked like it was trying to dance around rattlesnakes. Soon as they were a block or more away from the church building his horse stopped acting so skittish. Porter noted that to himself pondering the connection.

Despite what Mayor Palmer had said, Porter still had to satisfy himself that there wasn't a simpler explanation. He remembered plenty of strange things that had earthbound answers in his past and he aimed to verify those possibilities first. He followed the snake-like stream on up the valley, coming to a headwater where it sprang from the mountainside itself. Higher up he could see the snows that fed it and filtered through the tumble of boulders to its present point. He dismounted and knelt at the bank. Dipping a hand in, he found that it was cool and clean. He smelled the sweet water. It was cold, fresh and as good as anything he had ever tasted before. Near as he could tell there wasn't a contaminant that he could account for. His horse was pleased with it too.

He watched for anything amiss on the ride back and found nothing. It was a pleasant little high mountain valley. Good fields, blue skies and pleasant breeze all of it hardly seemed on the edge of town that many in Salt Lake had claimed was cursed. Taking a long circuit around the outer rim of the valley he hoped to come across some sign of trouble, perhaps a trail of bandits or some sinister witch-doctor up to no good. But the valley was as clean and downright boring as could be. Porter didn't so much as find a mountain lions track or the remains of any scavenger at all. This place was near perfect as the Garden of Eden itself.

Porter decided to make his way back to the outskirts of town again and set up room and board at Truman Ward's home as the man's son, Timothy, had suggested. Keeping a good pace through the fields, Porter was struck at the beauty of the place, but as he neared the town and the shadows from the looming mountains grew, the horse was again spooked but Porter retained control of the beast and made it to afore mentioned ranch house.

It was as Timothy had described with a stone fence across the front and a big stone box of granite to the side with a few sprouting garden greens. It was an odd stone thing almost like a sarcophagus rather than a planting box. Just beyond the sound of labored work brought Porters attention. A man worked, splitting timber.

"Morning. My name is Orrin Porter Rockwell and I understand you have a room to rent?"

"No," was the curt reply, as the man continued splitting wood and not bothering to look Porter in the eye.

"Are you Truman Ward?"

"Aye."

"Your son told me you had a room for rent and stall in the barn for my horse."

"Nope," answered the man, without looking up, still splitting logs. "Ye'd do far better to stay on that horse and ride on back to Salt Lake or wherever ye come from and forget this cursed place. No good can come of staying here. Specially after dark."

Porter was undaunted but waited a spell before answering, "I haven't ever turned my back on a body in need. Why don't you tell me what the matter is?"

Truman continued splitting his wood but did take a long sideways glance at Porter.

"Pa," broke in Timothy, "we still have Mr. Dentwieller's room available."

Truman Ward stopped setting up his logs for splitting and scowled at his son. "True enough, we do still have that room above the barn, but ye shan't be wanting it."

"Man's gotta hang his hat somewhere, even if it's just for a night or two."

Truman Ward shook his head and spat. Porter could now see that the man had quite the sweat going and in the brisk evening air, he didn't imagine it could be solely from splitting wood. "That room was the first one the wasting disease appeared in. For all I know it's still rife with the sickness."

"Looks like you've got something yourself," said Porter.

"Aye, I do. Nary a person in town doesn't have a touch of something. But far be it from me to open ye up to getting something too."

"Such as?" questioned Porter.

"Aye, ye're here because of the sickness aren't ye?"

Porter shook his head, "I came to find out why folk have gone missing round these parts. Too many have never been seen again. That Mr. Dentwieller, the Mason twins, a Miss Purdy, and a traveling performer out of Frisco."

Truman Ward dabbed at his beading forehead. "Aye, I remember them all. I'm not sure myself what's become of them. All of 'em young and in the prime of their lives, but this wasting disease is what's affecting us in the here and now. We've lost too many people already and more to follow I'm sure. That's what truly needs to be answered."

"I think I'll take the room regardless," said Porter.

"It's yours then brother, no charge," said Ward. "But ye can't say we didn't warn ye off."

"Much obliged," answered Porter.

Ward continued still sweating like it was a 100 degrees outside instead of fifty. "Timothy, show Mr. Rockwell the room and take care to feed and water his horse."

"Yes, Pa."

"Ye're welcome to have a meager supper with us. But when eventide comes ye best be indoors with the door bolted," said Truman, then he muttered under his breath, almost imperceptibly, "For all the good it will do ye."

Timothy showed Porter the barn and stall for his horse.

"Why'd your Pa say that?"

Timothy looked outside at his Pa still chopping wood and whispered, "After dark is when the crying and calling start. The best you can do is close your head up under your pillow and hope it goes away."

Porter shook his head but contained his own laughter—just barely. "Son, I ain't got where I am in life by burying my head in the sand."

"It's something terrible, Mr. Rockwell, Sir. When you hear it you'll know it's something awful and unnatural."

"What is it?"

"Ma and Pa tell me it's just cats or foxes yowling but taint nothing like those. It's always coming in the dark and carrying on a good portion of the night."

"You don't think it's an animal or you don't know?"

"It's not any animal I've ever heard. It's gotta a holler like a demon and it has kept us all up most nights. And then there are those red eyes I saw too."

"Red eyes?"

The boy nodded rapidly. "A few weeks ago, after I went to sleep the cries, they started up. Hungry like. Real close, like maybe they were right in our yard. My dog, he got scared and hid under the bed. Ma and Pa came and looked in on me and thinking me asleep, I heard them say they was glad I didn't hear those wicked cries and at least I was safe inside with my dog. They went back to bed but the cries kept up. I felt brave enough to try and look out my window since I knew my folks was right down below. I went to the window and it was terrible dark, but I saw a shadow out by the barn and two red eyes just looking up at me. They were red but dim like embers flaring. Then a I heard the cry again and something touched my bare ankle. I almost jumped out of skin, so scared I couldn't even scream—but it was just my dog licking my foot from under the bed. I looked back outside and those eyes were gone. I never told Ma and Pa."

Porter, pushed back his slouched cowboy hat asking, "Don't any of the men in town try to watch for this thing? Shoot it or something?"

"Well, a few of the men would gather together to watch for it, but they would always bunch real close together and nothing ever come of it. If they stood on one end of town, something would happen on the other end. The cries at the least."

"The cries, what do they sound like?"

The boy looked behind him in the gloomy barn saying, "It's loud and screeching, calling like it wants someone to come. Always just a reaching out of the gloom and taking hold of your dreams and turning them to nightmares."

Porter guffawed, "How you talk." The boy looked downcast at his comment, so Porter tried to turn it around asking, "When did this start?"

"Same time as the wasting sickness or thereabouts. All just after the earthquake back in November."

Porter rubbed at his beard. "Earthquake huh? Did that damage the town much?"

"No, not really though it did do a just a spare bit of damage to the pulpit in the church and the foundation stone."

Porter was perplexed. "Foundation stone? You mean like a corner stone?"

"No, it's inside the church. Old Dean Wallace he built the church around what everyone calls the foundation stone."

"Is there only one foundation stone or are they in all four corners?"

"I dunno, I've only ever seen part of the one the pulpit sits on top of. You'd have to ask someone older than me."

"I'll do that."

Porter rubbed down his horse, fed and watered her. Then he was invited into the Ward's home for supper. Mother Ward made a stew of chicken and had some corn and onions in the kettle as well.

Mother Ward started the conversation. "So, Mr. Rockwell, I've heard tell about some nonsense up toward Bear Lake you were involved in."

"Whatever you heard, I'm sure it was exaggerated."

Mother Ward insisted, "Something with the Godbeites."

"Godbeites?" snarled Mr. Ward, "Can't those leeches just leave it alone."

Porter made as if to reply but let the couple keep talking back and forth. It was getting dark out and Timothy looked apprehensively at the window. The red dusk was growing over the black razored edge of the mountains.

Porter leaned over and said to the boy, "I'm gonna want to see that church house and foundation stone tomorrow."

"Yes sir," nodded Timothy, "I'm sure we can do that."

Both parents were suddenly aware of the conversation again. "Ye don't need to be poking around in that church after hours. It's just for Sundays it is."

Timothy pleaded, "I just wanted to show Mr. Rockwell the foundation stone."

Mr. Ward nearly snorted out his soup with the objecting, "It's nothing! Just a big block of stone left here by the ancients. It's nothing."

"Anything carved on it?" Porter asked, as nonchalantly as he could possibly manage. "I saw some carvings on that stone in your front yard."

Mr. Ward could see that Porter wouldn't be assuaged from asking so he said, "Timothy—off to bed."

"But it's still light for another half hour," Timothy argued, as if he had a case in court.

"Mind the tongue or mind the belt, lad," said Truman, pointing at the loft.

Timothy shrunk away and disappeared up the steps in a flash.

Truman Ward continued, "Well, I'll tell ye what I know about it sure, but I don't want to hear any more questions afterward. Agreed? And keep the boy out of yer prodding's."

Porter agreed with a solemn nod.

"I'll speak this one time about the foundation stone and the church and that will be the end of it."

Mrs. Ward interjected, "It truly is a big fine building for such a small town. We're blessed to have it, despite things."

"Despite things?" questioned Porter.

She gave him a warm affirmation. "We treasure what we have, neither adding to them nor taking them away. We won't be galled by wicked spirits seeking to lead us from the righteous path."

Mr. Ward gave her a look for that remark but continued. "Well, old Dean Wallace, he founded the town. He came riding into this valley and made plans to buy lots from the Indians. But turned out he didn't need to as they didn't camp in this valley—ever. They said it was haunted or some such nonsense. As ye can see we have fine fields and water and everything ye could every need, right here. So Brother Wallace, he looks around, deems it good and gets a dispensation from Salt Lake to settle here and he starts to lay out the town. He finds that rectangular stone in the center of the valley and he thinks to himself that it would be a good stone to lay the foundation of the town on. Big as a giants coffin it is and t'was the original landmark for where the town would be built. That's why it's called that."

"Gotta be more to it than that," drawled Porter.

"There's a little more. See Brother Wallace, he was convinced the day would come that the town would blossom as the rose in the desert and he wanted a church big enough to last the ages. He built our church around that stone, but only after an old Indian came riding in and telling him we ought to leave the valley on account of it. That old Indian said it would bring bad medicine. I think he said it was a sleeping curse."

Mrs. Ward broke in again, "Brother Wallace used to be a Bishop in Nauvoo, and he thought if he built the church around that stone, that the gospel could keep the bad medicine contained."

Ward looked at her annoyed, but continued, "I'll say, we've lived here for thirteen years without any trouble. I don't believe the stone is connected to the bad dreams and sickness. It's just a stone."

"Bad dreams?" asked Porter.

Mrs. Ward added, "That foundation stone is mighty strange; animals won't go near it."

"Animals shouldn't be in a church anyhow!" thundered Mr. Ward.

Mrs. Ward said, "Some folk have said that you shouldn't fall asleep beside it. The sleeping curse."

Porter raised his eyebrows at that and asked, "Who would do that?"

She said, "I was told a Norwegian saint fell asleep alongside it back when they were still building the church and they let him lie there fallow and the like. Seems he woke up the next morning deranged and spouting about the horrors in the earth. They had to cage him up but somehow he found a knife and cut his own throat. He died the next day." She looked to her glowering husband asking, "Did I not speak the truth?"

Mr. Ward just looked away, unable to deny her tale.

Porter asked, "You said the ancients carved on the stone?"

Mr. Ward shook his head and went on. "All right then. The ancients, the Jaredites, we were told by Brother Isaac Morley, a carved

227

on it long ago. But that don't mean nothing. There, we've told ye all about it and we shan't talk of this again. Good night!"

"What about the crying and calling I've heard tell of at night?"

Ward shook his head, "Cats or coyotes. Nothing more. Good night, Mr. Rockwell. Remember, bar yer door for the evening."

Porter stepped outside and heard the bolt slam down behind him as he took one step from the door. It was full twilight now and a dark blue washed over the town. Most places you would see lanterns and candles blazing in windows but not in Wallaceburg. Instead, shutter and curtains were drawn tight and lamps were extinguished, as if no one wanted anything to know they were awake and inside.

The streets were deserted and there was no sound as yet. Porter stepped toward the barn and just as he was about to close the door, he thought he saw an unusually tall dark-haired woman in a deep blue gown, walking between the church and general store. She stopped and looked at him, her head almost reaching the hanging sign of the store. He thought to call out to her and ask why she would dare the night when no one else would, but then a gust of wind and an eerie cry from behind had him whipping around with his sawed off Colt.

He kept his pistol drawn for whatever was out there but spotted nothing. He turned back to look for the tall woman but she had suddenly vanished. He mused that she must have been returning home for the night just as he was.

He shut and barred the barn door and retired for the night. Sleep was difficult as that eerie crying and calling continued randomly through the night. Just as he would be drifting off to sleep, the crying would come again and tickle the weirdest shiver through him. Porter never could tell what made the awful sounds but he was sure it wasn't cats.

Once just before sunrise, he was sure someone tried opening the barn door, but as he roused himself and looked through the crossbeams to the outside he saw nothing but a wisp of black shadow. Sure his eyes had played tricks on him, he fell asleep just as the sun crept over the horizon.

By late morning Porter was awake enough to get up and stumble into town. He knew better than to expect to find a drink anywhere here but thought it couldn't hurt to try. His personal flask was almost empty. The general store did sell Valley-Tan whiskey and Porter bought their entire supply of three bottles. Unsure of where to go to investigate further, he stepped outside and into some clues. A couple of older gentlemen were speaking.

"Good morning, Brother Worby."

"G'morning, Brother Henslow."

"How'd you sleep last night?"

"Not well at all I'm afraid. Too much of 2nd Nephi chapter 10 I'm afraid."

"What do you mean 2nd Nephi chapter10?" asked Henslow.

"And you call yourself a scripture-reading Saint? Repent and go look it up," scolded Worby.

The older gentleman frowned but nodded and went his way presumably to read.

Porter despite having been a saint near his whole life was not the scriptorian type and had no idea what was meant by the reference, but he supposed that young Timothy Ward could tell him, so he went to fetch the lad and his scriptures.

As Porter strode on past the church, he wondered about the tall woman and looked about for where he had seen her standing last night. She had walked past where he stood even now and he noticed the height of the general stores sign and he was woefully shorter than it was. By his estimate the woman must be at least a foot or two taller than himself. That was something quite worth noticing.

"Excuse me, I mean no disrespect," Porter asked, a woman passing by, "but who is the big woman in town here?"

"Big woman? You must be talking about the widow, Eliza Lay. Though I expect that whoever told you that must have been speaking metaphorically."

Porter wondered briefly if the twilight had made the woman look larger than she had been or played tricks on his eyes.

"She lives right there," said the woman, pointing across the street. "You'll want to talk with her, she is the prophetess of dreams" said the woman, tugging on his arm. "Come, I'll introduce you."

Inside the widow's cottage, Porter sat in a small chair hardly big enough for a child. His knees loomed out and upward almost as high as his breastbone. He pulled a flask from his coat and took a quick pull, then sighed contentedly as the forbidden vigor splashed through his veins warming him all over.

The widow, who was very short, approached from the kitchen carrying a fancy teapot. She looked more like a tiny grey haired child. She was definitely not who Porter had seen last night. There would be no mistaking her for the incredibly tall woman.

The widow saw Porter's flask and giving him a curt smile said, "You really should quit your drinking, Brother Rockwell. At your age you can't afford to be breaking or even bending the Word of Wisdom. Health in the navel and marrow in the bones and all that. Try some of my dandelion tea. It will inspire you." She poured him a steaming cup.

Porter grimaced at the offering. "Afraid I haven't been able to resist my drink since I cut my hair for Don Carlos's widow all those years ago. But thanks' anyway for your hospitality," he said, pushing away the urine looking tea.

"Maybe you are too old to change," she said, with guilt-trip inducing resign.

"So what can you tell me about Wallaceburg?"

She leaned in close, almost whispering like she was telling him a great secret. "I've had dreams all my life, Brother Rockwell. I see things. I know the truth as it lies and what is beyond our regular mortal sight. I commune with those forces beyond the senses. Maybe sometimes I don't understand it right off, but I do eventually." She nodded with a pleased grin.

Porter sucked at his teeth, prepared to hear a lot of balderdash, call it good and bid good day to her, but the widow took his hand and squeezed.

"Brother Rockwell, something sleeping woke up in our little town. Something awful cold that has been resting here for a very long time. The spirits told me and I've had visions. Red eyes."

"Whad'ya saying? You fashion yourself like the Witch of Endor or something?" He chuckled to himself but she frowned terribly.

"This is no time for jokes. I've seen red eyes in my dreams floating and flying about town at night. Red eyes within a dark formless shape coming from the church at dusk and flitting in through windows and cracks in the walls. People are stared at by those red eyes hungry like and they get sick, they waste away and those red eyes—oh, they only grow all the brighter after a person gets weaker and sicker."

"Red eyes, huh? Anything else you can tell me? Any clue about what is really happening here?"

She slouched back, cross with him. "Brother Rockwell, we are a humble god-fearing people. We ask no one to support us or give us any undue help, but this is beyond what we can do and the Lord saw fit to send you here so I would ask that you conduct yourself appropriately and take of care of this trouble that is sore afflicting us."

"But what is it? I've seen nothing and you've told me even less!"

"Brother Rockwell, I've told you everything I know."

His salt and pepper brows furrowed and he stood looking at her. "Something I can understand?"

"I'm not sure what is a dreamlike metaphor and what is literal but I think you should look in the church for clues. I've seen those red eyes flying out of the church at night in my dreams for a reason."

"In your dreams. Red eyes. Right, they fly. I should have known."

She stood to look up at "You're awfully belligerent for a Saint, Brother Rockwell, especially considering all the things you've seen and done in your lifetime. I'd expect you to be a little more conducive to the strange realities and know to ask the right questions."

"All right, Little Sister. These dreams and red eyes—what's real and what ain't?"

Eliza Lay looked shocked. "Well, I don't know that. I'm merely sharing my visions with you. You're the one that needs to act upon them."

"Well then, earlier today I heard a couple of old gentlemen, a Brother Worby and Henslow discussing 2nd Nephi chapter 10. They seemed to relate it to last night. Any idea what that would be?"

She reached for her stack of scriptures and quickly thumbed through them. "It's right here, Brother Rockwell. 2nd Nephi chapter 10. There is a frightful amount of Isiah 34 repeated in it. '*And the satyr shall cry to his fellow.*' And comparatively in 2nd Nephi it reads, '*And the satyrs shall dance there. And the wild beasts of the islands shall cry in their desolate houses; and her time is near to come, and her day shall not be prolonged.*' I think this must be what Mr. Worby was on about."

"Satyr's?"

The widow nodded. "Foul things of old times still lurk in forgotten corners of the world, Brother Rockwell and I have no doubt that Wallaceburg is just such a corner."

"I guess I need to get some folk together, get some tools and take a look at the chapel and that foundation stone," he said, tipping his hat as he went out the door.

Late afternoon light washed over the town and the handful of folk gathered with Porter looked over their shoulders a time or two as the cool breeze licked at their necks and ears. There was Bishop Palmer, Henslow the organist, Thomason the woodworker, Jenson the blacksmith, Worby the bookish old man, and Mr. Ward pulling a block and tackle hoist. The Bishop unlocked the chapel doors and pulled them open with a great creak. A whoosh of stagnant air and dust fled outward, like phantoms escaping a stygian tomb. Inside, beams of sunlight angled down from three high windows toward the rear and shone down upon the pulpit.

With an ashen look upon his face, the Bishop said, "After you."

Porter arched his brows at him and stepped inside. The others gingerly followed, tools in hand.

Something flitted in a panic near the ceiling rafters, causing a shower of dust. It was captured by the sunbeams in a cascading vortex. Then all was still.

"There it is," said the Bishop, pointing toward the pulpit and foundation stone upon which it rested. "We've repaired it a score of times, but always the paneling is knocked away as if something pushed from the inside. But as you can see, tis only a crack an inch or so wide. Nothing could be in there. Could it?"

The wood paneling was indeed shattered and lay in splinters some few feet away from the pulpit. Exposed beneath the pulpit was what appeared to be a great white granite stone box with curious glyphs running along it. None of which made near the slightest sense to Porter, but then he had never studied anything of the sort.

Porter bent down to look at the gaping crack along the stone. "Dark as a box of smoke, in there ain't it," said Porter. He borrowed a lantern and held it up to the chink but could see nothing as the light did not penetrate the interior gloom.

"I repaired the paneling just last week," said Thomason. "Seems I have to do it again every Sunday morning before service.

"Every Sunday?" asked Porter.

"Yes. Even on a Saturday afternoon, it will be broken by Sunday morning."

The Bishop scowled at him. "True enough. I would have called him out on it except I watched him do the work myself."

"Why hasn't anyone ever opened it before?" asked Porter.

"Sacrilege, to tear apart our hard work from all those years ago," said Jenson. A chorus of agreement swelled from behind him.

Porter scratched at his beard trying not to swear or too terribly chastise them, but shook his head to himself. "Why not look into the matter here more?"

"We had enough troubles outside the chapel at night, them cries and missing folk, and the sickness too," said Mr. Ward.

"Seems connected to me," said Porter. "Should'a torn into this box long time ago."

"You don't know that. There's strange history here," said the Bishop, rubbing his hands and looking for the same support the townsfolk had given Jenson's comment.

"Maybe the foundation stone is the center of all your ills. It should'a been opened."

Thomason broke in, "No, we simply built around it. We never thought to try and open it. Far too heavy and as you can see until the earthquake and the exposed crack we didn't even know for sure that it was a box."

Porter held back both a chuckle and curse. "That's funny, cuz over at the Ward's place they have a similar enough type stone box like this. It's just missing the lid. So these have to be near enough the same thing. Made by the very same ancients. A tomb maybe."

"I suppose so," said Worby.

"Well, let's get after it," said Porter, as he tore off paneling with his pry bar. The others joined in, moving furnishings and pews to work. It took some time and the dying of the outside sunlight was painfully obvious to all save Porter.

Just as the last fingers of light fled from the church and the workmen were dependent purely upon their own lanterns, Thomason squawked in an unnatural cry.

Porter wiped his brow asking, "What is it?"

"I thought I saw something moving in there," said Thomason, backing away from the looming crevice.

"Where?"

"Inside the box. I saw it through the crack. Something hairy."

"Probably just a rat," muttered Porter, as he helped ease the pulpit from the rostrum. He didn't want them completely panicked before the investigation was done.

They drew off the pulpit and the rest of the flooring upon which it sat. From there they could see the exposed skeletal frame of cross beam rafters which had been built around the massive foundation stone, encapsulating it. Worse however was the dozen skeletal bodies moldering beneath all pressed up near the foundation stone. They were all bleached white bone, yet still in suits and ties.

"Heaven preserve us! Who are they?" gasped Thomason.

"Looks like all the missing folk. Dentweiller and Wilson. And that one there is Summers, I recognize his coat," said Mr. Ward.

"He's right," said Bishop Palmer. "It's everyone who ever went missing."

Henslow asked, "But how would they get in there?"

Porter snarled, and directed, "Let's tear out the rest of the flooring and open that stone box and we'll find out."

The demolition of that timber took little enough time and finally the lid of the stone box was free to be moved.

"I'm still surprised no one did this before," said Porter, with a grunt as he jammed his pry bar into the lip between box and lid.

"Something I never told you," said the Bishop, with cold sweat beading upon his forehead. "The old Indian that told Wallace not to stay in the valley also said we should never disturb the stone. We all swore to leave it alone."

Porter grimaced at that but looked to the exposed crack. "If something was trapped in there, it's already out."

"Nothing could fit through there," objected Henslow. Porter gave him a stern look and Henslow averted his gaze. "Oh, but the bones did somehow didn't they?"

"Let's do this," shouted Porter, as the mechanical hoist was moved into place. It took some doings to get the edges lifted up for the sake of purchase upon the stone lid, but they gradually managed by sticking pry bars under each corner and several men at a time lifting for all they were worth just to get the straps underneath.

"It's amazing what the ancients could accomplish," said Worby.

"This is nothing," countered the Bishop. "The ancients moved mountains, built cities and monuments to last the ages."

Henslow pointing at the stone saying, "Well look at the size of this sarcophagus, they must have been ten feet tall!"

"No one said this was a coffin," said the Bishop.

"Porter did," Henslow retorted.

"Man the jack," ordered Porter. "Watch yourselves in case the stone slips." He wanted them wary but not panicked, he had his suspicions already and unbuttoned the safety strap on his pistol.

They cranked on the hoist lifting the lid an inch when a raven cawed, startling everyone. The teeth on the hoist's safety gear slipped and the lid slammed back down.

Porter cursed aloud. Most of the men looked shocked considering they were in the chapel, but none dared say anything directly to him. "I'll work the crank. You two, get that lantern ready. Keep your bars ready."

The Bishop held the lantern, while Thomason and Jenson stood ready with pry bars in case the hoist slipped again. Porter and Henslow cranked down on the hoists bar and slowly the lid rose. Rank air splashed into their nostrils in pungent fervor. It smelled like death and Thomason was the first to glance inside. He gasped and staggered back.

"What is it?" shouted Porter, from behind the crank. The strap on the right end shifted, the raised lid blocked Porter's view.

Thomason shrieked, retreating toward the chapel doors. They slammed shut. Was it the wind or something else?

Jenson tried to swing his pick ax at but was knocked across the room as a throaty dry rasping announced its displeasure.

Porter let go of the hoists crank, dropping the stone lid. It broke against the stone box with a rumbling crack. Dust flew and two out of three lanterns winked out. The third was swinging wildly from the peg it had been hung on somewhere toward the front of the church.

Thomason threw himself against the chapel doors with a wail, but did his panic or something else keep him from opening that escape?

The swinging lantern gave only snatches of the macabre scene, as shadows swirled about in the gloom.

Bishop Palmer had stepped farther away against the wall, a look of sheer terror on his face. Worby and Jenson were on the floor apparently unconscious. Henslow held a pry bar behind Porter waiting for the old gunfighter to act. Mr. Ward was nowhere to be seen.

A black lithe form appeared. It was the tall woman Porter had seen the night before. She stepped away silently from the stone box. Any hope Porter had about dropping the lid on this mother of fear vanished. Turning slowly, she took in the scene and the aura of fear expanded greater than it already had. The swinging lantern slowed until it cast an even weaker glow in the murk.

Thomason still scraped at the doors but they would not budge.

Porter had to admit the colossal woman was alluringly beautiful despite the fear threatening to engulf them. Her voluptuous figure was contained by a scandalous black gown which revealed more of her ivory skin than the bawdiest of dance hall girls ever showed. The pale skin almost glowed in the lamplight while her lips were the most uncomfortable kind of red. Her long hair, dark as a ravens wing, cascaded down her exposed spine in wavy rivulets. Curious gold adornments wrapped about her wrists and waist while a tiara gleamed upon her frozen brow. Her nails like talons were painted crimson.

"Who are you?" asked Porter.

"I am that I am," she said, with haughty sarcasm. "My name was forgotten before your peoples even learned to sail the golden seas."

"Try me," Porter challenged.

"I am Lilitu." She swiftly glided closer with steps that made no sound. Her black skirt giving no indication of legs striding beneath it at all. "I sensed *you* from afar. I knew you would come from the moment I awoke."

Porter leveled his Colt at her but she caught his wrist in an icy clamp. "I have waited for a man such as you, with such vitality. Someone to share the dark eons with. Someone whom I might draw greater sustenance."

"I ain't interested," he said, straining to escape her iron-like grip.

The giantess loomed over him, she stood almost two feet taller than himself. She ran a great hand along his bearded cheek, Porter jerked away but could not yet escape.

"I have almost finished with this meager place. I can feel that there is yet much more to sup upon not far away. Come with me and we shall tread the world down in our feasting."

A pick ax suddenly burst through her chest. She released her hold on Porter and wheeled, eyes aflame in wrath. Porter backed away, letting circulation return to his wrist.

Mr. Ward let go of the handle in shock that she still stood. Lilitu backhanded him across the room. His body crumpled doll-like over the side of pews three rows back.

Thomason screamed, still straining at the sealed door and the final lantern was abruptly snuffed out. He whimpered near the doors. He cried out once and then silence.

Another man groaned in the dark. A moment of surprised panic was met with a sudden gurgling from somewhere in the gloom.

Dark clouds shifted and faint blue moonlight streamed from the windows high above and washed over Lilitu. She no longer bore any resemblance to a living woman but was instead a towering skeletal ghoul. The ribs stood out barren like a washboard belying the emptiness inside her. A slightly elongated skull bore hellish red witch-fire in the eye-sockets while blood stained fangs protruded from her grinning maw. With long taloned fingers she plucked the pickax from her back as if was not of the slightest consequence. She let it drop to the floor with a crack breaking the harsh silence like a bare foot through the ice.

"There is a price for eternal life," she said. "But I paid it willingly. Join me and become my dark prince."

Porter unloaded his Colt .45. The bullets smashed and splintered bone, but aside from scant fragments flying away there was no discernable effect and she did not slow her charge but came straight at him with talons extended.

Porter emptied his six-gun and swung it at the gaunt demon as she grasped him in a crushing embrace. Her mouth opened wide and bore down toward his exposed neck. Red eyes leered in lustful hunger.

"I command you in the holy name of our Lord to leave this place and never return!" shouted Bishop Palmer.

The red eyes flashed but stopped just before the fangs could sink into Porter's neck. A low chuckle like something echoing from deep inside a cavern rumbled out of that wretched mouth. "You have no power over me, for this was *my* home first."

The Bishop looked confused. "What did it say Porter? That was all Greek to me."

Porter could barely breath let alone answer. He struggled to release her death grip but could not escape.

Making the sign of the holy priesthood and raising his right arm to the square, Bishop Palmer tried to rebuke the demon. He clutched a bottle holy oil for anointing's in his left hand, unscrewing the lid with his forefinger and thumb.

"Begone, worm," she croaked, as her bony hand shot up flinging the Bishop away but as she did so, the oil he held flew into the air and came splashing down across her offending forearm. She screeched in awful pain, releasing Porter. Smoke wafted from the holy searing. She stumbled back toward the stone box.

The bottle of precious blessed olive oil audibly rolled away into the black beneath the row of pews.

Gasping for air, Porter stumbled away. "Get the oil!" he coughed.

Someone was moving in the dark and Porter knew it wasn't Lilitu because their footsteps made noise. Then there was a wretched gasp as the life was sucked out of someone.

Porter scrambled beneath the pews hunting for the lost bottle of oil. His left hand found a dripping trail granting hope like a candle in the blackness of despair. Crawling beneath the rows, his fingers caught the edge of the round glass, but only succeeded in rolling the bottle farther away. A smear of oil trailed invisible into the gloom.

A great foot slammed down on Porter's back, stealing the breath from his lungs.

"Shunning my kisses?" Lilitu asked. "I danced for Akish and even he could not resist my charms." She grabbed Porter's coat rolling him over onto his back.

He stole back a precious breath before her foot returned, crushing the air from him. With the moonlight having retreated back behind clouds, once again she looked like a woman. A beautiful evil woman grinning at him with long dripping fangs.

"I have never been rejected before," she said.

"Get used to it," said Porter, as he ran his exposed hands through the trail of oil upon the floor and then grasped her leg. Holy fire erupted across her leg at his touch and she screamed a deafening wail loud enough to wake all the ancient buried kings. Smoke exploded up her scanty black gown as she tried in vain to extricate herself from his death grip but the holy fire did not burn him.

She kicked and screamed and slapped at the gunfighter but he held on with the tenacity of ages. Lilitu finally succeeded in knocking Porter away as the last of the holy fire died out. She stood before him in the bony form of a giant skeletal vampire.

"You don't deserve the honor I would bestow upon you. I'll drink your blood and feast upon your marrow," she snarled.

The chapel doors slammed open as the widow Eliza Lay and some few others entered with lanterns and rifles. Porter was on the ground as were several other drained bodies. The townsfolk opened fire upon Lilitu but again with scant effect. She roared at them taking three steps forward.

"Pitch some blessed oil on her!" shouted Porter.

Lilitu paused in her attempt to destroy Porter. If a look of panic could be seen upon that deaths head, it surely flashed across that white boney face.

Someone behind the widow passed her a flask of olive oil. The widow tossed it to Porter. He caught and splashed it over the shocked skeletal face of Lilitu.

She burst into flames, shaking and crying aloud in a dead language none but Porter could understand.

The fire caught the sheet music and curtains, then the pews and torn broken wood from the façade of the rostrum. Everyone but Lilitu fled from the burning chapel. Some even hurriedly retrieved the dead.

The townsfolk made no effort to put out the fire, instead most began singing hymns to drown out the awful cries of Lilitu.

Porter stood guard at the open doors, watching, making sure that Lilitu was consumed along with the chapel. He prayed silently that the burning pyre would contain her evil night-striding soul once and for all.

By morning the chapel was but a smoking ash heap. The foundation stone was found smashed apart by the falling roof timbers. Most amazingly, everyone who had been afflicted by the wasting disease suddenly felt much better. The fevers were gone and strength returned to their bodies.

Porter felt his job was done and he mounted up to leave. His horse was no longer skittish about the town square and that was sign enough to him that his job was done.

As Porter was trotting out of town, Bishop Palmer, his arm in a sling, waved him down. "We can't thank you enough. I was wrong, we did need a man of your skills and I'm eternally grateful."

Porter nodded. "Right back at ya for bringing blessing oil to a gunfight."

"Yes, well. Why don't you stay on? Help us rebuild. You'll always have a place here."

"Much obliged at the offer but I already got a place to hang my hat and it needs me."

"Til we meet again then, Brother."

Porter tipped his hat. "Til we meet again."

Afterword

Nothing has fascinated me so much since I was a child, as the unexplainable and supernatural unknown. Monsters and dragons, angels and demons, aliens and fairies, spirits and ghosts all dwell there like old friends. I've always hungered to delve into these mysteries and terrifying realms and to *know*.

The older I get and the more I understand, the more these mysteries only deepen and yet tantalize further with wide shadowy arms and always I must answer them.

Fiction grants refuge to explore these dark places and learn that which forever eludes us in the daylight. These tales are cathartic for me and a home for that insatiable need to tread grim lands that no longer exist . . . or do they?

Much thanks for reading and I hope you enjoyed these weird western tales of Porter Rockwell, one of my personal heroes.

David J. West
Utah
Summer 2016

About the Author:

David J. West writes dark fantasy and weird westerns because the voices in his head won't quiet until someone else can hear them. He is a great fan of sword & sorcery, ghosts and lost ruins, so of course he lives in Utah in with his wife and children.

You can visit him online at:
http://www.kingdavidjwest.com/
https://twitter.com/David_JWest
http://david-j-west.tumblr.com/

Also by David J. West

Heroes of the Fallen
Bless the Child
Weird Tales of Horror
The Mad Song: and other Tales of Sword & Sorcery
Fangs of the Dragon
Whispers of the Goddess
The Hand of Fate
Space Eldritch
Space Eldritch 2: The Haunted Stars
Whispers Out of the Dust
Gods in Darkness
Redneck Eldritch

Reviews are always appreciated, thanks for reading.

Made in the USA
Charleston, SC
03 October 2016